Pieces of Stone

DATE DUE

YOU CAN WRITE YOUR NUMBER HERE TO REMEMBER WHAT YOU HAVE READ			
			PRINTED IN U.S.A.

Pieces of Stone

. . .

L. M. Kaye

ISBN: 1516856732
ISBN 13: 9781516856732
Library of Congress Control Number: 2015913081
CreateSpace Independent Publishing Platform
North Charleston, South Carolina

Dedication

. . .

To Greg and Jared
Thanks for always having my back

Contents

CHAPTER 1

• • •

SOMETIMES DREAMS TAKE US TO places we'd never choose to be in our awake hours. And with them, they drag the rest of our faculties into places where sometimes, no matter what we do, we can't win. Like when you're trying to outrun some ominous force, knowing the whole time that you can't. Even though it never catches you, there is *never* a doubt in your mind, not even for a *minute* that it eventually will. And *that* is the minute, those seconds frozen in time, when a nightmare is born.

Adrenaline burned hot, sending fiery spikes into her chest fueled by the expectation that they'd be caught. But being dragged away, or worse, wasn't an option. The thin material of her hospital scrub pants was no match for the thick, thorny shrubs and weeds that tore mercilessly through them. Pain coursed through her already injured shoulder as she raced through the woods.

The right way to go…left—no—right. Stay low, but keep running.

She fought to keep focused, scanning her brain for any memory of where the path began. With every stand of trees came the hope that maybe the way out was just beyond them. The full moon both helped and hindered the trek, illuminating their every movement each time they left the safety of the trees.

She continued to grip the flashlight, even though it was useless now, for turning it on would surely pinpoint their location. If only she could remember if there was another way out, but it was so long ago, and everything looked different, especially in the dark. Her mind careened recklessly, leading her thoughts into dangerous territory.

What will happen if we're caught? What if we don't make it out? What am I willing to do to save us? No! Stop thinking...keep running.

The roar of the river was getting louder, which was a sign they were going in the right direction. The sound of the rushing water covered the noise they made as they pushed through the dense growth, snapping twigs under their feet.

They ducked down when they made it to the side of the structure and sat with their backs against it. She squeezed the hand that she held in hers as she worked on catching her breath.

Almost there now.

The path was just beyond where they sat, but they'd have to cross a clearing before making it to the tree line. From there, they could follow the old road. She dug down deep, past the thumping in her chest, past the icy fear, and just listened.

Silence. Nothing. Only the wind moving through the trees.

Maybe she'd put enough space between them and the threat. She wanted to believe that. But knew better. She pushed herself up onto her feet and glanced sideways, looking for movement. Nothing but trees swaying in the wind.

Time to move.

She clutched the flashlight, which could now be used as a weapon, and they made a run for the tree-lined ridge that led to the road. Halfway there, a sense of relief softened the adrenaline rush, but she forcefully pushed it down.

A crunching sound to the left forced them to pause. Her breath caught in her throat as she watched the bushes move. And then they were still. Without any further warning, the trees came alive, and a large shadow jumped into the clearing. A deer. It shot off to their right and was gone. A loud breath escaped her lips, fully deflating her lungs.

The hill came into view, and she positioned her finger over the on button of the flashlight. But before she could turn it on, her worst fear materialized. About twenty feet before the hill, a figure emerged from the woods. This one was not a deer. As she heard the familiar voice, she closed her eyes, paralyzed by exhaustion, and wished that it was all nothing but a bad dream. Only it wasn't.

Six Weeks Earlier

He watched them as they casually strolled around the property, smiling and holding hands, as if everything in the world was right. He saw how easily they laughed and joked with each other. He strained to hear their words, but the wind easily stole the sound away. He was an excellent observer, and blending in was a skill he had finely honed.

They both agreed that the freshly painted house, with its new front porch and recently paved driveway, finally had the curb appeal it had been missing. It sat on a little more than three acres and had a split-rail fence that defined the lot and added to the country setting. With the addition of a little landscaping, the place would be an easy sell.

The town of Morrison, only eight miles north of Emma's condo in Clare, offered quiet country living yet wasn't too far off the beaten path for commuters who headed west daily in order to make their living. Dozens of families in these neighboring towns had thrived there for two or three generations. Everyone knew everyone. David Thompson was one of those people.

The six-foot-two, muscular businessman put his arm around Emma. "I should have this house ready and back on the market by June."

She tipped her head, sending her shoulder-length tawny hair toward her high cheekbones, and looked at him over her sunglasses. Her eyes drank in the way his golden hair blended with his tanned skin, and she almost lost her resolve. "Another sales pitch, David?" The words dripped with sarcasm.

"I'm only saying that it's a great house. A sweet deal, too, I may add. I know you just started looking," he said. "But can't you see yourself sitting up there on that porch, writing your next book?"

Here we go again. God, he's persistent, thought Emma. "Too hard to maintain." She crossed her arms. "It would take days just to clean it, and I don't have enough time now as it is for writing. I'm thinking about just staying at the condo." She turned to face him.

He leaned in close and looked down at the feisty five-foot-five woman who stood in front of him. "Suit yourself." By now, he knew Emma Simms well enough to know that she wasn't easily persuaded. He walked her to her car just in time to see his brother's truck come flying down the winding driveway, leaving a plume of dust in its wake.

"Emma." Paul tipped his head to her and then handed David a folder. "Here are those quotes for the renovation on Nolan Street."

David flipped through the paperwork. "Wow, a little higher than I'd hoped."

Paul shrugged. "Well, I'll tell Sal we won't need his guys. We'll finish it ourselves."

"That'll trim the cost, but it'll take us longer." He shook his head. "I don't know. The people are anxious to get in there."

Emma glanced at the quotes. "Scratch the painter. I can do it if it'll help."

"Thanks," David said. "Are you sure you'll have time before your classes end?"

"They're workshops, and I don't give any exams. Anyway, my weekends are open."

David placed both of his hands on her hips. "Good, I'll get to see you more," he said and moved in for a quick kiss.

Emma turned her head and stepped sideways, avoiding his lips. "Nice seeing you, Paul," she said before she slid into her car.

"Dinner tonight?" David asked through her open window.

"Can't," she said, not even trying to hide her irritation at his public display of affection. "I have things to take care of before we go away this weekend."

The man watched until she drove down the street and turned the corner. He was glad to see her go. After all, she had more important things she should be doing.

Emma hated the fact that David was right. She looked out the window at the cornfields and open land. This *was* what she was looking for. It was *so* quiet, and it offered something she didn't have at her condo. Privacy. She could imagine herself sitting on that porch, and yes, it would be an awesome place to write. David knew she was just being her oppositional self, yet his smile never faded or even dimmed, for that matter. They say opposites attract. Irritation took root in her craw. She was the one buying a house, and *she* didn't want to be *told* what to do. She didn't need *any* help from him or anyone else. And besides, he knew she didn't appreciate being groped in front of others. And there it was…that familiar argument beginning in her head again. The fact that he was always so…nice, only made her feel like that much more of a bitch.

Five minutes later, she turned down the unpaved road her sister lived on. The houses were older in this part of town but nicely maintained. They had the character that the newer houses lacked. Some were over a hundred years old. If they could talk, she was sure the wealth of information they held within their walls would surely be able to fill a hundred novels. The road was shaded by a canopy of trees, and it turned and twisted for about a half mile before it wound its way to her sister's house. It was an old Victorian home that her sister and brother-in-law bought when they were first married nine years ago. It was here where she met David after they hired him to renovate their kitchen last year.

As soon as her foot hit the ground after getting out of the car, her eight-year-old nephew, Jeremy, ran toward her, his thick auburn hair bouncing with every step.

"Aunt Emma! Aunt Emma's here!" he yelled to his mother, who was on the porch.

"Hey, Jeremy," Emma said, handing him a white bakery box. "I have those cookies you liked last time."

"Thanks!" Jeremy said. He hugged her and grabbed the box. "Hey, Dad!" he yelled, and ran back to the house. "Look what Aunt Emma brought me!"

Emma watched him disappear through the front door.

"Don't eat too many. It's almost dinnertime," Kate yelled through the screen door.

It startled Emma sometimes how much Kate resembled their mother. Both had waves of auburn hair and those brown eyes that took on a more golden hue when they laughed. But most of all, they both moved in an effortless, graceful way that exuded femininity. Emma considered herself to be more of a tomboy. As a child, she preferred climbing trees and building forts with the neighbor boys instead of playing with dolls like her sister did. She walked up the steps and onto the porch.

"Hi, Kate," she said, and hugged her sister. "I just wanted to pop in for a minute. I know you're seeing patients tonight."

"I don't have to be there till after six. It's good to see you. Come, sit down." Kate pulled out a chair at the small patio table for Emma and then sat down in the one next to it. "What are you doing out this way?"

Emma took her seat and swung her feet up on the porch railing. "David wanted me to take another look at a house he's been working on not far from here."

"Are you thinking about buying one out this way?" Kate could barely contain her excitement. "It would be great having you so close."

"Maybe," Emma said, as more of a question than an answer. "I've been meaning to come by for a while, but it's been so busy."

"I thought you liked it that way."

"Come on, now. Don't start," said Emma. "I haven't even had time to write."

"I'm sorry. That was sarcastic." Kate changed the subject. "So what are you doing this weekend?"

"David's taking me to Chicago."

"Sounds exciting," said Kate.

"I guess," Emma said, avoiding eye contact.

"What? You don't want to go?"

"I do," Emma said, not sounding the least bit convincing.

"Maybe it'll help if you talk about it," said Kate. "Is everything all right with you and David?"

"Who wants to know? You? Or the you who's a shrink?"

Kate jerked her head toward Emma and looked at her out of the corner of her eye.

Emma felt only slightly ashamed and said quietly, "Everything's good."

"I'm your sister, and I care. I want to help if I can."

Emma let out a forced breath. "I can't get used to it. It's always been just me, and now that...there's David...it's us. It's as if I disappeared or something."

Kate reached over and patted Emma's knee. "That's one way of describing the progression of a relationship, I guess. But you won't disappear."

Emma groaned, jumped up, and leaned against the railing, facing Kate. She wasn't going to have this conversation...again. "Look, it works for you and Derrick, but..."

Kate leaned toward her. "Emma, David is good for you...it *is* working. Don't run away again."

Emma threw her hands up. "Let's not do this."

Kate stood up and took a step toward her sister, looked directly into her eyes, and said softly, "I just hate to see you throw away another relationship without a good reason."

The words stung. "I'm not throwing anything away." Emma turned, her back now to Kate. "It's just...casual. Why does it have to be more?"

Kate opened her mouth to say something but stopped when Jeremy and Derrick came out to the front porch.

"Can you stay for dinner?" Derrick asked. "I'm about to throw some chops on the grill."

Jeremy hopped up and down. "Please, Aunt Emma, please, can you stay?"

Emma wanted to leave before it got too heated. Again. And she didn't want to make Derrick uncomfortable, either. Again. His fair complexion took on a putrid shade of pink when she argued with Kate in front of him. "I can't today. I just wanted to bring you some goodies." She grabbed Jeremy and started tickling him. "I have to get going."

Jeremy waved to Emma until she drove around the first bend in the road.

On the ride home, Emma thought about her conversation with Kate. She couldn't hide anything from her sister. She could talk to Kate…except about men…well, relationships, actually. Who did Kate think she was? She didn't have to explain herself to Kate or anyone else. After all, she was the one who called the shots after their mother died. Kate was only fifteen then, and being responsible for another person was hard enough, especially when you were only nineteen years old yourself. Yes, she could take care of herself just fine, thank you! Kate had no idea what it was like. She only had herself to rely on, and she liked it that way. Not only did they survive, she made a good life for both of them. Kate would have had more student loans to pay off if it weren't for her. What was their last argument about? Oh yeah, Kate called her stubborn and said she was unable to compromise. Why should she? The world wasn't as bright and shiny a place as Kate seemed to think it was.

Her mind was forced back in time to a place she didn't like to visit. That Sunday afternoon in July. She'd argued with her mother the day before and had stormed out of the house, slamming the door so hard that it knocked a picture off the wall. She couldn't even remember what they'd fought about *that* day. When she got home the following day, around one o'clock, she was relieved that her mother wasn't home waiting for her. She called out for Kate, but she wasn't there, either.

After grabbing some cold pizza, she went to the garage to get a can of soda. Her mom's car was there, so she assumed someone had picked her up. When she got back to the kitchen, she saw her mom's purse hanging on the back of a kitchen chair. She must be taking a nap. Her mother admitted to feeling "down" lately, and that's what she did when she felt…that way. Slept.

Emma finished eating and went to bed. She could hardly keep her eyes open because she'd stayed up half the night watching a vampire movie marathon with Allison. Two hours later, she woke up and lay staring at the ceiling. She wondered if she'd have to endure another yelling match. No sounds. The house was quiet. She got up and went to her mother's room. She was still asleep. Something about the way she was lying didn't look right. She went into the room and told her mom it was time to get up. When she didn't get a response, she pulled the covers back and tried shaking her. Her arm was…cold. They said it was an overdose.

She blamed herself. Maybe if she hadn't argued with her so much, or maybe if she'd helped her more with the house and bills. The "maybes" could have gone on forever. Whether her death was an accident or not didn't really matter. You had to be tough and look out for yourself, or you were toast. Plain and simple.

Forcing herself to return to the present, Emma turned the radio up, way up. She didn't want to think anymore. At the last second, she pulled the steering wheel hard and made a left on the next street. She knew where she should go.

• • •

What was she doing there? Why was she wasting so much time with *him*? She was above him. He knew the truth. She was pushing his hand. He would have to show her. The man was deep in thought when the receptionist called his name.

"She'll see you now," said the woman behind the desk.

He smiled at the receptionist, thanked her, and went in for his six-thirty appointment.

• • •

Allison was sitting on her porch, having a drink and a cigarette while talking on her cell phone. Her coal-black curly hair was in a ponytail on top of her head. She used to wear her hair like that in high school. Hell, she still looked as if she could be in high school. That youthful, breezy way about her had followed her into her thirties. That, and her perpetual optimistic attitude, made Emma smile or sometimes want to strangle her. She saw Emma's car and started jumping up and down like a little kid. Merlin, Allison's black Labrador retriever, greeted her on the driveway.

"Em, get over here! Can't remember the last time you were here." Into the phone, she said, "Got to let you go. My girl's here. OK. Bye, now."

"Hope I didn't interrupt anything," Emma said as she petted Merlin.

"Naw," she said, waving her arm in the air, "that was just Eric. He's one of my wholesalers. What's up?"

Emma looked puzzled. "Eric? Thought you were seeing James or Joe or…"

"Jason," said Allison, "his name is Jason, and I do see him sometimes, but oh, you haven't seen Eric!"

"I can't keep up with you."

"Well, my friend, it's a good thing you don't have to. Hey, do you want a drink?"

Emma let out a short laugh. "You have no idea."

"Wicked day?" Allison asked.

"Yes, and I think I was the witch."

"A rum and Coke can usually turn it around for me," Allison promised in her high-pitched singsong way. "Be right back."

Emma saw the pack of cigarettes on the porch swing. "What the hell," she said, and slipped one out of the pack. It was something she did occasionally when feeling stressed out or if she'd had a few drinks. She'd quit years ago but lately had been finding one in her hand a little too often. She stood at the porch railing and looked around. It was an unnaturally balmy evening for the second week of May. The smell of lilacs wafted through the air. By the middle of summer, this yard would be in full bloom, and the smell would be intoxicating. It wasn't hard to see why Allison's flower shops were so successful.

"Be careful with this one," Allison warned as she handed Emma her drink. She sat down on the porch swing.

Emma plopped herself down next to Allison. Merlin hopped up next to Emma and put his head on her lap.

"So, what happened?" Allison asked.

Emma took a big swig of her drink and told her friend about her visit with her sister. "I know better than to have that conversation with her.

She thinks she can tell me what to do. She likes being married and thinks everyone should be. She thinks I'm a spinster or something. I'm only thirty-six!"

Allison put her arm around Emma. "Well, you won't get that from me."

"That's what I love about you."

"How's your book coming along?" Allison asked, and lit up a cigarette.

Emma exhaled the smoke and watched it float into the air. She laid her head on Allison's shoulder. "What book?"

"So then...what have you been doing?"

"Still running the writing workshops and spending way too much time with David. I've got some ideas, and I'll get something started soon."

"A man is keeping you from writing? It must be love."

"No one's keeping me from anything. I spend time with him because I like to."

"You spend time with him because he's hot," teased Allison.

"Whatever," Emma said. She held her glass up. "Now get me another drink."

Four hours later, Emma finished watching a movie at Allison's, even though her friend had fallen asleep halfway through it. Sometimes she felt more at home here than at her own place. Her condo was more of a blank canvas. It lacked decor; *functional* would describe it best. This house was cozy with a lot of textures drenched in earth tones. Allison had a good eye for that sort of thing, but her first love was growing things. She was always giving plants and flowers to Emma. Only thing was, you had to take care of them and water them. Another good reason for not having a dog.

She looked around while she put her shoes on. If she could find a house like this one, she'd buy it, but then she'd have to ask Allison to decorate it. She even wrote about it in her last book, which was a mix of sorts. It consisted of her experiences growing up in a single-parent household with a parent who suffered with depression and then with raising her sister after her mother died. The characters were based on real people, but the story was tweaked here and there. She attributed its success to the fact that most people could relate; either they had screwed-up lives or knew someone who did.

Emma took the blanket from the back of the couch and covered Allison with it. She slipped the half pack of cigarettes in her purse and said good-bye to Merlin before quietly letting herself out the front door.

• • •

The cloudless day couldn't even hold a candle to David's mood. The warm breeze blew through his hair as he made his way down the busy sidewalk. He was sure he could have found a closer parking spot, but he was in such a good mood that he decided to take a leisurely stroll through the only place he had ever called home. The town of Clare was what many people would call quaint. There were no modern strip malls, just small businesses and a few mom-and-pop stores. David was committed to supporting it and chose to shop locally, rather than give his business to the larger retailer just two towns over. The city landscape had remained virtually unchanged since he was a child, and a handful of the businesses had been owned by the same families for decades.

He stopped for a brief moment to talk to a couple sitting under the awning at a coffee shop before making his way to his destination next door. David was glad that time hadn't stolen the town's charm. Some of the buildings had been remodeled, and the one he was entering now was one his company had made improvements to a few years back. His father retired shortly after they finished this job, and David had been in charge since then.

He looked through the glass showcase at Jovan Jewelers, even though he'd already made his choice two weeks earlier. It was perfect, the one-carat diamond solitaire with its simple yellow-gold band. Emma didn't wear much jewelry, and what she would wear was pretty simple. He had given her some garnet stud earrings for her birthday in January. They were her birthstone, and she said she loved them. He liked how they looked against her golden-brown hair. When she wore them, she usually pulled her hair back and said it was easier to show them off that way.

He realized he was taking a chance by asking her to marry him. She'd always made jokes or changed the subject when it came up, but they had been seeing each other exclusively for almost a year, and he wanted to make it permanent. The economy was definitely on the upswing, and his construction company had no shortage of work. Emma's book sales were doing well, especially on her last one. She'd been looking for a house, so why not buy one together? After all, the word *practical* described her perfectly.

The clerk came out from the back room, handed David the paperwork and receipt, and apologized that it wouldn't be ready till the end of the next day. When he left the store, he was so preoccupied with thoughts of the upcoming weekend that he didn't notice the man watching him from a bench across the street.

• • •

Emma had just left her morning workshop and was exiting the student center of Monroe Community College when David called her on her cell phone.

"Hey, babe, let me take you to lunch."

"Can't." She stuffed the last of a cold burger in her mouth. "I'm on my way to a meeting about the summer workshops. If I don't go, I can't sign up to run any."

"I hear you chewing. What awful thing is it now?"

She rolled her eyes. "It's all I have time for." She didn't appreciate being questioned about her food choices—or anything else, for that matter.

"All right, how about dinner?" David asked.

"Sure. Your place around six?"

David teased, "I'll cook something nutritious, something green, maybe."

"That's all right. I'll pick up something on the way."

"If you insist," he said. "Can't wait to talk about the trip."

After they hung up, David's mind swung back to their weekend trip to Chicago where he planned to propose. He'd made reservations at a restaurant his brother had recommended. He couldn't wait to give her the ring.

• • •

The man paced, clenching his fists. He could picture David, smiling and looking so smug coming out of the jewelry store. What was he doing? Making plans for happily ever after? There was no such thing. Just some fairy tale you told children. Some got to hold on to it longer than others. David Thompson was old enough to know better. He was a fool, and he would pay for that kind of foolishness.

• • •

Emma checked the clock and decided to critique one more paper from the workshop before she left for David's. She wondered if she'd taken on too much with running two workshops and helping David with remodeling projects. Meanwhile, she wasn't getting any writing done. Her book sales still generated enough money for a decent income, and she had money tucked away for a substantial down payment on a house, if she could only make up her mind about moving, and where. Just a few months ago, she was investigating housing prices down south, thinking about leaving the cold behind. That was still definitely an option. A half day's drive or a short flight wasn't really that far away.

She needed to commit and start another book. Millie, her agent, wanted her to get serious and set a deadline. Millie was the only one who could get away with making demands on her. Not that she would meet any of those demands, but she wouldn't dismiss her from her life if she did.

Part of the problem *was* that she was spending too much time with David, but he was hard to say no to. And he was fun. That was the first thing that had attracted her to him. Well, that wasn't entirely true. The way his muscles pulled at his shirt when he moved and those soulful blue eyes that melted her on the inside might have had something to do with it. She mentally added a few other things to that list. He was *so damn* distracting. She finished her critique, grabbed a sweatshirt, and headed out to pick up some Chinese food on the way to his apartment.

Forty-five minutes later, she used her key and let herself in. "Hello," she called out, and put the carryout down on the kitchen counter.

"Out here, babe," he said.

As soon as she left the kitchen, she stopped and did a half-circle turn, taking in the orderliness of his place, and wondered why it irritated her so much. A laugh escaped her throat when she thought about what he'd think if he could see hers right now. Housecleaning wasn't high on her priority list. Most days it wasn't even on the list. She found him sitting on the balcony and leaned down to kiss him.

He gave her an exaggerated frown. "Here's the girl who turned down my lunch invitation."

She put her hands on her hips. "I had a meeting I couldn't get out of."

"Maybe I should sign up for one of your workshops."

Emma bent down and playfully whispered in his ear, "Then I could give you some private one-on-one time."

David reached up, took a lock of her hair, swirled it around his finger, and then tucked it behind her ear. "I would hope so." He kissed her and then jerked his head back. "Hey, did you come by here earlier today?"

"No, why?"

"I made a list of things I needed to take care of, and now I can't find it. I know I left it on my desk."

"Maybe," she said, brushing her lips against his, "it was the other girl you gave a key to."

"I'm sure that's it." He pulled her down hard onto his lap.

"I picked us up a feast on the way here. Hope you're hungry," she said.

"I am," David said. His eyes locked on to hers.

She guessed he wasn't talking about the egg foo yong or wonton soup. She kissed his cheek, got up, took his hand, and led him to his bedroom as the Chinese food cooled in the kitchen.

Just inside the doorway to his bedroom, David wrapped his muscular arms around her. Emma wiggled free, walked out of her jeans, and playfully jumped on the bed. She rose up on her knees, lifted her shirt over her head, and threw it at him. He caught it, and a smile spread across his face as he watched her slip out of the tiny thing that was her bra. His eyes washed over her creamy, flawless body in the soft light that came in through the window. She lay back and ran her hands over his velvety bedspread. He peeled off his shirt and lay down next to her, propped up on his elbow. His fingers caressed the side of her cheek and glided down her neck and then between her breasts before moving down and resting on her belly. His touch alone sent her on a roller coaster that threatened to render her helpless. He nibbled on her lips teasingly, his hand finding its way under the elastic of her panties, taking his time once his fingers found the prize. His hand lingered there, and her body arched toward him. With her eyes closed, she breathed him in, almost allowing his heady scent to lull her into submission. At least, that's how she saw it.

"I love you," he whispered.

The part of her that was allergic to vulnerability cringed.

Those three little words packed a punch, one she intended to dodge. She opened her eyes and looked at him straight on, putting her hand to his mouth. The tenderness of only a moment ago was extinguished, leaving in its wake something else entirely. The look in her eyes went from dreamy bliss to one of determination. In one swift move, she pushed him over and rolled on top of him, pinning him to the bed. Surprise was etched on his face. She hungrily engulfed his mouth with hers. Her fierceness only spurred him on.

His lips latched on to hers as their bodies locked. He dragged his mouth from hers to breathe and let his hands wander down her back, over her curvy behind, separating her legs. His voice was thick, gritty, when he said her name. His body temperature spiked, fully awakening her need.

A pulsating heat started in her inner thighs, quickly rose, and spread out, devouring her entire lower half. Her hips moved, needed to move, and she pushed against him, feeling the hardness through his pants.

His lips traveled hungrily over her neck, tasting her as he made his way to her ear. She pulled back and placed her hands on his chest and sat up, still straddling him. He held her hips in his strong hands and pressed her tightly to him. Her legs felt weak, but she found the strength and rose up on her knees, reached down, and with urgency, unzipped his jeans. He moaned at the instant release of built-up pressure. She tugged his jeans off and threw them on the floor.

Effortlessly, he flipped her onto her back and nuzzled his face in her hair, the rich smell of her now-dewy skin filling his senses. His hand wandered down, feeling the wetness through the silk of her panties. She pushed them down and kicked them off. He kissed her harder, more greedily, as their bodies fought to be closer. They moved together, first frantically and then in a more steady rhythm, sticky with sweat but still clinging to each other as every nerve in her body wanted to scream...did scream. He gasped quietly when his body shook, releasing the last of his energy.

When she came to her senses, David was on his side next to her. His blue eyes had taken on a darker hue mixed with a twinge of concern. They had that look that she'd seen in them before, as if he saw right through her. She was naked, but that wasn't the kind of vulnerability she felt at the moment.

"What's wrong?" he asked in a soothing tone.

"Not a thing." Emma jumped up, grabbed her pants, and strode to the bathroom. "I'll get dressed and see about our dinner." She shot him a wide smile and shut the door.

David put on some shorts. "Take your time. I got this." He opened his mouth to say something else but just looked at the closed door for a moment, turned around, and went to the kitchen instead.

• • •

That same evening, about thirty miles out of town, the old woman was watching television when she heard a vehicle approaching the house. She glanced up at the wall clock; it was seven fifteen. She'd never cared for visitors to come calling unannounced. The car didn't stop near the walkway that led to her front door. Instead it veered off between one of the outbuildings and her garden shed. No one ever did that anymore, and definitely not without her permission.

She turned off the lamp next to the couch so she wouldn't be seen so easily through the window. Peeking through the curtains, she carefully scanned the yard, but there was no movement or any sign of a car. On her way to the kitchen, she stopped at the hall closet and took out the old shotgun she kept hidden behind the winter coats. She heard the creaking sound the old deck boards made when someone walked up to the back door. Then came the knock. Cautiously, she walked through the kitchen with her eyes planted firmly on the back door. The knocking started again.

"Who is it?" she yelled through the door. Using the barrel of the gun, she pushed the window curtain over a few inches. Then she saw him. She reached for the dead bolt, unlocked it, and swung the door open. "You scared me half to death!" she said, holding her hand over her chest. "I didn't expect you today, and why so late? Oh, never mind." She waved her hand in dismissal. "I was just about to make some tea. Would you like some?"

The man stepped into the house. "That would be nice," he said. He turned and locked the door.

"Go and make yourself comfortable in the living room," she said, "and I'll get us that tea."

"I'll get it," he said, reaching up to get the teacups out of the cupboard. "It's the least I can do for just showing up like this."

The old woman smiled at him. "All right, then, I'll go and get those papers I was telling you about." As she walked out of the room, she said, "Don't forget, two sugars, please."

He reached for the sugar bowl and took out three cubes. After checking over his shoulder, he pulled a small bottle out of his pocket, opened it, and sprinkled some powder into one of the teacups. He put two sugar cubes in with the powder. After pouring the tea into both cups, he stirred the one with the sugar in it. He took a sip and dropped the last cube into it to mask any bitterness. He stirred and sipped again. *Perfect.*

● ● ●

Emma emerged from the bedroom wearing only a skimpy tank top and a pair of shorts she'd left there last week. He'd offered to give her some space in his closet a few months ago, but she'd declined, sure that it would be taken as more than just a practicality. One pair of shorts and a tank top wouldn't hurt anything. He'd already set the table and served up the food when she walked into the kitchen.

David shook his head. "How am I going to keep my mind on food with you dressed like that?"

Emma walked up behind him, wrapped her arms around him, and buried her face in his wavy blond hair, breathing in the remnants of his cologne. Then she sat down and dug into the fried rice. "I am starving," she said.

David leaned over and kissed her. "Can't wait to get you out of town tomorrow. I've got some surprises."

Emma took another bite before asking, "Like what?"

"Maybe some dinner reservations." He nodded his head and tried to look serious. "Do you even know the definition of *surprise?*"

Emma looked at him. Sometimes the little boy in him came shining through. He was so damn sweet and *good.* What did this beautiful man see in her? She was so drawn to him. She stopped smiling and looked down at her food. That *feeling* was what scared her.

David watched her smile slip away. "What is it?"

"Nothing," she lied.

He continued to watch her face for a few seconds but said nothing.

Emma felt his eyes on her, searching, but was relieved when he didn't question her any further.

● ● ●

The old woman rambled on with insignificant conversation. The man found it difficult to look interested. He hadn't heard a word she'd said in over five minutes, but she seemed to be none the wiser. His concentration had taken a hit. The whispers were getting louder, *mocking* and *accusing* and *blaming*. Always *blaming*. They were more real to him than this flesh-and-blood being in front of him. It was futile to ignore them, and they were probably right about the nature of her intentions. She was stringing him along, using him, as everyone else did.

He watched the woman sip her tea in a birdlike manner before setting it down on the coffee table. She handed him copies of the paperwork she'd had him sign the week before.

"Now you can take care of things around here without all the nonsense of having to check with me first." Her words were slightly slurred. "You know what I...you know..." She abruptly stopped talking.

He became immediately attentive.

"For the life of me," she said, looking down at her hands, "I can't seem to remember...what I was going to say."

"You were saying that I know what you want done around here."

She looked at the man, blinking several times. She wiped her eyes with her napkin and tried to focus again. She started reaching for her teacup but then stopped and sat back. "Don't know what's come over me. I feel a little...woozy." She leaned back and rested her head on the back of the couch. "I think I just need to rest a minute."

The man sat completely still, silently watching her face and listening to the *whispers*. She closed her eyes. He sat next to her for another five minutes in the company of a voice that only he could hear.

Sounds, fading in and then out...whispers...one, maybe two...a hissing, almost words.

But he knew what they meant. He always did.

After putting the teacups in the sink, he went back into the living room, took a throw pillow from the couch, and sat down next to her. Holding the pillow with both hands, he placed it over the old woman's face and firmly pushed down. He was amazed at how easy it was. There was no resistance, no movement at all, actually. A few minutes had passed before he realized the whispers were gone. He let the pillow fall to the side and sank back into the couch, listening to the blare of silence in his head. He took no pleasure in the act. It had to be this way. He walked through the kitchen and out the back door to get the plastic tarp he'd left on the porch. After spreading it out on the floor, he lifted the woman up and laid her down on one end of it. He rolled her up in it, hoisted it over his shoulder, and went outside. With the body draped over his shoulder and a shovel in the other hand, he walked through the yard and headed past the outbuildings, past the barn, and into the field. He picked up his pace so he wouldn't run out of daylight. He knew enough about the old woman to know that no one would be looking for her.

CHAPTER 2

• • •

THANK GOD IT'S FRIDAY. HER mother used to say "TGIF" to her and Kate when they were little. At the end of the week, she'd write it on a napkin and pack it with their lunches for school. It's funny how you remember all those little things, all the bits and pieces. That same feeling was in the air now. A weekend to play, to recharge her batteries, but it wouldn't change her mind about asking David to slow things down a bit. He'd understand; after all, he was always so understanding.

Emma checked the time and then looked around her condo and saw it for what it was. A mess. She grabbed the laundry basket and started throwing things in it as she ran through the living room. It was heaping by the time she reached the bedroom, which didn't look any better, so she gave up and went to the kitchen. Dishes were piled in the sink and a dirty frying pan still sat on the stove. She threw the dishes in the dishwasher and wiped off the counters. There. No sense in starting out the weekend with him razzing her about her housekeeping, or lack of. David was organized in every part of his life and should just be grateful he didn't live with her. When she was almost finished packing the last of her things for the trip, she glanced over at her laptop sitting on the bedside table. For just a fleeting moment, she considered packing it, too. No, she'd put off starting another book for this long; what was another weekend going to hurt? She called David on his cell phone, and he answered on the first ring.

"Ready?" he asked.

"I am," she said, and threw her new lingerie into the suitcase.

"I have a quick stop to make, and then I'll pick you up."

She heard the smile through the phone. "What are you up to?"

"Gotta go. See you soon."

• • •

The man waited. It wouldn't be long. He pulled the note out of his pocket and unfolded it. It read: "Jovan's 5:30, flight 9:25." Near the bottom of the piece of paper was something about reservations for Saturday night. Going into the apartment had been extremely risky, but he had to. It couldn't go any further. David had proved to be too time-consuming.

The older blue Bonneville idled at the curb just a few doors down from the jewelry store. The man watched for David's green pickup truck. The minutes ticked away, giving the whispers time to kick his thoughts into overdrive. *Snickering and sneering*, throwing belittling digs at him, getting *louder and louder*, leaving little space for him in his own head.

With his mind swamped in doubt, he questioned his capabilities to follow through. His thoughts raced. Maybe David wasn't coming. Maybe plans had changed. The sound of his heartbeat thundered in his ears, and he pulled nervously at the neckline of his shirt. He flipped down the car's visor and checked his reflection in the small mirror. Sweat dripped freely from underneath his baseball cap. He wiped his forehead on his sleeve. By the time he looked up, the green pickup was parked across the street, and David was already heading into the store. Panic sliced deep, and he had to force himself to breathe. With his hand grasping the handle of the knife, his brain screamed: *Focus, focus, focus!*

Time slowed as he kept his eyes glued to the glass door of the building. A car pulled along the curb in front of him. Just as two men got out of the car, David stepped out of the building. The man reached for the door handle. *Too late!* By the time he'd reach David, the two men would be standing right next to them. Now he would have to wait.

A stinging urgency slammed into him. The voice in his head growled the command. He put the car in Drive and gripped the steering wheel with both hands. He pulled away from the curb and took aim. The man stepped down hard on the gas pedal just as David stepped off the curb and was putting a small box in his jacket pocket.

$$\bullet \quad \bullet \quad \bullet$$

Emma walked to the window for the tenth time. Still no sign of David. She called his cell phone; it went to voice mail. She dialed her sister's number from her landline.

"Hi, Kate. You're not in the middle of dinner or anything, are you?"

"No, Derrick's working late, and Jeremy went to a friend's house. I thought you were leaving tonight."

"We are. I'm waiting for David to pick me up, and he's running late." Emma hesitated. "Anyway, I wanted to say I'm sorry about the other day."

"No need. I'm sorry. I was being intrusive again."

"Look. Let's not argue about who's sorrier. The point is, I'm not ready to settle down. I may never be, but if I am, you'll be the first to know."

"Deal," said Kate.

"Listen, when I get back…hang on a minute, Kate, I got another call." She answered her cell phone, feeling sure it was David. "Hi, where are you?"

"Emma, this is Paul."

"Hi. I thought you were David. He's running late and—"

Paul blurted out, "David's been in an accident."

"An accident? What kind of accident?"

"Don't know. I got a call from Riverside Hospital. They said I should come right away. They wouldn't tell me anything else."

"I'm on my way," said Emma. She picked up her house phone. "Kate, I've got to go. David's been in an accident."

Fifteen minutes later, Emma pulled up to the emergency-room entrance and parked in a handicap spot. As soon as the automatic doors slid open, she spotted Paul and his wife, Lena, talking to a nurse at the end of the hall. She ran over to them.

"What happened? Where's David?" She looked from Paul to Lena and then to the nurse.

"They're working on him. We don't know anything else," said Paul.

An older woman in light-blue scrubs approached the group and stood next to the nurse.

"I'm Doctor Wells, and I'm on the team that's taking care of David. He's sustained some very serious injuries. He has swelling on his brain, and we need to operate to reduce the pressure in his head." She stopped to let the news sink in. "We feel that surgery is his best chance." The doctor motioned to the nurse. "She'll show you to the waiting room. I'll find you when we know more." She turned and disappeared down the hallway.

They followed the nurse in silence to a small room just steps away from where they saw the doctor last.

"You can wait here. There's someone waiting to speak with you," said the nurse. She nodded to a uniformed police officer.

"I'm Officer Parks. I was the first to arrive at the scene."

Paul spoke first. "So it was a car accident?"

"Actually," said the officer, "it was a hit-and-run. He was crossing the road on Eighth Street near Rollins Road when he was struck by a car."

"A car hit him?" Paul raised his voice. "You got the guy who did it, right?"

"No, but we do have two witnesses and a description of the car," said Officer Parks.

"So the bastard hit him and just kept going?" Emma asked.

"That is the story we got from the witnesses," said the officer.

Paul spun around and slammed his fist into the wall. "He better hope you find him before I do!"

"I understand you're upset. We're actively working the case. We will keep you informed."

The three of them sat in the small, windowless room for two hours. Emma called her sister and told her she'd call when she knew more. Paul decided it was time to call his parents, who were in Maine visiting relatives. He promised to bring back some coffee and went into the hall.

• • •

The man parked the blue Bonneville in the barn behind an old tractor and some farm equipment. He cut through the backyard between the outbuildings and along the side of the shed and went in the back door so he wouldn't draw any attention to his presence. He was confident that no one had seen him come or go since he'd been there. It was the perfect house. The tree-lined drive and overgrown shrubs and pine trees provided the perfect cover. He was sure that no one would ever suspect he was there.

He entered the dimly lit kitchen. The bottle of whiskey he brought with him the night before beckoned, and he decided to allow himself a small celebration. He took a glass from the cupboard and splashed an ample amount of the honey-colored liquid into it. Leaning against the kitchen counter, he sipped the drink while he relived the day's events. The muscles in his neck loosened as the alcohol soothed him. He had accomplished what he needed to, but just barely. Distraction almost won. Then, just like the flip of a switch, he changed gears.

It came out of nowhere, just like always. First *sounds*, then *an echo* that turned into a whisper. *It* could get louder, meaner, as if *it* was looking for a fight. It was happening more and more again. The tone was mocking somehow, even though he couldn't always make out any words. A voice from the past, alive once again, to berate him and make him feel small. He was taking those damn pills—most of the time, anyway—but *they* were starting to sneak through.

Then came that aching, burning feeling.

It always started with a tiny flutter deep within his gut, swirling, churning, growing, and increasing in speed and size. It became so strong he thought he would implode. Finally, the rage festered and seeped out.

He hurled the glass at the wall.

The sudden crash sent shards of glass flying, and the sound stilled his mind, throwing him back to reality. He grabbed the bottle and slid down to the floor. Tipping the bottle up high and fast, he poured the comforting liquid down his throat, hoping to quell the lonely battle deep in his soul.

• • •

Paul returned to the surgery waiting room with coffee and sandwiches. Lena told him there was no word yet on David's condition. Emma stopped pacing and sat down next to Lena.

"My parents are going to catch the first flight they can. My mom's a mess," Paul said, putting the food and drinks down on the table. He picked up one of the sandwiches and put it in front of Emma.

Emma sat on the edge of the chair with her hands folded and her elbows on her knees. She thought about praying but couldn't remember how. She looked up when she heard the doctor's voice.

"He's in stable but serious condition. Hopefully we'll be moving him to the ICU in about an hour."

"Will he be all right?" asked Lena.

The doctor's expression took on a more serious look. "We'll know more when he wakes up."

The woman had kind eyes. Emma wondered how often she had been forced to sit in this same spot. The news wasn't good. She knew she was really saying, "*If* he wakes up."

"Can I see him?" asked Emma.

"As soon as he's in ICU, they'll come get you," the doctor said.

Paul asked about David's other injuries. They learned he had a couple of broken ribs and a broken leg. After the doctor left, the three of them sat in silence, as if talking about it would make it real.

The waiting game continued for another hour and a half before a young male nurse said he could take two of them in at a time to visit. Paul and Emma followed him to the intensive care unit while Lena stayed behind.

The ICU was a large open area with a circular desk in the middle. Three people wearing dark-blue scrubs were looking at clipboards and checking monitors. Rooms were situated along both sides, and the patients could easily be seen through large glass windows that framed the front of each room. The walls were a bland gray that blended in well with all the stainless-steel medical equipment that filled the area. The only noise was the continuous buzzing and beeping of machines. The smell of disinfectant and bleach was heavy in the air, except for the occasional whiff of urine. They followed the nurse past several rooms before he stopped in front of one of them.

Nothing could have prepared them for what they saw. Emma barely recognized him. His face was swollen and badly bruised. The entire right side of his head was covered in gauze and bandages. Wires and tubes were coming out from underneath the blankets. As they approached him, Emma felt numb. She touched his blond hair that was visible only on the left side of his head. She wanted to hold his hand, but it, too, was covered with bruises and bandages. Her hands moved nervously in front of her before she let them fall to her side.

Paul bent down next to David's ear. "Hey, bro, I'm here. You get better, you hear me?"

The nurse reminded them that they should only stay for fifteen minutes every hour. Emma stayed ten minutes longer and left so Lena could be with Paul.

She counted the minutes till the next hour when she could see him again. The waiting room was cold, and the smell of pine cleaner and burned coffee was making her sick. She was exhausted and let herself sink down into the chair but couldn't get comfortable on the stiff furniture and was up pacing again. She wanted a cigarette and was disgusted when she found herself biting her nails, a habit she thought she'd broken years ago.

Five hours had gone by since they first saw him. Each time they went to his room, she hoped there would be some kind of improvement. The doctor said she didn't expect him to wake up for at least twenty-four hours and encouraged them to go home. The nurse promised to call if anything changed.

• • •

Waking up with a jolt was how the morning started. First she felt relief that it was only a dream. A bad one. Then it all came roaring back. David. The hospital. Emma sat up and looked at the clock. Eight o'clock. Remembering the nightmare of the day before, she couldn't believe she'd been able to sleep at all. The last thing she remembered was setting the alarm clock for seven. Damn. She must have forgotten to turn it on. She jumped out of bed, grabbed her cell phone from the nightstand, and called the hospital. They said there had been no change in his condition. Ten minutes later, she stepped out of the shower and heard the phone ringing.

"Honey, how are you?" It was Allison. "Kate called and told me about David. How is he?"

"He's in bad shape, still unconscious. I'm getting ready now to go back to the hospital."

"I'm so sorry, Em. Hey, I have something for you. Can you stop by?"

"Maybe later," said Emma.

"Please, I'm on the way and it'll only take a minute."

Emma didn't have the strength to argue. "Sure, I'm leaving in five minutes."

She towel-dried her shoulder-length brown hair and then examined her face in the mirror. Her eyes were puffy with purplish bags under them. She thought about where she should be this morning. In Chicago. With David. She'd be wearing her new lingerie. If her eyes were puffy, it should have been because she drank too much wine. She tossed those images away and put her hair up in a clip. She threw on jeans, a T-shirt, and running shoes, and then grabbed her purse and ran out the door.

Ten minutes later, she climbed the steps to Allison's porch. Before she even stepped a foot in the house, she could smell bacon and something else. Her stomach growled. Allison was an excellent cook. She grew up working in her parents' Italian restaurant in town. Emma had worked there awhile, but cooking wasn't her thing. She remembered her own father cooking for her when she was little. Then he got sick—depressed, actually—and left.

"Couldn't handle a family" was how her mother put it. Emma hadn't seen him since she was seven. She wondered if he had a family now. Maybe he cooked for them.

"Breakfast's ready," yelled Allison. She set another plate down on the table.

"This," Emma said as her eyes passed over the food on the table, "is what you meant when you said you had something for me?"

Allison pressed her lips together, looked down, and then shyly looked up at Emma. "Would you have come if I said it was breakfast?"

"No!"

"So in my defense, I think a lie was called for."

Emma's eyes narrowed, and she turned around to leave.

Allison was in front of her in an instant. "You're already here. Sit down and eat. Please."

Emma stole another quick look at the scrambled eggs, bacon, and cinnamon rolls on the table. She sat down and took a bite of the eggs. Her appetite surprised her, and she shoveled in the food.

"I was worried about you, Em," said Allison.

Emma looked up and finished chewing. "I'm still mad at you." After a few more bites, she stood up. "I've got to go."

Allison packed a few cinnamon rolls in a bag and handed it to Emma. "Call me when you can. Take care of yourself, sweetie."

● ● ●

The hospital was busier than it had been the previous night. She maneuvered around visitors and hospital personnel in the halls and almost plowed down a small child in front of the gift shop. When she got off the crowded elevator on the second floor, Lena was standing outside the waiting room, talking on her phone.

"He's still the same," Lena said. "Paul's with him now. You go in. I have some calls to make."

Emma checked in with the nurse and went to David's room. Paul was sitting in a chair next to the bed with his hand on David's arm. He was talking to him but stopped when he saw her. He turned his head away and wiped his eyes with the back of his hand.

"There's been no change...I just keep talking to him..." His voice cracked, and he took a deep breath. "Lena said she heard that they can hear you."

Emma walked over to Paul but couldn't think of anything to say, so she hugged him. Then she bent down and kissed David's forehead. The confident, sweet man she knew lay so still before her, and she couldn't remember a time when she felt so utterly useless. If only she could fix him and turn back the clock so this horrible thing never happened to him. He didn't deserve this. She wanted the bastard who hit him to pay for what he did. Waves of anger, sadness, and something...else, hit her at the same time. She put her head down on the bed next to his.

Five hours later, David's parents arrived at the hospital. Lena had left to run some errands for Paul. Even though tragedy had struck, there were still employees to pay, permits to apply for, inspections to pass, and deadlines to meet. Lena had been the company's secretary, bookkeeper, real-estate broker, and only human-resources person since David took over the company.

Emma sat with Paul in the waiting room, trying not to listen in on a conversation between a doctor and a visitor. The woman wiped at her eyes with a tissue several times while nodding that she understood whatever it was he was telling her. It was obvious that it wasn't good. She imagined the torment and helplessness David's parents must have been feeling, seeing their son in his current condition. Even though his mother didn't hide the fact that she loathed the idea of her son dating her, Emma still felt for her now. Everything about the woman was abrupt, rude. David seemed immune to it. Either he ignored it, or he didn't notice it. Maybe this was how families were supposed to act. Maybe *this* was normal. The only thing Emma knew for sure was that she didn't want any part of it. Even growing up, everywhere she looked, she only saw dysfunction. Somebody's parents were splitting up, or somebody's mom had a boyfriend. It seemed everyone was either screwed up or was still dealing with the remnants. So far, the definition of *normal* eluded her. David's mother thought he belonged with Amanda, the daughter of a friend of hers. He'd dated the girl briefly but said she was plain boring. Maybe that was what normal was.

Paul's cell phone rang. He answered it and hesitantly stepped into the hall. He looked back at Emma several times during the conversation. She couldn't help but notice how much he looked like David, just a little younger.

"That was the police. They want us to come to the station. Said they had a few things they want to talk to us about."

"Right now?"

Paul shrugged. "Said it wouldn't take long. I'll tell the nurse to let my parents know where we went."

Twenty minutes later, they arrived at the Clare Police Station. It was located on the east side of town, across the street from the river. A soft-spoken woman escorted them to a back room and told them to have a seat and that the detectives would join them shortly. The room was small, rectangular, and windowless. It looked like an afterthought, as though it had been thrown into the building plans at the last minute, or maybe it was simply meant to be a storage room. In it was a square table with chairs and a file cabinet with a coffeepot on top of it. They sat down just as two men in street clothes walked in. One looked to be in his early forties. The other was quite a bit older with a shaved head. The latter held his hand out to shake Emma's and then Paul's hand. The younger man closed the door.

"I'm Detective Sommers," said the older man, "and this is Detective Allor. First, let me thank you both for coming. I know you're going through a rough time right now, but this won't take long."

"What's this about? Did you find the person who did it?" Paul asked.

"No, but the two witnesses were able to give us some information that may help," said the older detective.

The younger detective approached the table and remained standing. "They gave us a description of the car. It was an older-model, dark-blue Bonneville." He carefully looked from Paul to Emma before continuing. "Do either of you know anyone who has a car like that?"

Emma shook her head in slight frustration. "What are you saying? Do you think we might know the person who did this?"

Detective Sommers took the seat next to Emma, his hands folded in front of him. "One of the witnesses said he saw what could have been a look of recognition on David's face just before he was hit. He said he thought for a brief moment that David might have been raising his arm to wave at the person in the car."

Paul stood up, and the chair skidded out behind him. "That's impossible," he said, throwing his arms up. "Why would someone he knew do this to him?"

"That's what we're trying to figure out. We need to be thorough," said Detective Allor.

Paul paced the small room while Emma tried to wrap her mind around the latest development.

Detective Allor turned to face Paul. "Was he having problems with anyone at work or in his personal life?"

Emma shook her head in disbelief. "No, he doesn't have any enemies, if that's what you mean."

"This is a small town," said Paul. "We grew up here, and everyone likes David."

Detective Sommers stood up and handed Paul his card. "I'll let you get back to the hospital. If either of you think of anything that may help, give us a call."

When Emma stepped out of the small room, the other detective handed Paul a small box. "I told you I'd release it as soon as I could."

Paul thanked him and stuffed the box into his front pants pocket.

On the ride back to the hospital, Paul didn't look at her once. She had the feeling he was holding something back. He pulled into a parking spot, let the truck idle, and stared straight ahead.

After a full minute of uncomfortable silence, she asked, "OK, what is it, Paul?"

He continued to stare, his gaze unfocused.

"Was it what that detective said? I think he's wrong. I don't think someone did it on purpose. I think he—"

"He wanted to marry you," Paul blurted out.

Emma was confused for a moment but instantly rebounded. "He did talk about that once in a while, but we—"

"No," Paul said, forcefully shaking his head, "he was going to ask you to marry him this weekend." He took the small box out of his pocket and held it out toward her. "If Lena was in your position, I'd want her to know how I felt."

She looked at it but didn't take it from him.

He put it down on the seat between them and went back to staring out the window. "He called me right before he walked into Jovan's Jewelers to pick it up. That's what he was doing on that street the night he was hit. He told me he made dinner reservations at that restaurant me and Lena like in Chicago, for last night…he was so…happy."

No words could sum up what she felt. At least not any words she thought Paul would want to hear. The only thing she could think about was running. Her stomach knotted as she released her seat belt, opened the door, and got out. She turned back to Paul and stood with her arms crossed tightly in front of her.

"I'm sorry. I need to go."

• • •

On the other side of town, the man was still reeling from the news about David. He saw him fly through the air. He saw him hit the ground. Tough son of a bitch. At least he was out of commission. For now. Right now he had other things on his mind. There was still so much to do. He needed to get to a hardware store and pick up a few essentials.

• • •

The phone rang again. Emma checked the caller ID. It was Kate this time. Allison called twice, and the workshop coordinator left a message. Millie, her agent, wanted to arrange a book signing. She rolled over on her bed, wishing everyone would leave her alone. The only thing she knew for sure was that she was a horrible person. If David had proposed, she would have said no.

She was finally on the edge of sleep when the phone rang. She checked the number; this time it read "Unknown." She answered it, thinking it was the hospital. There was noise in the background, but no one spoke. "Hello," she said again. Silence—and then the person hung up. Now that she was wide awake, she decided to call Paul to see if anything had changed. There was no answer. She decided against leaving a message. Her stomach growled, but she was too tired to get up and get something to eat. She reached for the quilt, pulled it over her head, and fell asleep.

CHAPTER 3

• • •

Two WEEKS FLEW BY, AND nothing much had changed. David was still in intensive care, but there was talk of him being put on a step-down unit. The doctors said it wasn't uncommon for victims of a head trauma to remain in a coma for this length of time. They told the family that he was strong, and only time would tell. Emma was grateful that she was able to replace herself at the workshop, and she opted out of the summer session. The days of trying to budget her time were gone.

Lena came by in the morning to let Emma know that some of the Thompsons' relatives were coming from out of town to see David and that Paul was going back to work. Two of their renovation jobs were within fifteen minutes of the hospital, so Paul thought he should make himself useful. They had fallen way behind on Nolan Street.

"Paul could use your help," Lena was saying. "I know you've put everything on hold for now, and you've got to be awfully tired of dodging *her*."

Yes. His mother. "I'm not actually dodging her." Crap. "Well, maybe I am. I did say I'd help, didn't I?"

Lena squeezed Emma's arm. "Take a little break. You'll know if anything changes. David would want us to do this. This family really needs to move in. They've already put in some hours themselves."

"You're right," Emma said. "Tell Paul I'll be there this afternoon."

• • •

The sun was hot when Emma parked her car at the Nolan Street house. It was the second day in a row that the humidity was unusually high for this time of year. It was only June 1, and it wouldn't be considered "the dog days of summer" for at least a month. She hoped the air was on.

The two-story house was just outside Clare city limits in the neighboring town of Lowry and sat on a double lot that backed up to a small park. It had a newer, detached two-car garage next to it that was connected by a paved sidewalk. The house had dramatically transformed since she'd seen it last. They had replaced the windows, the front door, and the roof. Frank, David's crew leader, was going over some plans with two other men in the driveway. He had been in the business for over thirty years. She liked Frank. He was a rather large, rugged-looking man with warm eyes.

He flashed her a smile as soon as he saw her. "Emma, good to see you," he said, taking both of her hands in his. "So sorry about David. The wife and I are praying for him. He's a tough guy, you know."

"He is." She followed Frank into the house. Looking around, she noticed that most of the drywall was already finished. "The place looks great, but Lena said it was behind schedule."

"We'd be much further behind if it wasn't for Sal's crew. We had to call them back. Luckily they weren't busy. His guys are here, and he'll be back tomorrow."

"So I hear you need a painter?" asked Emma.

"We do. The kitchen's ready. The cabinets are gonna be installed in a couple days, so you should probably start in there."

For an eighteen-hundred-square-foot house, the kitchen was rather cramped, but it had a spacious dining area with high ceilings and a set of French doors that led outside. It looked out over a fenced-in yard that had tasteful established greenery and, from the looks of it, perennials. That was something Emma had known nothing about before she met Allison. The Simms had moved around quite a bit when she was young, and that had remained the status quo well into her teens. They'd never even stayed in one place long enough to keep a garden until then. That's when she met

Allison, her first real friend, in eleventh grade. She remembered how appalled her friend was by that "no garden" thing and took her to a nursery and bought her three plants: one jalapeño and two tomatoes. She promised to teach Emma how to make salsa before school started back up in September, and since it didn't involve any actual cooking, she was able to master it.

She pictured the backyard she had as a child. It was a lot smaller than this one, but there was a field right behind it. Her father gave her a butterfly net the summer he left. She spent hours with that net, catching butterflies in the field. She kept looking for him that summer, everywhere she went. The day her mother told her that he wasn't coming back, she took her butterfly net and went out to the field, found the biggest rock she could lift, and smashed it until nothing remained but pieces. She was deep in daydream mode when she heard a high-pitched woman's voice.

"Hello," the woman called out again when she entered the kitchen.

Emma turned and saw a petite brunette woman carrying a very small, very blond little girl.

"Hi," said the woman, holding her hand out to Emma. "I'm Joyce Swanson, and this is Missy," she said as she bounced the child on her hip.

Emma put her hand out. "Nice to meet you both. I'm Emma."

"My husband and I were so sorry to hear about David. Paul said you two were close."

"Thank you."

Joyce looked around the room. "My babysitter's sick. Otherwise I'd be working here today. I'm waiting to hear from my sister. Hopefully she can watch Missy for me this week."

"I'll be here as much as I can," said Emma, "unless something changes with David."

There was a drawn-out silence between the two women.

"Sorry," said Joyce when Emma caught her staring. "I'm sure you get this a lot, but I've read your books. I really enjoyed your last one. I know parts of *Lost Days* were about your experiences, and I can relate. My childhood was similar. You expressed it well. When's the next one coming out?"

"I don't have a date yet," said Emma. Guilt had taken up residence in the back of her head and poked out whenever someone asked about that. It didn't help that Millie, her agent, had been badgering her on the subject.

Just then, Paul walked into the kitchen. "I see you two have met."

"Hi, Paul," said Joyce. "We were just talking about her book." She turned to Emma. "It was a pleasure meeting you. We'll get out of your way now. See you soon." They left through the kitchen doors.

"Detective Sommers called this morning," Paul said, "and wanted to know if we'd thought of anything that may help."

"I take it they have nothing new?"

He looked down at the floor. "Nope."

Emma sighed. "Does it really matter if they find him? It doesn't change anything."

Paul's features visibly hardened. "It would for me."

• • •

Painting was something Emma never expected to excel at, but here she was, helping David's company complete yet another house. It was kind of a thrill to see it all come together, from the beginning to the end, and become a home. This house in particular had been so run-down that she'd never imagined it could turn out so fresh and beautiful. David was an artist in his trade. He always saw what was possible and took such pride in his work, never taking shortcuts. Lena was right about taking a break from their vigilance at the hospital. David would want that. Anyway, it gave her something to focus on, and she actually enjoyed it. Paul said he appreciated the help but avoided any lengthy conversation with her. They never mentioned the ring or talked about that afternoon in his truck. It was just as well. With the majority of the kitchen done, she put away the painting supplies, grabbed her purse, and headed home for a quick shower before heading back to the hospital.

Half an hour later, Emma stood looking into her empty fridge, realizing she hadn't been to the grocery store in over two weeks. She went to the cupboard and took out two cans of tuna. Damn. No mayo. It didn't matter, anyway, because the bread was moldy. She'd have to stop and get something on the way to the hospital. David said she'd starve to death if it wasn't for fast food. Sadly, he was right.

Emma opened a soda and started going through her mail. She came across an envelope that was postmarked from a small town up north, in the upper peninsula of Michigan. Her name and address was handwritten, and she recognized the penmanship. She had received several letters in the past with the same handwriting. There was only one person who sent letters from there. Her father. She tossed the unopened envelope in the trash and went to take a shower.

When she got to the hospital, she was told that David was no longer in the ICU. Even though his condition had remained the same, he was deemed stable enough to be moved to the step-down unit. Some of the monitors had been removed, and the bruises on his face were starting to fade. He didn't look as swollen, and he looked more like himself.

His dad was reading the newspaper to David when Emma walked in. She said hello to his mother who managed a polite, yet fake, smile, and then immediately got up and started gathering her things. It made Emma wonder if Paul had told them about the ring and David's plans. If they knew, she was glad they hadn't brought it up.

After the Thompsons left, Emma pulled the chair closer to the bed. She told him about meeting Joyce and Missy and about the progress on the house. Then she told him that she needed him. It was the first time she'd ever said those words to another person. With her head resting next to his, she let herself do something she never did in front of anyone. Cry.

• • •

At seven thirty the next morning, it was already muggy. Emma found the heavy air hard to breathe after stepping out of her air-conditioned condo. The sky was hazy, and according to the weatherman, it wasn't going to let up until it rained, maybe tomorrow night. She hadn't planned on leaving so early, but sleep seemed to elude her on a regular basis these past few weeks. She wondered if Joyce had found a sitter. A few workers were already unloading supplies when she arrived just before eight.

She went straight to the kitchen and opened the pantry. What she saw sickened her. Paint was every which way. Every inch of the floor was covered, and some of it had splashed up the walls. The two paint cans were placed neatly on a shelf, with the labels facing forward. It didn't make any sense. Everything about it screamed intentional. But why would anyone... do this on purpose? She took it all in. Then she saw it. Realizing she left her phone in the car, she ran to the front door, opened it, and ran squarely into Paul.

"The paint!" She stopped and took a breath. "You have to see!" She spun around wildly and ran back to the kitchen.

Paul looked confused but ran after her. When he reached the pantry, he stood next to her, looking in. "What the hell?" was all he said.

They both looked up at the wall. Above the shelf where the paint cans were placed, someone had used the green paint to write the word *WHY*.

When Frank arrived ten minutes later, Paul showed him the mess and then called Joyce. Emma waited outside for her until she arrived. The spilled paint was disturbing enough, but the painted question was downright creepy. Even though it wasn't a threat of any kind, Paul called the police to report it. Joyce refused to believe it was anything sinister and just wanted it fixed.

When the police left an hour later, Frank questioned the workers who had arrived earlier. The kitchen doors were unlocked, but no one had entered the kitchen before Emma did. They were probably left unlocked by accident the previous night. Paul thought it best to err on the side of safety and change the locks. Frank decided to rip out the floor that afternoon, so there was no point in sticking around. Emma and Joyce called it a day.

Emma stopped at the local market on her way home. She put a few basic items in her cart and decided to call Allison. She needed a diversion, something to take her mind off David and the paint incident. There was no answer, so she left a message: "Hey, Allison, if you're not busy, come on by. I'm planning on staying in the rest of the day." She grabbed a bottle of wine and got in line at the checkout.

The humidity hung thick in the air. She walked into her condo, kicked off her shoes, and glanced up into the mirror in the foyer. Her normally straight hair had taken on a wavy, fuzzy look. She put the groceries away and headed to the bathroom to put her hair up. She splashed water on her face and changed out of her sticky clothes. While she was throwing away the empty plastic bags from the groceries, the discarded envelope caught her eye. She threw the bags in on top of it and started to walk away. She stopped, mumbled to herself, turned, and went back to the garbage. *Why not?* It had been a very strange day, and to keep the momentum going, she reached in and dug the envelope out.

She poured herself a small glass of wine, sat down at the kitchen table, and opened the envelope. It was more of a note than a letter. It was short and to the point. It read: "Hope all is well with both of you. Please call me. I, myself, am not well. There is something I should tell you." It was signed, "Your father, Peter Simms," followed by his phone number. Wow. This was nothing like the ones she had received in the past. They were always more lengthy. He usually asked more questions and offered more useless information. She tossed the note on the kitchen counter, took her glass of wine, and went to the living room. As she was flipping through the channels on the TV, Allison knocked on the door. Emma hugged her and then went to the kitchen to get the bottle of wine and one more glass.

• • •

When Emma arrived at the Nolan Street house the next day, the kitchen looked totally different with the newly installed cabinets and counter-tops. The workers had just finished and were packing up their tools when Emma arrived around two. She glanced briefly at the pantry door but quickly looked away. Together, she and Joyce would try to tackle the rest of the painting.

She heard the door slam and assumed it was Joyce. Before she turned the corner to the living room, loud voices filled the air. Two men were nose to nose in a heated argument near the front door. One was older with tanned, leathery-looking skin and graying hair. He was short and stocky and had his finger in the face of a tall, much-younger man. A third man was standing off to the side of the pair. The two men both took a step backward when they saw her.

The shorter man approached Emma and extended his hand. "I'm Sal. My crew's working here." He looked back at the two younger men before continuing. "We were just discussing work ethic. We didn't mean to scare you."

Emma hesitated for a second but accepted his hand. "I'm Emma."

Sal turned back to the men and in a quiet but stern voice said, "Next time you don't feel like showing up on time, you're done."

They nodded at Sal and went outside. It was obvious who was in charge. Sal apologized to Emma again. "It's hard to find good workers. Some can't follow simple directions and that's if they even show up." He nodded politely. "It was nice meeting you." He excused himself and went outside.

Joyce arrived twenty minutes later and was pleased with the kitchen despite the setback of the day before. Emma helped her unload some boxes into the garage before they started painting. She mentioned the argument she'd witnessed between the two men. Joyce rolled her eyes.

"So I take it you've seen it before?" asked Emma.

"Everybody's seen it before," said Joyce, matter-of-factly. "Sal's the boss, and he makes sure everybody knows it."

"I got the impression he was about to fire them when I walked in."

Joyce laughed out loud. "I wouldn't doubt it. There's always a new face or two around here."

"I suppose he just wants the work to get done," said Emma.

"And so do I," said Joyce.

When the painting was done, Emma helped Joyce carry some of the boxes from the garage into the kitchen. Everything was coming together for Joyce and her family. It was difficult to not be envious.

"I'm going to head out and get to the hospital," said Emma. "It looks as if you've got everything under control."

"I wish you could stay and meet my husband. He'll be here soon."

"I'd like that, but maybe another time," said Emma.

• • •

Later that evening, the man looked into the full-length mirror, adjusted his baseball cap, and assessed his outfit: a long-sleeve jersey, casual khakis, and running shoes. He liked what he saw. There was nothing in his presentation that would be the least bit memorable.

From his backpack he retrieved the pill bottle, dumped a few pills into a plastic bag, and took them to the bathroom. With the bottom of a glass, he carefully ground them into powder and then tucked the bag into his pocket.

Swish, swish, swishhh.

His head shot up, and his eyes sprang wide open. He listened, sure that he'd heard something coming from the staircase. As he stood at the bathroom sink, he was flooded with an overwhelming feeling that he was being watched.

Maybe he forgot to lock the back door.

He spun around to face the doorway and lost his balance. He reached back and steadied himself against the bathroom sink, holding his breath as he listened for even the slightest sound. Catlike, he slunk to the door and peered out into the hallway. Nothing. He turned back and was spooked by his own reflection in the mirror. Creeping closer, he studied his face. It looked odd, different somehow. He didn't trust it. Without taking his eyes off the mirror, he reached for the bath towel that hung over the shower curtain and covered the mirror, tucking the towel securely behind it.

He retreated to the bedroom and found the pill bottle. With trembling hands, he tossed two pills into his mouth, threw his head back, and swallowed them. They would quiet the racing thoughts and keep the whispers away—or at least give him the strength to ignore them.

Time to go.

The ground was dry from lack of rain, and dirt kicked up around his feet, causing a dust cloud on the dirt path that led to the barn. Five feet past the shed, he paused and looked out to the field where he'd buried the old woman. Shame and regret stung him, but...he had no choice.

I could have handled it, but...they...kept picking and picking and picking!

He leaned forward into the wind and went into the barn. He opened the Bonneville's trunk and threw in some of the items he had purchased from the hardware store. Feeling satisfied that he had everything he might need, he got in the car and drove it out of the barn, down the drive, and then turned left on the road and headed west. A storm loomed on the distant horizon.

The man hadn't been familiar with too many cities in this general direction until quite recently. He'd taken several test runs to get acquainted with the lay of the land, and he was confident that in the shady streets of the city he would find exactly what he was looking for.

About an hour later, the man was coasting down the dimly lit street. Occasionally, he could see some movement between the abandoned buildings. He'd read somewhere that this had been a budding neighborhood with undeveloped potential before the housing market fell into the toilet. Many small businesses had either folded or moved away. Houses sat abandoned, and crime was on the rise. Now, the only establishments that still seemed to thrive were the local bars and pawnshops.

It had begun to rain, and not many people were hanging around on the corners like there had been the last time he was there. Some young men were gathering in the doorway of a pawnshop, and a few people next door were standing beneath the overhang of a barber shop. A man and woman were arguing in front of a liquor store. People walked by without giving the couple a second look. No one paid him any attention as he rolled to a stop at the curb. In this part of town, it was obvious that people minded their own business. Except the girls. They lingered near corners, walking with purpose but going nowhere, under the peering eyes of passersby. Two girls stood in the small doorway of a boarded-up building.

They both looked to be in their mid-twenties but could easily have been much younger, considering that their lifestyle had a way of adding on the years.

No, someone a little older.

The clack of heels sent his attention to the sidewalk on the opposite side of the street. A woman strolled back and forth a little way down the block. She was holding a sweater up high over her head to deflect the rain that was coming down harder now. Her short dress was even shorter with her arms raised up so high. He imagined her in a suit jacket. Watching for a few minutes more led him to believe that she had no specific destination in mind. He knew what to do, so he turned the key, put the vehicle in Drive, and was just about to pull out onto the street when a silver SUV blew past him. It stopped at the curb in front of her. She strolled over and leaned in the passenger-side window while laughing and twirling her long hair around her finger. The driver pushed the door open, the woman slipped in, and they drove away.

The man slammed his fist down hard on the steering wheel several times.

"Damn!" He cradled his hand. The pain proved gratifying, real. The flutter started. "Breathe," he said out loud. *In through the nose, out through the mouth.* He could hear *her* say it. *She* always said the right thing. The swirling sensation in the pit of his stomach came under his control, and he was glad he'd taken the pills. They took the edge off and rounded out the racing thoughts, which made it easier to shift gears and put the anger back down. He scanned the sidewalk for any sign that his outburst had been observed. A couple of older men had just walked past his car and seemed unconcerned. The rain had driven the bulk of the people indoors now. He was pretty much alone. He needed a drink.

Looking out to where he first saw the girl pacing in the rain, a flashing neon sign called out to him. As soon as he got out of the car, he could hear yelling in the distance. He glanced up and saw a commotion ahead. A broad-shouldered man with a shiny head and thick neck was throwing another man out of the bar. The intoxicated man yelled some obscenities, tripped, and fell off the curb, landing face down in a puddle on the street.

He got up and began walking down the sidewalk, yelling out at no one in particular. Watching the unsteady man stumble down the street helped lighten his own mood, lessening the tightness in his neck and chest. He glanced through the bar's window and saw a pretty good crowd. It would be easy to blend in.

He walked through the double glass doors and noticed there was a baseball game on a large flat-screen TV near the bar. The announcer was talking about extra innings. He approached, pretending to be interested in the game. After ordering a draft, he looked around. A group of older men was having a loud conversation about a new starting pitcher for Saturday's game. On the other side of him, a woman was rambling on about something to a man who was busy checking out a woman at the next table. A group of younger people was toasting one another and doing shots. Not quite the sort of place you'd go to for a quiet dinner, but absolutely perfect for what he had in mind.

He was feeling more relaxed now, even though it had been a wasted evening so far. He finished his drink and was about to leave when he looked in the mirror behind the bar. That's when he saw her. She had walked in alone and was still standing at the door, shaking the rain out of her long reddish hair. She couldn't be more perfect, with her delicate features and thin build. It was as if she was purposely sent to him. When she walked over to the bar and sat two seats down from him, he no longer doubted it was fate. If something was handed to you, you'd better take it. He signaled the bartender for another drink.

He watched her indirectly through the mirror behind the bar. She took off her jacket, hung it on the back of her seat, and quickly became interested in the ball game. She ordered a gin and tonic. He wondered if she was meeting someone here or just killing time. His pulse kicked up a notch, and he was thankful that he already had one drink under his belt. It wasn't anger that made his heart beat faster this time, but excitement. He checked her hand for a ring. Nothing.

Looking into the mirror, this time at himself, he saw how his curly brown hair rolled out from under his cap. His already dark eyes looked even darker peering out at him from under the brim. He'd noticed how women looked at him and saw how they'd smile at him when he let his gaze linger. It never went further than a one-night stand. Nope, relationships weren't his thing. They went bad, usually quickly, just like everything else.

He had an idea. Getting up, he leaned toward the bar and told the bartender he needed to use the restroom, and he'd be right back. Turning to his right, he knocked the woman's jacket off the chair and bent down to pick it up. He slid it back onto the chair.

"Miss, your jacket fell," he said, and leaned in a little closer to her.

She turned and smiled. "Oh, thank you."

He smiled back and then continued to the restroom. The men's room was empty, so he took the small plastic bag out of his pocket and stuck it just inside the left sleeve of his shirt. He used the urinal, washed his hands, and then splashed water on his face. He looked directly into the eyes that looked back at him from the mirror. Showtime. He left to go back to his seat.

By the time he got back to the bar, the ball game had ended. The alcohol gave him the confidence he needed, and the words rolled right off his tongue. "Crap, I missed it!"

"The other team got a walk-off home run," the woman said.

Not giving a damn who won, he feigned disappointment. "I thought we had this one wrapped up."

"Well, I guess the other guys refused to get beat up like they did the other day." She gave him a quick once-over and held out her hand. "I'm Gwen."

"Nice to meet you, Gwen. I'm Luke." He let his hand linger, feeling certain that she had deemed him harmless. He grabbed a handful of nuts out of the small plastic bowl on the bar.

"Have you ever eaten here?" Gwen asked.

"No," he said, cautiously looking around. "I'm not sure I'd want to."

She laughed. "Safer to stick with the free peanuts."

"I take it you've never been here before?" he asked.

"No, I'm not from around here. I thought I would surprise a friend, but he wasn't home."

"Well, his loss," he said, putting on his most charming smile. "So, just killing time then?"

"I guess. Just got laid off from my second job this year. Thought maybe my friend had some connections."

"What kind of work do you do?" he asked.

"Accounting. But right now...anything that pays the bills."

He nodded his head in agreement. "I hear ya. I'm in the same boat. Lately I've had my hands in a little of this and a little of that."

"Yeah, it's hard all over," she said, holding up her almost empty glass.

"Let me get you another drink."

"Why not," Gwen stated. She excused herself and went to the restroom.

He waved to the bartender and ordered her another gin and tonic. He couldn't believe his luck. He removed the small plastic bag from his sleeve and cupped it in the palm of his hand. When the drink arrived, he asked for another slice of lime. As luck would have it, the bartender moved to the opposite side of the bar to wait on a newly arrived customer. With his hand slightly shaking, he dropped the powder into her drink, squeezed the second slice of lime into it, and mixed it with the straw. The only thing left to do was wait for her to return from the restroom.

An hour later, a man wearing a baseball cap helped a slightly tipsy woman into her jacket and out of the bar. In this neighborhood, that sort of thing happened every day.

CHAPTER 4

• • •

TWO DAYS LATER, EMMA LOOKED out of Kate's kitchen window and watched Jeremy pull the string back on the bow. His father stood behind him, positioning his arms while helping him find the right stance. His round, small face looked solemn as he focused on the blue-and-red target straight ahead of him. Slowly, his father backed away while Jeremy continued to hold his position. He let go, and the arrow shot high and flew over the top of the target. Jeremy turned toward his father with his shoulders slumped forward in defeat. Derrick approached his son and tousled his shaggy brown hair. Together, they ran to retrieve the arrow.

The interaction touched Emma in a way she hadn't seen coming. She wondered if she would ever see a child of her own learning something from his or her father. From David. And there it was. She'd been so adamant about not wanting commitment. Her mind replayed conversations she'd had with an old boyfriend and with her sister. She was so convinced that she didn't need anyone.

She finished drying the dishes while Kate sat at the kitchen table addressing envelopes. Derrick's family reunion was less than three weeks away, and the fliers needed to be mailed. Kate and Emma always joked about the Nelson reunion. Actually, they were a little jealous of them. The Nelsons were part of a large family with aunts, uncles, and lots of cousins, many of them still living in town. Derrick still saw them on a regular basis. There would be no reunions for Emma and Kate. It was just the two of them.

"How's he doing?" Kate asked without looking up.

"Well, he's not giving up."

Kate laughed. "I'm not surprised. He really wants to win that kid's archery competition at the reunion. How about you? Are you coming? You know you're always invited."

Emma glanced at Kate and then back out the window. "Not sure."

Kate stared at her sister's back for a few seconds and then went back to stuffing envelopes.

Emma stared out to the yard. "Do you think it's too late?"

Kate looked up. "Too late for what?"

"For this, what you and Derrick have."

Kate got up, walked to the window, and stood next to her. "Of course not. Where's this coming from?"

Emma shrugged and shook her head.

Kate put her arm around Emma. "You've been through a lot. It makes us think about…life."

"I look at you," Emma said. "You have a great husband, a great son, you're a great doctor—you have it all."

"You've been spending way too much time sitting in a hospital with nothing else to do but think." Kate sat down and got back to work. "This might be a good time to start your next book."

Emma looked at Kate. "Maybe you're right. I've been putting it off."

"You can still sit with David while you're doing it."

Emma nodded. It was good advice. "I always knew you'd make a great doctor."

Kate's progress came to a halt when she saw the clock. "Which reminds me, I have two patients to see at the clinic tonight. I'll have to finish this later," she said, scooping up the envelopes from the table.

"Go ahead. I'll finish cleaning up," Emma said, and started putting the dishes away. "It's the least I can do after eating all your lasagna."

Right after Kate ran upstairs to change, Emma heard the back door slam, and Jeremy came barreling into the kitchen.

"Mom! Aunt Emma! I did it! I hit the target. Not in the middle, but I hit it!"

Derrick was just steps behind his son. "Yep, he's getting the hang of it."

Jeremy, bubbling over with excitement, sprinted down the hall and then up the stairs to tell his mother.

Derrick sat down at the table and picked up one of the fliers. "You're coming, right?"

"Don't count on it. Nothing personal," said Emma.

"Kate said she'll drag you there if she has to."

Emma growled, "I don't doubt that she would."

Jeremy ran back into the kitchen and grabbed his father's hand. "Come on, Dad, I wanna shoot it again!"

The two of them went outside just as Kate reached the kitchen.

"So when will I see you again?" asked Kate.

"I'll stop by next week."

"Come for dinner again. It was nice having you here."

"Sounds good. Hey, have you gotten one of those letters lately?"

No clarification was needed. Both sisters knew what that meant. Over the years, they had both received letters from their father. Not on their birthdays, not on Christmas, just at random times.

Kate looked up from her chair where she was putting on her shoes. "No."

"Well, I did. It was more of a note than a letter, actually," Emma said. "Short, sweet, and to the point."

Kate's posture stiffened, and she shifted in her chair. "And the point being...what?"

"He said something about not being well and about having something he needed to tell me."

"We're big girls now," Kate said nonchalantly. "Maybe we should see what he wants."

Emma went on the defensive. "I don't care what he wants! Where was he when Mom died? We could have used some help then! He didn't care then. Why should we care now?"

"I don't want...this...to bother us anymore. Maybe it's time we dealt with it. Maybe we should see what he wants. Get closure."

"It's obvious to me! He's either playing games, or he's sick! Either way, I don't give a damn!" She was out of breath, her eyes were wild, and her face was flushed.

And for once, Kate seemed to have no idea what to say. She burst out laughing. It was the kind of laughter that makes your face hurt. She couldn't stop.

Emma's chin dropped, and her mouth flew wide open. She looked at Kate in disbelief. "You find that funny?"

Trying to catch her breath but unable to stop laughing, Kate held her finger up and managed to say, "Wait."

Emma stood there with her hands on her hips, waiting for Kate to calm down. This was not anywhere near the reaction she'd expected.

With her eyes watering from laughing so hard, Kate said, "I'm sorry, you looked so…flustered."

"Well, I'd rather look flustered than crazy."

"Just think about it. That's all I ask," said Kate. "Maybe it would be good for us both to get that closure." She stood up and walked toward Emma with her arms wide open. "Now hug me. I have to go, or I'll be late."

• • •

The receptionist at the Oakwood Clinic greeted Kate with a smile. She liked the way Dr. Nelson treated her patients. She'd heard another resident make negative comments about some of the people who came to the clinic. Her son came to see the doctor after he was diagnosed with a depressive disorder. He didn't have insurance, and Kate let him pay what he could afford. Since he'd been seeing her, he was doing well and had even been able to hold down a job. He liked their visits, and the medication she prescribed for him was working. She would definitely recommend Dr. Nelson to anyone.

"Nice to see you, Doctor," she said.

"Sorry I'm a little late," Kate said, looking around the empty waiting room. "Hope I didn't keep anyone waiting."

"Your first appointment had to cancel, but I was able to reschedule your seven o'clock one. He should be here soon."

"Thanks, Amy. I'll be updating some files. Send him in when he gets here."

Kate sat in the shared office that she used about two nights a week. It was bare-bones, as far as decor went. There was an old file cabinet in the corner and a large old desk that had seen better days. One drawer was broken and had been duct-taped shut a few years back. There was an area with two somewhat comfortable, high-backed chairs that Kate had actually picked up at an estate sale four years ago. She thought it too formal to sit behind a desk and expect people to open up to you.

The clinic was where she had done her internship, and she'd hoped to continue working there after, but spending cuts in mental health had nearly forced the clinic to close. She and a few other doctors decided to keep it running. They volunteered some of their time and oversaw the internship program. The clinic helped many people who otherwise wouldn't be able to afford treatment. Her mother dealt with depression as far back as she could remember. She couldn't afford treatment because she had two girls to support and found it difficult to make ends meet. Kate's father, whom she couldn't even remember, also battled depression. Mental illness could destroy a family, and she had seen it firsthand. Maybe her mother would still be alive if a clinic like this had been available then.

Ten minutes later, Amy knocked on the door and informed Kate that her client had arrived. Kate closed the file she had been working on, stood up, and walked to the door to greet him.

"Hi. Come on in. I want to hear about your week."

Luke came in, smiled at his doctor, and closed the door.

"Have a seat," she said, motioning to the two chairs to the left of the desk.

He sat down and folded his hands in his lap. He told her his week had gone better than he had hoped and that he'd met someone a few days ago.

"That's good," she said. "Tell me about it."

"We met by accident. We started talking, and one thing led to another."

Kate leaned forward and nodded her head, encouraging him to continue.

"She reminded me of someone," he said as his eyes took in Kate's wavy auburn hair. "Actually, a lot like someone I know."

"I'm happy for you. It's a start, and everything has to have a start."

He looked down at his hands before continuing. "It's still not easy."

"Remember what we said about that? The old adage?"

He remembered. "Anything worth having requires a little work."

"Right," said Kate.

Luke thought about it. "I'm sure it'll be worth it."

"Remember, life is all about putting the right pieces together," Kate said.

He nodded. That was exactly what he was doing. "So you think I should continue with it?"

"Absolutely. You're allowed to be happy, to make a life for yourself."

She was right. She always seemed to know what she was talking about. He needed someone on his side. He was glad it was her.

"What about Phil? Aren't you two friends?" she asked.

He didn't think of his coworker as a friend, really, although he pretended to be so Phil would get him the job with Sal. And he hooked him up as a client of Kate's. Some would consider that to be a friendship.

"Yes, we are," he lied.

"How's your anxiety level? Is the medicine helping?" Kate asked.

"It's better. The breathing exercises help. The medicine's good, too."

"So you're taking it as prescribed?"

He said he was, but he thought he needed another script.

Kate opened his chart to check. "It says here that you have enough medication for a couple more weeks." She closed his chart. "We can reevaluate that on your next visit and see if it needs to be adjusted."

Luke put on his best smile to hide his disappointment. "Sure." After all, he wasn't lying. He had just been…sharing it lately. He'd just have to cut his dose down a little more.

Kate skimmed through his treatment plan. "What activities are you interested in?"

"I like driving. It calms me. I like to read."

"Reading is good," said Kate. "What do you like to read?"

"Everything—nonfiction mostly."

"That can be very interesting," said Kate.

He waited for her to continue, to mention Emma's book, but she just changed the subject. It hit him like a slap in the face. He'd certainly offered enough of his personal information—or rather, some of it. Still, he felt she had snubbed him in a way. It wasn't right. He hid his irritation with her. It was something he had become very good at.

The rest of their session involved the usual talk about his...family. He didn't see how talking about his parents was relevant. They were gone, in the past, and they should stay there. It was the future that he was working on now. Yep, the doctor was right. He did deserve to be happy.

Kate opened his chart again and took out a piece of paper. "One more thing," she said, and handed it to him. "This is part of the initial paperwork I had you sign. This paper gives me permission to talk to the doctor you used to see. It can help me with your treatment plan. Would you like to sign it now?"

He picked it up and examined it. He'd told her some things about his earlier life and his hospitalizations, so why not? "Sure." He took the pen from her and signed his name.

When their session ended, Kate saw him to the door and told him to see Amy to set up his next appointment. She went back to the desk to prepare for her next client. Luke was guarded, and she knew he wasn't telling his whole story. He'd suffered from neglect as a child, and still had a rough time connecting with anyone, but at least he was dealing with it. There were things about her own childhood that she hadn't fully dealt with. Maybe it was time to do just that. She decided she would call Emma on her way home tonight.

• • •

Voices…the TV…maybe a radio. Someone talking. What were they saying?

She opened her eyes but could only manage to keep them open for a few seconds at a time.

Blurry, spinning…so nauseous.

She blinked several times, trying to focus.

Too foggy.

Gwen tried to sit up, but the pounding in her head was too intense.

What happened? Am I sick? Can't remember. Is it morning? Night? Where am I? On a bed…but whose bed? The bar. I was at a bar. The man, what was his name? Why can't I remember?

Then she remembered having a drink. Or two. Not enough to feel *this* way. As the fog started to thin, she tried to swallow, but her throat was too dry. Her tongue felt like cotton and stuck to her lips when she tried to moisten them. On her left, she could make out a table with a…bottle on it. She pushed aside the heavy blanket that covered her. When she stretched her arm to reach for the bottle, she bumped something else with the back of her hand and heard it hit the floor. Determined to get the bottle, she rolled onto her side. Her body seemed weighted down, and it took all of her strength to swing her legs off the side of the bed. While trying to ignore the pounding in her head, she pushed herself up into a sitting position. The room spun wildly. Gwen planted her hands on either side of her and waited for it to stop.

Now she could see that the bottle was half-full of something orange. She picked it up and fumbled with the lid.

Damn! Why don't my fingers work?

When she was finally able to get it open, she took several large gulps, some of which dripped down the front of her shirt.

Orange pop. Did I put it there?

So many questions she couldn't answer. As she took in her surroundings, she saw what she had knocked off the table. It was a small lamp.

Looking up behind the bed, she saw a window near the ceiling. It was made of glass blocks, and light was coming through it. The room was like a box with cement walls. It smelled musty, and the air was damp.

OK, I'm in a basement. Whose basement? His basement? What was his name? Luke. How'd I get here?

Directly in front of her was the door. She drank the rest of the orange pop and stood up.

Time to go.

The first step was easy. When she tried to take another one, something tugged at her and she almost tripped. Gwen looked down in disbelief. Something was tied to her ankle. Her eyes followed the cord to the foot of the bed. She was tied to the bed.

What kind of game is this?

Confusion transformed to panic. She backed up to the bed, eased herself down, and pulled at the material around her ankle. The knot was too tight. Adrenaline surged through her, and she tried desperately to slip her ankle out of it. She looked around for anything that she could use to pick at it but found nothing. The voices she thought she heard before were starting again. She stilled herself, held her breath, and strained to listen. The floorboards creaked, and she heard two men talking. As she listened for a few minutes more, she realized it wasn't two voices but one man talking—no, arguing—with himself.

What the hell is going on?

She was overcome by nausea and lay back down on the bed. Fear flooded every cell in her body as she pulled the blanket up and listened.

• • •

Bad thoughts piled up in his head, and he couldn't shake them loose. The faint whispers echoed in the distance and would eventually surround him. There was nowhere to hide. He dumped the remaining pills out of the bottle and counted them. There wasn't enough left to keep *them* at bay for very long. Two days' worth were wasted on the old woman, and now he had someone else he needed to share them with. He put two pills in his mouth and washed them down with the rum he found hidden behind some canned green beans in the pantry. Booze gave the medicine a kick, and he needed it now that *she* wouldn't write him another script. He'd figure something out. He always did.

• • •

At that very same moment, Emma set her laptop down on the bedside table in David's hospital room as a code blue was called on the overhead speaker to the room next door. Within minutes, the sound of pounding feet slapped the tile floor, getting closer and closer, until frantic voices seeped through the wall behind Emma.

Earlier, she saw a woman in the next room sitting in a chair exactly like the one she was sitting in now. It just as easily could have been David that those people were racing to get to. She didn't know the woman, yet they had so much in common. She held David's hand and waited out the crisis that was taking place just feet from where she sat. At first there were several voices, and then there was no sound at all. Then only a woman's voice, sobbing. It was hard not to feel guilty for being thankful it wasn't her in the woman's place.

Emma turned the volume up on the small TV that hung on a metal arm next to the bed. She flipped her laptop open but couldn't concentrate. The conversation she had with her sister about their father's letter came to mind. It wasn't the first time Kate had talked about seeing him. When Kate was little, she'd make up stories about all the things they'd do together when he came home. Back then, part of Emma wanted to believe it could be true. It never happened. When Emma was twenty-one, he'd sent her a letter asking if they could get together the following summer. By that time, she was independent and had built a strong wall around her and Kate. It was safer that way. She never wrote him back. She was in the middle of that daydream when Paul walked in.

"What was all the commotion a little while ago?" he asked. "They wouldn't let anyone come down the hall."

"There was an emergency in the next room," Emma said. "I don't think it ended well."

Paul pulled a chair up to the bed and sat next to his brother. It had become a daily ritual for him to tell David what was going on in the business. Emma was listening to Paul's report when her cell phone rang. It was Kate. Emma told Paul good-bye and walked into the hallway.

"Hey, Kate, what's up?"

"I've got an idea," Kate said.

Emma knew immediately that it wasn't going to be good.

• • •

The next morning, Emma stopped at Nolan Street and told Paul she had agreed to go up north with Kate to see their father. He was surprised. He knew a little about her childhood and told her he didn't see the point of it.

"Believe me, I don't, either, but I'll be back by Sunday—Saturday night, if I can help it," she said. "If anything changes with David—"

"I'll call you."

On the way out, Emma ran into Joyce. She was arranging boxes in the garage. Sal and one of his workers were helping her scoot a larger one out of the way.

Joyce was surprised to see her. "Did Paul tell you we'll be moving in about a week earlier than we expected?"

"That's great news."

"Hey, I'd like to thank you for helping with the painting. Can I take you to lunch this weekend?"

"That's really nice, but I'm going out of town with my sister for a couple days. We're leaving tomorrow afternoon."

"Sounds like fun. Where are you headed?" asked Joyce.

"I wish it was for fun. Actually, we have some rather unpleasant family business to take care of up north. In the upper peninsula."

Both women jumped when a large box came crashing down on the garage floor directly behind them.

"I'm so sorry," said the worker as he bent down. His hat fell off, spilling out his curly dark hair. "I tripped."

Sal walked back into the garage when he heard the loud bang. "If anything's broken, we'll take care of it," he said, and then glared at the worker.

Joyce looked at her writing on the top of the box. "Nothing breakable in here. Just some metal canning pots."

The worker apologized for scaring them, and put the box back in its place.

"Maybe we can have lunch next week," said Joyce.

"I'd like that."

• • •

That night, Luke threw a few things in a bag and set it down by the back door of the farmhouse. He rummaged through the fridge and took out some cheese and a half gallon of lemonade. After getting a box of crackers and a half loaf of bread from the cupboard, he put it all on a tray to carry to the basement. He stacked the magazines that he'd found in the old lady's bedroom next to the food. Next, he crushed more of his medicine and some over-the-counter sleeping pills into powder. He put the mixture into the lemonade and gave it a good shake.

He checked on her, using the peephole in the door, before sliding the tray in. She'd be able to reach it when she woke up. He put some other supplies in the room as well. There was nothing he needed from her just yet, so he closed the door and went back upstairs.

Luke cracked open a beer and guzzled more than half of it. He swallowed one of his pills and put another in his pocket for later. His anger at Kate for not giving him another script had intensified. After all this time, he thought they had a better relationship than that. Right now, there was nothing he could do about it. There were other things that needed his attention.

It had been years since he'd been up north, but the latest development warranted some action. On the way out the back door, he grabbed the bag he'd packed and headed to the barn. He tossed his bag onto the passenger seat and drove down the driveway. It would be dark soon, and he knew he'd have to drive through the night. He didn't need this right now, but he was left with no other choice.

CHAPTER 5

• • •

ON FRIDAY EVENING, THE HIGHWAY was packed with travelers making the trek up north for the weekend. They had been on the road four and a half hours, and Emma regretted letting Kate talk her into such a ridiculous idea. What could they possibly gain by this trip? It was nothing but a waste of time. She stared out the window, pretending to listen while Kate rambled on about absolutely nothing.

"And Derrick called her, and she said she wasn't coming because of what his aunt said to her at the reunion last year. Can you believe that?"

Emma sensed that Kate had stopped talking when she mumbled, "What?" but continued to stare out the window.

"I said, 'Did you see the comet that landed on the road?'"

Emma mumbled, "Yeah."

"Emma?" Kate said. "You haven't heard anything I've said, have you?"

Emma looked at her sister but didn't apologize. Finally she said, "This was a mistake."

"Look, we made the decision to do this. Can't we just make the best of it?"

"There is no 'best of it' that I can see," Emma said, holding her cell phone in the air and trying to get a signal. "I can't even make a damn call."

"If anything changes, Paul said he'd let you know."

She gave up on the phone and threw it into the backseat.

"Emma, we'll be home day after tomorrow. How about we enjoy the scenery, if nothing else?"

Emma purposely ignored the pleasantries that Kate was trying to feed her. "I just hope you're not going to be too disappointed."

Kate kept her eyes on the road. "I have no expectations."

She slapped Kate's leg. "Well, of course you do. You think a quick visit to 'Daddy' and you'll have all kinds of answers." She let out a chuckle. "I know you."

"Ouch."

Emma crossed her arms. "Tell me it's not true."

"It's not. Anyway, isn't this why we didn't tell him we were coming? So we could catch him off guard?"

"I guess," said Emma. It was the first thing they had been able to agree on all day. She wanted to end the conversation on a good note, so she turned the radio up a little. The Mackinac Bridge appeared over the treetops in the distance straight up ahead.

Silence was never one of Kate's strong suits. She liked to talk, and started spurting out facts about the bridge as they approached it.

"The Mighty Mac," Kate stated, "is fifty-seven years old and five miles long, and it's the fifth-longest suspension bridge in the world, but it's the longest in the western hemisphere." She gave Emma a look that said she thought she couldn't live another moment without that information.

Emma just wanted her to stop talking. "What—are you a member of the bridge authority or something?"

The sarcasm didn't slow Kate down. "Did you know that it is solely maintained by tolls and fees collected right here on the bridge?"

Emma rested her head against the car window and looked up at the huge wire cables that ran the length of the bridge. She wondered if Kate would shut up if the cables snapped and they plummeted seventy-five feet into the cold, deep water below.

Kate slapped Emma's arm. "Come on, can't you just lighten up?"

"Will there be a quiz after this lesson?"

Kate started laughing. "Jeremy did a report on it last year. He'd be proud that I still remembered all of it."

They crossed the Mackinac Bridge just before sunset and decided to find a motel and some food. They would drive the last hour or so in the morning. Emma wished she had left the envelope with his address on it in her trash. She hoped he wouldn't be home.

● ● ●

About two hundred and fifty miles south, in the basement of an old farmhouse, Gwen opened her eyes. It took a minute, but the reality of her situation thundered back. The room seemed to sway, reminding her of summers spent on her aunt's boat. How long had it been since she'd heard him talking to himself? There was no light coming through the little window above the bed now. Great. It was too dark to see anything. She was thirsty again and needed to pee. Then she remembered the lamp. She slid off the bed and reached around until her hand found it. She felt for the switch and turned it on. What she saw sent a chill through her, even more than the dampness in the room had managed to do. There was a tray on the floor near the door. On it was a plastic jug, some food, and—books? *He* was here. And he was planning on keeping her here. How long, and for what?

● ● ●

The next morning, the sun was bright, which didn't help the fact that Emma had the mother of all headaches. She'd tossed and turned all night and was unsure if the motel bed was to blame—or just the sheer dread she felt for the day ahead. In the car, she flipped the visor down and laid her head back on the headrest while Kate programmed her GPS.

"There," said Kate. "We should be there in just over an hour."

Emma rolled her eyes. "Goody."

For the first time since they'd left home, Kate's expression said she'd had more than enough of Emma's oppositional attitude. "Emma, what makes you think it's going to be so horrible?"

"How could it be anything else?" She took a deep breath. "Anyway, it doesn't matter." She closed her eyes and mumbled, more to herself, "I'm just going for you." Then she opened her eyes and looked hard at Kate. "What is it you really hope to get out of this?"

Kate's lips formed a tight line and then relaxed. "You remember him. I don't. Maybe I…just want to meet him."

Deep down, Emma knew she couldn't hold that against Kate. She did remember him. She sat up a little straighter and tried to ignore the pounding in her head. "Let's do this then."

• • •

The shoreline of Lake Michigan stretched for miles and miles. Large rocks dotted the sand until the rolling waves crashed over them and then, seconds later, receded again. Cars were parked on the roadside, and people walked over the sandy, grassy hills that led to the water where they would set up camp for the day. It had been a long time since she'd seen this endless coastline.

Emma remembered that summer before her childhood changed forever, when they'd stayed in a cottage somewhere on this long stretch of highway. She remembered playing on the beach and jumping into the waves. Her mother chased her and slathered sunscreen on her that smelled like coconut, and they ate sandwiches that they'd packed in the picnic basket with the broken handle. Her father would swim with her and pretend to be a sea monster looking for lunch. She would squeal and laugh as she ran to her mother to be saved. Little did she know that it was all about to end. Kate was too young to remember any of it.

After checking the screen on the GPS, Kate said, "Looks like we turn right at the next road. It shouldn't be too far from there."

"OK," Emma said in the most pleasant voice she could muster. She knew that she was done giving Kate a hard time. After all, she was only there to protect Kate, just as she'd always done. There was comfort in knowing that soon the whole unpleasant experience would be over, and they could finally put this part of their lives in the rearview mirror where it belonged.

The town of Ellington sat nestled between two major lakes. The main road curved around the smaller lake and went straight through the town. Fishing was obviously a high priority in the area, due to the fact that four of the nine businesses on the main street were bait shops or sporting-goods stores. The souvenir shops were packed with tourists, and the ice-cream parlor had a line that started outside the building. Golf carts and ATVs appeared to be the chosen form of transportation for the locals. The scene would have looked inviting and festive to Emma, if only their reason for being there could have been something different.

After turning right on the next street, they were only moments away. Most of the houses were small and looked like summer cottages. It was obvious that some had been vacant for quite a while. The grass hadn't been cut, and the yards looked as if they could definitely use a good cleanup. A little further down the street, they came to a larger house that was situated near the road. Behind it was a row of smaller dwellings. One of them had the address on it they were looking for. There was no sign of a vehicle or any other indication that someone might be home. A single pot sat on the porch and looked as if it had flowers or a plant in it at one time, but now it was just some dried-up vines. They pulled into the shared driveway. Kate made the first move and got out of the car. She looked back at Emma.

"Are you coming?"

The two women walked up the steps and stood on the small porch. Kate knocked on the door. Nothing. She knocked again, this time a little harder. Still nothing. Emma was definitely breathing easier, reveling in relief. The feeling was short-lived.

"Hello," came a voice from somewhere behind them. "Can I help you with something?" An older woman wearing a bright, flowered bathrobe and flip-flops sashayed toward them. Kate stepped off the porch and met her on the sidewalk.

"Great," Emma said, and reluctantly followed.

"We're looking for the man who lives here. Do you know him?" Kate asked, pointing back at the small house.

The woman stared at the sisters, obviously sizing them up. "Who's asking?"

"We just want to talk to him. Do you know where he is?" Kate asked.

"I'm the landlady. I'm not sure I should say," she said matter-of-factly.

It was clear she wasn't planning on being cooperative. Emma stepped forward. "We're family. I'm Emma, and this is Kate."

The woman's eyes narrowed. "Family, huh? Peter never mentioned any family. And now they're coming out of the woodwork."

Emma pulled the letter out of her pocket and held it out to her. "Actually, he's our father."

The woman's chin dropped, and she looked at Emma suspiciously while reaching for the letter. Her eyes scanned the handwritten note. "Well, I'll be damned. You think you know someone..." she said, shaking her head.

"Do you know when he'll be back?" Kate asked.

The woman's face softened for the first time. "I don't know. He's been sick awhile."

"So is he in a hospital?" asked Kate.

"He was. He thought he'd be coming back a week or two ago, but he called last week to say he was being moved to a rehab facility."

Not that she cared, but Emma asked anyway, "So what's wrong with him?"

"I take it you haven't seen him for a while?" asked the woman.

"No," said Emma, "not for a very long time."

The woman hesitated a minute. "He liked the bottle—liver problems, I guess. Hasn't drunk in a few years, but that sort of thing has a way of catching up to you."

"Do you know where we can find him?" asked Kate.

"I have the name of the place and the phone number written down." The woman turned and pointed toward her house. "I'll go get it for you."

Emma wanted nothing more to do with the situation. "Do you really want to go through with this?"

"Yes. We've come this far. Let's finish it."

The woman returned a minute later and handed Kate a piece of paper. "I'm Lorraine Moore. I put my number on there, and here's the information I gave to his brother yesterday."

Kate looked at Emma questioningly.

Emma said, "He doesn't have a brother, as far as we know."

"I didn't know he had daughters, either, till today." The woman shrugged. "That's what the guy said, anyway. I've been renting to Peter for years, and he rarely had company. As I said, he never even mentioned any family. There was a lady friend, though, who came by now and then. Haven't seen her in a while."

"Thank you for your time, Miss Moore. You've been very helpful," said Kate.

"When you see him, could you let him know that I'll be needing his stuff out if he's not back in a couple weeks? He's a good renter, but I gotta make a living, ya know?"

"We understand," said Kate.

As they got back into the car, Kate asked, "Brother?"

Emma shook her head. "Don't ask me. Mom said that he only had a sister who left home when she was eighteen."

• • •

Evergreen Rehabilitation Center was located two miles north of the highway in the town of Hillsdale. The main street looked as though it had been a business district back in its day. Now the buildings were more than a little worn out, and some were in desperate need of structural repair. The three-story brownstone building that housed the center looked as if it had been built around the same time as the other buildings but had been lucky enough to warrant the attention the other structures hadn't.

They parked near a fenced-in area that was full of tables and chairs. A wrought-iron fence bordered the courtyard and was connected to a breezeway, which consisted of mostly windows. People were sitting at the tables, some were in wheelchairs, and still more people were being ushered out to the gated area. A woman was handing out books and magazines while a man pushed a small cart around, filling cups from a pitcher and passing them out.

Kate and Emma entered the building through the main entrance and stepped into a spacious lobby that had high ceilings with elaborate wood-work designs. It made Emma think of an old hotel. Furniture was set up in small groupings, some with tables in the center. On one side of the lobby, a group of people was visiting a man who was hooked up to a portable oxygen tank. On the right side, an elderly woman pleaded with a younger man and little girl to take her home with them. At the back of the room was a reception desk and double doors directly next to it. A woman was sitting behind the glassed-in area, talking on the phone. She smiled and signaled to them that she'd be with them in a minute. After she hung up, she slid open the glass window.

"Can I help you?" she asked.

Kate spoke first. "We're here to see Peter Simms."

The woman's eyes grew large and round, and she stared back at Kate without blinking. After a few seconds, she snapped out of her trance and stood up so fast that her chair rolled back and hit a metal file cabinet. She politely asked them to wait, scurried through a side door, and was gone.

"That was odd," said Kate.

"I'd say she looked surprised to see us," said Emma.

Five minutes later, they were beginning to think that the woman had forgotten about them, when the double doors next to the desk swung open. Out came a short, stocky woman with bright red hair, dressed in a dark suit jacket and skirt, followed by a tall, thin man in his forties. The duo approached them as if they were on a mission. The woman's expression was dour but seemed to mix with concern as she got closer.

She held her hand out to Emma and then Kate. "I am Sonja Westmore, nursing supervisor of the facility, and this is Detective Mark Billings."

As soon as the introductions were made, Kate looked at the man. "Detective?"

He stood silent and let the woman speak.

"I am going to have to ask about the nature of your business with Mr. Simms."

Emma got right to the point. "We're his daughters."

The woman gave them a weighted stare while she opened a manila folder that she had tucked under her arm. She skimmed through it and then looked up. "I'm afraid neither of you are listed in his family history." She closed the folder and looked at them, apparently waiting for an explanation.

"It doesn't surprise me we're not," Emma said. "He hasn't seen either of us since we were very young."

"It's just the timing..." the woman said, turning to the man as if hoping he would finish her sentence.

He took a step forward. "What Sonja here is saying is that there's been an incident involving your father."

The girls were confused but waited for him to continue.

The detective motioned toward the double doors. "Would you mind coming with us to Sonja's office? I have a few questions I'd like to ask you both."

"I'm sorry, but we don't know anything about him," insisted Emma. "He doesn't even know we're here."

Kate was digesting the conversation when she suddenly spoke up. "Wait." She held up her hand. "You said there was an incident. What exactly does that mean?"

The woman scanned the lobby. "Please come with us. This really isn't something we should discuss here," she pleaded.

They agreed to follow the pair through the double doors. The inside of the building didn't look as old as the lobby. It had probably been renovated within the past decade or so. They followed them to another wing that looked more modern and held several offices and what looked like a large conference room. They were directed into an office at the end of the hall. Two desks were in it; one was empty, but sitting at the other was a young woman who looked up as they entered. Sonja asked the woman to give them some privacy. She gathered some paperwork and left the room.

Sonja touched the back of one of the chairs in front of her desk. "Please. Have a seat," she said, and took hers behind it.

"What's this about?" asked Kate. "And why are you here?" she said, turning her attention to the detective.

"First, I need to see both of your identifications before we can continue," he said.

Kate reached into her purse for her driver's license, and Emma followed suit. The detective remained standing and took a picture of each of their licenses. He handed them back and then took a seat at the side of the desk. "I'm sorry to inform you that Peter Simms passed away yesterday afternoon." He let the statement hang so they could absorb the news. "And I'm here because he didn't die from natural causes."

Kate's jaw dropped.

Emma faced him. "What exactly did he die from?"

Sonja looked at the detective. "They're not on the release of information form. I'm not sure where we even stand legally…"

Emma stood and pointed her finger at Sonja. "You're the one who brought us back here. Either you tell us what's going on now, or we're leaving."

The detective stood. "Please, sit down, and we'll tell you what happened." He nodded at Sonja, encouraging her to continue.

The woman let out a ragged-sounding breath and relaxed into the back of her chair. "All right, first let me say that we've never had anything like this happen here before."

"What happened?" Emma asked.

"He died from asphyxiation," said Sonja.

"Asphyxiation?" asked Kate.

"Yesterday afternoon there was a bingo game in the activity room," Sonja said. "One of the staff wheeled him in there. He seemed to like going to the activities, so they took him in, wheelchair and all. When she went back to get him, well, he wasn't there."

"Where was he?" asked Kate.

They listened to Sonja's story about how a doctor entering the facility from an employee entrance noticed him sitting in his wheelchair. As the doctor got closer, he could tell something was wrong. Peter was leaning over to one side of the chair, and his oxygen tubing was draped around his neck and shoulders. He wasn't breathing, and the doctor tried to help him, but it was too late. When she finished the story, she was out of breath and looked exhausted.

The story was horrible, but Emma felt no personal loss. He was just a sickly man who died in a nursing home. When she looked at Kate, she saw something much different. She rested her hand on Kate's shoulder. "Are you all right?"

Kate shooed her hand away and twisted in her chair to face the detective. "So you're saying someone murdered him?"

"Yes, there's enough evidence to suggest that. We've ruled it a homicide," he said.

Sonja looked up and blurted out, "He couldn't have been there very long. We do rounds every fifteen minutes, and there's always staff in the halls."

"We're not going to sue you, if that's what you're thinking," Emma said.

The detective changed the subject. "I guess I'm interested in why you chose to visit your father now, after all these years, and the day after he was murdered."

Emma leaned forward. "He sent me a letter. Said he had something he needed to tell me."

"He didn't say what it was?" Detective Billings asked.

"No. He left his phone number and asked me to call him."

"Did you?"

"No."

"Then how did you know he was here?"

"We showed up at his address today, and his landlady told us where to find him," Emma said.

"Yes," he said. "I'll have to speak with her and see who else knew he was here."

Kate spoke up. "She told someone else yesterday."

The detective perked up. "And who was that?"

"His brother," Emma answered.

"Where can I find him?"

"You can't," said Emma. "He doesn't have a brother."

"So any idea who it might have been?"

Emma was tired of this game and refused to hide it. "What didn't you understand when we said we knew nothing about Peter Simms?"

"All right," he said. "I'm sorry, but there's something I have to ask. Where were you both yesterday afternoon?"

Emma's body visibly stiffened. "About four hundred miles south of here, at home. Any more questions?" She stared at him, daring him to say something.

"Look," said Kate. "It was my idea to come see him. Granted, what happened to him is awful, but it has nothing to do with us."

The detective was persistent. "I'm sorry, but you have to admit it's odd that you arrived here the day after..."

Emma was on her feet again. "I think we're done here," she snapped.

"Just one more thing. I'd like you to look at a surveillance tape and tell us if you recognize anyone on it," he said.

Emma wanted to leave. As far as she was concerned, the situation no longer warranted any more of their time. "Look, we don't know anyone who lives here. We can't help you."

"Please don't make me insist," said the detective. "It'll only take a few more minutes."

Emma shifted from one foot to the other.

"Sure, show us the tape," Kate said.

Ten minutes later, they were sitting in the security office watching a surveillance video. The picture was a little grainy, but it probably never mattered before now. The town didn't look like a place that had to deal with more than maybe a stolen golf cart or an occasional rowdy tourist. The video showed people entering and leaving the building through the main entrance.

"We're not watching the whole thing," said Emma.

"No. I'm skipping ahead," he said. "There. This is the part I want to show you."

The monitor showed a group of people entering first. After them came a couple with two children; a minute later, two men; then an older woman using a cane; and then a man wearing a dark baseball hat.

"Anyone look familiar?"

"We don't know any of those people," said Emma.

"Is one of them a suspect?" asked Kate.

The detective hesitated. "We have all of them on tape as they left for the day, with the exception of the man wearing the cap. He must have left through an employee exit. We're interested in talking to him. Another patient who usually sits with Peter saw him leave the room with a man yesterday. No one saw him after that, not until the doctor found him."

Emma stood up first. "If there's nothing else, we need to go. We have a long ride ahead of us."

"Oh, in case I need to reach you?" said the detective. "And any other family we should notify regarding collection of the deceased?"

"Not that I know of," said Emma.

Kate reached into her purse and handed him one of her business cards.

Five minutes later, with the sun in her eyes, Emma found herself just about running to keep up with Kate in the parking lot. Kate hit the button on her key fob, popped the door open, and got in the passenger seat.

"Sure, I'll drive," Emma said sarcastically, and got behind the wheel. When she pulled out of the parking lot, she snuck a peek at Kate, trying to gauge her mood, but her face was impassive. Dread, which had hovered over her head constantly since they'd left home, swooped down again. She tried to dodge it. Talking about feelings wasn't her strong suit. It was Kate's. And she wasn't talking. Emma had driven through and out of the small town before she had the nerve to say anything.

"I need to know if you're all right."

Kate stared out her window at the lake and then down at her hands before speaking. "A day late."

It didn't answer the question, but at least she was talking. She tried another angle. "Want to get something to eat before we head home?"

Kate went back to staring at the lake and didn't answer.

Emma drove along the coastline for another twenty minutes before she found a market. The sign advertised smoked fish and homemade pastries. She swung the car into the parking lot. "What do you have a taste for?"

Silence.

"All right, then," Emma said. She hopped out of the car and turned back, resting her hands on the roof. She searched her brain. Nothing she could say would make it all better, but she could probably manage to make it worse.

"I'll be right back," was the safest thing she could think of.

● ● ●

Luke sat up and swung his legs off the couch. He knew he'd drunk too much last night because the light hurt his eyes, and he needed to vomit. Saliva pooled in his mouth, and his stomach muscles began to contract. He staggered to the bathroom, fell to his knees, and hugged the toilet bowl. His stomach let loose, and he heaved up mostly liquid. His mind did a backflip to the previous day. It sickened him. He bent over the toilet again. After the second wave passed, he stood up, leaned over the sink, and splashed cold water on his face. He cupped his hands, filled them with water, and rinsed out his mouth. The putrid aftertaste almost caused the event to repeat itself. He got back to the couch using the walls to steady himself.

Sleep evaded him, so he stared at the ceiling. It was too bright in the living room to sleep, anyway. He thought about how he'd sat outside the old man's house and that neighbor who walked up to his truck. It amazed him how gullible people were. Did that guy really think he'd want to rent one of those dumps? And the lady giving out information so easily. And Peter. Luke only wanted to talk to him…If only he had been more…reasonable. He used to understand…He used to talk about how they could all be together. *It was all a lie!* He was no better than everyone else who'd lied to him. He saw it in Peter's eyes and the ugly way the old man's face twisted when he said to stay away from them. He pointed at Luke and said there was something wrong with him, that he was unstable. Then everything slowed down, and Peter's voice echoed, as if it was in a tunnel. Luke's arms felt numb, and his knees wobbled. Then he saw hands, *his hands, wrapping and wrapping…tighter and tighter. Quiet!* And then everything was quiet.

He closed his eyes and put his hands over them. It happened, and he couldn't take it back. The walls were closing in. And then he thought about Sal. He could lose his job for calling in sick again. He needed to be there, to keep an eye on things. He rolled onto his side and faced the back of the couch, his body slowly rocking. *Breathe, breathe.* At least he didn't have to be anywhere today.

• • •

Emma emerged from the market with a bag of smoked fish, crackers, and cheese curds. She also picked up a box of chocolate walnut fudge for Jeremy. She'd left her sunglasses in the car again, and was squinting as she walked through the parking lot. When she slid into the car, she announced, "Lunch." Kate wasn't in the car. Emma dropped the bag on the seat and jumped out. Thinking that Kate must have gone into the market, she started heading back. Just before she reached the door, she turned and checked the parking lot again. She saw Kate across the road, standing at the edge of the water. While waiting for the traffic to clear, she thought, now what? When she got to the beach, she stood next to Kate. The wind whipped freely, with no houses or structures standing in its path, and was able to drown out all sound from the street. Kate sat down in the sand.

"Now I'll never get the chance," Kate said.

Emma sat down next to her. She wasn't feeling what Kate was. She'd outrun the past a long time ago. Or did she? "Maybe," Emma said, "you don't need that chance."

Kate looked at Emma, tears running off her chin. "I just wanted to know..." She anxiously wiped at her eyes, and grains of sand blowing in the wind began sticking to her wet face. "I thought...maybe if I met him, I could understand..."

"Maybe there's nothing to understand," said Emma. "I know you think there's a reason for everything. Maybe there isn't always one." She watched the seagulls hover low over the sand, looking for an easy meal. "Maybe everyone just does what they know how to do. I mean, the past gets under your skin, but you know how you want your future to go. Me? Maybe I can be good leaving the past where it is, but I'm not so good with the future." The vulnerability of admitting it washed over her. "But what do I know?"

"Aren't you curious about what he was like or...heredity...mental health?"

"You mean because Mom checked out and Dad got himself murdered?" Emma regretted it the second it left her lips.

Kate choked back sobs and tried to talk at the same time. "What does that say about us?"

Emma wanted it all to be simple and had always managed to keep her life that way. She put her arm around Kate and gave her a squeeze. "We're not them. That's all. We're not them."

They sat there looking out over the water, taking in the vastness and rhythm of the waves as they watched seagulls swirl in the air and fly away until they turned into nothing but dots against the distant sky.

Forty minutes into the drive home, they approached the road they had visited just hours before. Emma slowed the car and turned left instead of heading straight to the Mackinac Bridge.

"Why are you turning here?" Kate asked.

"I have an idea. The landlady said she wanted his stuff out, right? Well, what if I tell her what happened? Offer to pay to get his stuff out?"

"And why would you want to do that?"

"So she'll let us in his place. Maybe we can get a feel for what he was about. It might not be good. I mean, he got himself killed, and we might not like what we find."

Kate needed only a second to think about it. She knew Emma was right. He was gone, and this was a chance to see into his world, good or bad.

A half hour later, the landlady walked out of the main house with Emma in tow. Emma signaled to Kate to follow them. The woman said she was sorry about what happened to her renter, said he seemed like a nice man, and let them into his house before returning to her own.

They stood in the doorway, getting their first glimpse into the life of a man they didn't know. The place was tiny and would work better as a summer cottage than it would a year-round residence. The kitchen and living room were actually one room. To the right was the bathroom, built to scale, and next to it was the bedroom. The room was barely large enough for a double bed and a dresser. Emma took one step into the bedroom and hesitated. The man had few possessions. An alarm clock, a dish with coins in it, a stopwatch, and a shiny ceramic plate with an impression of a small hand on it were the only things out in the open. She picked up the plate and turned it over. The letters *E. R. S.* were scraped into the bottom. Emma Rose Simms. She put it down as if it was hot.

She opened the top dresser drawer. It was filled with clothes. The second one was more of the same. In the bottom drawer, she found a few towels, and underneath them was a white shirt box. Next to it were several loose pictures; some were black and white. When she opened the shirt box, she froze. Right on top was a picture of a little girl and a baby. There was no doubt about who they were—her mother had a picture just like it. The baby had a full head of reddish curly hair, and the little girl paled in comparison, with her ordinary thin brown hair that fell barely past her chin. It made her laugh because her hair didn't look much different now.

She thumbed through the pictures and found more snapshots of the same little girls, but one in particular got her attention. A family picture. Kate was sitting on their mother's lap, and Emma was standing between their mother and father. His arm was around her shoulder. She and Kate were wearing red velvet dresses, her mother was wearing a cream-colored dress with ruffles around the neckline, and her father wore a white shirt and a plaid vest.

Underneath the pictures were a few newspaper articles. On one, the headline read, "Free Clinic to Remain Open." She knew as she skimmed through the first paragraph what she would find. A name. Her sister's. The clinic where Kate had volunteered. She was being hailed as one of the doctors who saved the program and supervised the new residents. Another paper was behind it, fastened by a paperclip. She flipped it over and saw a picture of Kate and Derrick. It was an engagement announcement that Derrick's mother put in their church paper. Under that was another newspaper clipping, this one about her. It was an article outlining an interview she'd had with a local paper right after her first book came out. She put all the clippings back in the box and picked up the silver stopwatch. Her fingers worked the watch stem and found it still worked.

"Hey," said Kate, as she stepped into the room. "He had good taste." She tossed a book to Emma.

Emma caught it with one hand, and with the other, she slid the stopwatch into her pocket. She knew what book it was before she flipped it over. It was her book, *Lost Days.* A few pages had been folded over to make a bookmark. She opened it to that spot and saw it was the chapter that told the story about the summer he left. It made her pause a moment before she dropped it on the bed. She picked up the white shirt box and handed it to Kate.

"Take a look at this."

Emma's fingers traced the round shape concealed in her pocket and wondered why she took it. As Kate leafed through the box, Emma's cell phone rang. It was Paul. The connection was poor, and then she lost the call. "I'm going outside to call him back," she said to Kate.

Kate went through the box, looking at the pictures and then the newspaper articles. She carried it to the living room just in time to see Emma come flying through the door as if she was being chased.

"We have to go now! David woke up."

CHAPTER 6

• • •

KATE PULLED INTO EMMA'S DRIVEWAY at 9:35 p.m. They had made it home in record time without getting a speeding ticket. The trip up north had been emotionally draining, but as she hopped into her car, Emma's energy level was high, fueled by excitement about seeing David. The feeling that life would soon get back to normal gave her the zest that had lain dormant these past few weeks.

She walked through the hospital corridors with a renewed sense of purpose. So many things went through her mind as she dodged several groups of people. She would finally be able to tell David the things she should have said before. After getting off the elevator on the second floor, she made a right and could see David's room at the end of the hall. Lena was standing just outside the door and started walking toward her. They met just a few feet from the room.

Lena stopped directly in front of her. "Wait," she said, as Emma tried to see around her into the room. "He started talking only a few minutes ago, and he's still not really with it."

Emma smiled and took another step, trying to dodge her, when Paul came out of David's room.

"Emma," he said softly, putting his hands on her shoulders, "you can't go in just yet."

"What are you talking about, Paul?"

"He doesn't remember everything," he said.

Emma shook her head in dismissal, got around Paul, and made it into the room before he could stop her. David was propped up in the bed; his father was leaning over, talking quietly to him. His mother was sitting in a chair near the foot of the bed.

"David." She ran to the bed, bent down, and hugged him. She pulled away and looked at him. That's when she saw it. There was no emotion in his eyes. He was just...looking at her. "David?" she asked.

He pulled away a little and then cocked his head slightly to get a better look at her.

"It's me."

He shook his head. "Sorry..."

She sat on the side of the bed, motionless. Paul was behind her and put his hands on the sides of her arms, encouraging her to stand up. She stood, put her hand over her mouth, took a few steps back, and bolted out of the room. When she made it halfway down the hall, she stopped, and leaned against the wall.

Paul caught up to her a few seconds later. "I'm sorry. I tried to tell you."

"He doesn't know me," she said, looking straight ahead and focusing on nothing. "He doesn't know who I am, does he?"

"He's confused. He's talking about things that happened a couple years ago. He doesn't even know why he's here. He thinks that we're still building my house. Mine and Lena's house. Emma, we moved into it almost two years ago."

It felt as if all the air had been sucked out of her lungs. When the initial blow subsided some, she asked, "What did the doctors say? Will he be able to remember?"

"They said to give him time," Paul said.

"All right," she said in the most convincing voice she could muster. "He woke up. That's what matters, right?"

"I don't know. Maybe we should go back in and tell him everything."

Emma shook her head, hard. "No, that's not what he needs right now." The pressure continued to build in her eyes, but she was determined to pull herself together. "He must think I'm some kind of nutcase, waltzing in there like that."

"I'll think of something to tell him."

"Thanks." On her way to the elevator, she heard Paul call her name but kept walking.

• • •

Sunday evening, Allison answered the door and motioned for Emma to come in. She was on the phone doing "the thing" she always did when she flirted. It was a high-pitched, over-the-top laugh that Emma loved to imitate and that Allison always swore she didn't do.

Allison pointed her finger toward the kitchen and then ran up the stairs, taking them two at a time. Emma went in and tossed her purse on the kitchen counter next to a slow cooker. She lifted the lid and took a whiff of the apple concoction. It smelled strong of cinnamon and made her instantly hungry, so she scooped some out with a wooden spoon. While it cooled, she noticed a bouquet with pink carnations and smaller purple-and-dark-pink flowers in a vase on the kitchen table. Fresh flowers may have been a common sight in this house, but this one had a small card attached to it. She stepped closer to the table to read it. It said, "Thanks for the coffee."

"Aren't they pretty?" Allison said as she snuck up behind Emma.

"Are they from Jason?"

"No." Allison reached for the flowers and took out a carnation. "They're from someone else." She tucked the flower behind her ear.

"Coffee, huh?" Emma asked, finally tasting the apple dessert.

Allison took the spoon from her and dropped it into the sink. "So far, anyway. He's this guy I met at the coffee shop next to my store. He came by to fix the lock on my back door. It's been sticking awhile, and we were talking about…Oh, listen to me ramble on." She looped her arm through Emma's and led her to the living room. "Let's go sit down."

Emma lay down on the couch and closed her eyes.

"You look awful," said Allison. "Kinda pale."

"Thanks."

"First David and then your father," Allison said. "So much crap for one person. What a coincidence that it happened the day before you got there."

"Well, who knows what he was into?"

"How's David?" Allison asked. "Is there any change today?"

"I just talked to Lena. She said he's been sleeping most of the day."

"Well, he's been through a lot. Give it time. I'm sure he'll get his memory back."

"Hope you're right," Emma said. She propped herself up on her elbow. "Thanks for inviting me over."

"You might want to hold off on that thank-you till after dinner. I'm trying out something new."

"If you cook it, I'll eat it."

"Good," said Allison. She pointed to an envelope on the coffee table. "I got an invite to Derrick's reunion. I guess they liked my meatballs last year. You going?"

"I hate those family things. How about you?"

Allison shook her head. "Can't. I have a convention. I'll be out of town till Monday. I think you should go, though."

Emma shot her a look. "Did Kate put you up to this?"

Allison looked away. "I saw her at the grocery store this morning," she admitted.

"Not you, too. Why does everyone think they know what's good for me?"

"This thing with David's been tough on you, and we care about you. Is that so horrible?"

Emma sat up and crossed her arms. "I'm fine, really."

"I know you think you are…"

"Look, I'm not some fragile flower that's going to dry up and blow away."

"I know, but it's good to get out," said Allison, "to be around people."

Emma pointed over her shoulder toward the kitchen. "Don't you have something you should be stirring or chopping or something?"

Allison put her arms up and surrendered. "OK, OK, I get it." She got up and went to the kitchen.

Emma followed Allison and had just started setting the table when she heard her cell phone ring. She dug into her purse and fished around for the phone. By the time she found it, the call had gone to voice mail. After she listened to the message, she stared at the phone, shaking her head.

"What happened? Is it David?" Allison asked.

"No. My condo was broken into."

• • •

Allison arrived at the condo just minutes after Emma and had to park in the street. A police car occupied the extra spot in the driveway. By the time Allison walked through the front door, Emma was already talking to her neighbor and a police officer. The neighbor was explaining how he'd noticed the door opened at an unnatural angle.

"Everything inside looks all right," Emma said.

"Maybe they were scared off by something and never actually made it in," the officer said. "I'd still like you to take a more thorough look around and make sure."

Emma walked from room to room with Allison behind her, and nothing seemed out of place. They'd made it to the kitchen when Emma stopped and abruptly backed up.

"It looks a little disorganized in here," Allison said when she noticed Emma hesitate and step back.

"Funny." Emma gave her a sideways glance.

"Oh, I thought maybe the place was, what do they call it? 'Tossed,' right?"

Emma ignored her and took two steps toward the kitchen counter. "The frog."

"The what?"

"My frog cookie jar," said Emma. "The one I bought from that flea market. You said it was ugly, but I bought it anyway."

"Well, if they had to take something..." Allison said, trying to lighten the mood.

"My TV, my jewelry, laptop, anything. But a cookie jar?"

The officer appeared in the kitchen doorway. "So is anything missing?"

Allison answered for her. "She thinks they took her cookie jar."

"Was it valuable?" he asked.

"Only if you consider a green ceramic frog valuable," Emma muttered. "The cookies in it cost more than the jar."

The officer completed the report and offered to give Emma the name of someone who could come over to look at the door. She told him she had someone she could call.

"This is bizarre, Em. Are you sure you didn't move it or something?"

"No," Emma insisted, pointing to the empty spot. "It's been there, in that corner, since I got it." She dialed Paul's number. He said he'd be right over.

Allison insisted on staying. Emma went to change into some sweats and left Allison digging around in her fridge. Knowing that someone was in her condo wandering around, touching her stuff, was awful, but most of all, she was pissed. Why would anyone take such a worthless object? The neighbor said there had been only one break-in since he'd lived there, and it happened years before she'd moved in.

When she got back to the kitchen, Allison had cheese slices on the cutting board and was buttering bread. A glass of wine was sitting on the kitchen table.

"Sweetie, you seriously need to go shopping," Allison said, putting the cheese sandwiches in the frying pan. "Get some real food to cook. Oh yeah," she said, flashing Emma a fake smile, "forgot you don't cook."

Normally, Emma would have reciprocated the banter, but her heart wasn't into it. She sipped the wine while she watched her friend take over her kitchen. Allison's movements were fluid, gliding from one cabinet to another with ease, almost like a dance. She knew that she had never looked like that in her kitchen—or any kitchen, for that matter.

"Stay at my place tonight," Allison flatly stated.

"No. Paul will get it buttoned up till morning." Emma heard the creak of her broken door, and then Paul called her name. She went to meet him and found him already examining the door.

"Wow, that's a lot of damage," he said. "Not a very bright thief, though. He could have gotten in with a lot less effort, if you ask me. Was anything taken?"

"Only a hideous cookie jar," Allison said as she came up behind them. "Can I make you a grilled cheese?" she asked Paul.

"No, thanks, I ate at the hospital. Of course the door will need to be replaced, but for now, I'll just secure it. Anyone see anything?"

"No. My neighbor noticed the door was open when he went out to walk his dog. How's David?"

"He's weak, tires easily."

Emma hesitated. "Does he remember anything?"

"No," he said, and looked away. "Well, I'll get started."

Back in the kitchen, Emma finished her wine and stared at the sandwich. The past few days had been quite disconcerting. She poured herself more wine and started laughing. "I have the worst luck. I mean, I travel hundreds of miles to see someone I really don't know, just to find out he was murdered, and then I come running home to see someone I care about who doesn't recognize me, and now some idiot bashes my door in!" She took her wine and stomped off to check on Paul.

Paul put the last of his tools in the toolbox. "No one's getting past this, that's for sure. Maybe you should stay somewhere else tonight."

"I told her that, but she's too stubborn," Allison piped in from the kitchen.

"I'm good, really," Emma insisted.

"The door's standard size, and I have a few in my barn. I'll send someone over tomorrow morning to replace it, but you better check with the homeowners' association."

"I will. Thanks."

After Paul left, she told Allison she was going to bed. She didn't need anyone feeling sorry for her, but more than that, she couldn't tolerate anyone hovering over her. She'd been indulging in too much self-pity as it was since David's accident, and decided that enough was enough. Permanence was fleeting, anyway, and getting too attached to anyone or anything was plain insane. It was time to make a change. Tomorrow was the day she would start writing another book.

• • •

He turned the radio on. Better. He was tired of hearing her yelling, trying to get his attention. He thought about just dropping her off somewhere. She wasn't Kate and couldn't take Kate's place. He wasn't thinking straight when he brought her here. Now he wished he'd insulated the basement ceiling when he was remodeling this house. The old woman didn't want to spend the money. If she only knew how much work he'd done on his own initiative. Supplies weren't an issue. He stole what he could and bought what he couldn't. They never noticed when materials at one of the jobs disappeared a piece at a time.

If it worked out the way he wanted, tomorrow he would get to be with Emma, alone. The only thing left to do was get to the job site early enough. He was sure he could get Paul to send him. They would be face-to-face. She would have to look at him, and maybe she would sense what he already knew. Their connection. He'd done what he needed to do and was positive no one saw him at her condo. If it was going to happen, he needed to sleep. Timing was everything. He closed his eyes.

It felt like flying...floating...a strong wind, warm on his face. It smelled... green, sweet, as if someone just finished cutting grass. The sun was hot, dancing on the pavement, making a puddle of water appear on the road up ahead. It would always magically disappear when he got close to it. He brought his head back into the car, his mom smiling, sitting in the driver's seat, laughing with him as they sped down the highway.

Luke sat up, leaned against the headboard, and silently wished he hadn't woken up. Remembering only made his heart heavy. He got up and went to the window, opened it, and breathed in the night air, trying to change the channel in his brain. He went downstairs, still in a brain fog, and stumbled to the kitchen. The solution lay in the bottle of whiskey he'd left next to the kitchen sink. He opened it and poured the comforting liquid down his dry throat, hoping to wash away the dream. The wooden clock above the kitchen doorway, in the shape of an apple, told him he still had four hours to sleep. It was a good time to take one of his pills. He'd already missed a dose and needed to be at his best in the morning. Maybe now he could sleep without those dreams.

• • •

It was eight o'clock Monday morning, and Emma had just finished getting dressed when she heard someone knocking on the back door. She ran to her closet and tripped over a pile of dirty clothes, regained her footing, scooped up a pair of flip-flops, and managed to slip them on as she hopped her way to the kitchen. A man wearing carpenter pants, a T-shirt, and work boots stood on her back deck. Before she reached the door, she recognized him as one of the workers from the job on Nolan Street. She opened the sliding glass door and let him in.

The man stepped into the kitchen. "Morning, Miss Simms. Did Paul tell you he was sending someone over?"

"Yes, he called a little while ago. Hope this didn't take you away from something important."

"No." He gave her a confident smile. "I got to work early today. I have time." He pointed past Emma toward the hall leading to the other room. "I'll need to get the old door out first."

"Of course. This way."

He followed her to the living room and immediately went to work removing the bolts from the door. Twenty minutes later, he unloaded the new door from one of Paul's work trucks. "It shouldn't take too long. I've installed quite a few doors." He turned his attention to his work.

"Great. If you need anything, I'll be in the kitchen."

A little more than an hour later, Emma was typing, backspacing, typing, and backspacing some more. The words weren't flowing as they usually did, and the enjoyment wasn't there, either. Her last book had a life of its own, and the ideas flowed easily. It was the best of both worlds—some parts real, some parts imagined. She scanned through her notes, hoping something would grab her. She cursed out loud, ripped the pages from the notebook, crunched them into a ball, and whipped them at the garbage can. And missed. They landed on the floor at the feet of the man who was installing her door. He picked them up and dropped them in the garbage.

"Thanks," she said, her face flushed. "How's the door coming?" she asked without looking up.

"By the looks of it, better than it's going in here."

"Having a hard time getting started is all." She threw the notebook down next to her computer.

"Working from home?" he asked.

She stood up and pushed in the kitchen chair. "You could say that." She went to the coffeepot and poured herself a cup. "Coffee?" she asked him.

"No, thanks." He took a few steps closer. "Paul says you write books."

She let out a loud breath. "Used to, anyway."

He took another step toward her. "What kind of books do you write?"

"A mixture of sorts."

"How so?"

"Some characters are molded after real people I know," she said, looking at him for the first time since he came into the room. "And some I make up."

"So you've had an interesting life?"

"Interesting? No. Different, maybe." She sipped her coffee. "I write about life, struggles. Something everyone has."

"Looks as if it all turned out well for you," he said, taking in the spacious condo.

"Oh, I don't know about that." She looked down into her cup.

"Well, I should head out," he said. He stepped closer and handed her two keys for the new door.

She looked up into his face. His mouth hung half-open, giving her the impression he was about to say something. The few seconds of eye contact was bordering on uncomfortable. Before she looked away, she couldn't help but notice a jagged line near his temple. He caught her stare and reflexively adjusted his hat, letting a few thick brown curls tumble over the scar.

"Tell Paul I'll settle up with him tomorrow," she said. "I'm sorry. I didn't get your name."

He smiled, held out his hand, and said, "Luke."

Emma shook his hand. "Thanks for fixing my door, Luke." She followed him to her new front door.

Right before he stepped outside, he stopped, turned abruptly, and blurted out, "Maybe you're just trying too hard."

His sudden stop caught her off guard. She found herself less than a foot from his face. "What?" she asked.

"Your book." His eyes smiled. "I'm sure ideas will come to you. Soon."

She watched him walk down the sidewalk and get into the truck before she closed the door. Back in the kitchen, she sat down in front of her laptop and thought about what he'd said. What did he mean? It didn't matter. He was just some carpenter. What did he know, anyway? And there she was, bitchy Emma. Usually *she* only showed up when the other person hit a nerve or tried to tell her what to do. But just maybe the book could be something new, something completely different. Getting lost in new characters might prove to be a much needed distraction right now.

• • •

He sat in his truck in front of the renovation property, waiting for Sal and the rest of the crew to arrive. He looked at the shiny new key he held in his hand. A piece of her life. Now he could come and go and not have to break anything. Destroying her front door was easy, but getting Paul to send him to fix it was a gamble, one that had paid off. Now he could see what she was up to whenever he wanted.

The way she smelled lingered in his senses. She knew his name. He could still feel the warmth of her hand. There weren't even words to describe the strong connection they had. The time was getting near. The other room in the basement was ready. He would put in a solid day's work and then get to the *real* work.

CHAPTER 7

• • •

EMMA WAS RUDELY JOLTED FROM concentration by the phone. Only three hours into writing, and she'd already nailed down two new characters and wanted to be invisible awhile longer. She recognized the number and was somewhat relieved that it was only Joyce. Not that Joyce was to be considered less than anyone else, but right now she didn't want any heavy conversation. She didn't get that from Joyce. Still, she let it go to voice mail.

With her thoughts interrupted, she poured another cup of coffee. The stirrings of purpose had sprouted, and some lost fervor had returned. She took the hazelnut creamer out of the fridge and poured a generous amount into her coffee. While sipping the rich, sweet drink in front of the sliding glass door, she looked out over her small but semiprivate patio and was pleased. It looked inviting. Then she realized she couldn't take any credit for that. It only looked that way because of the pots of flowers Allison gave her and the wrought-iron table David made her buy. The art of decorating was, in a way, the same as a dog marking its territory. This place was supposed to be temporary, so the need to put down those kinds of roots was a huge waste of time and money. Last year at this time, she'd hoped to have moved somewhere south by now. Then David came along. She grabbed her phone and went outside. She remembered that day David had dragged her to the store to buy a patio set. He said he appreciated her rather simplistic decorating style but insisted on some basic equipment and a table and chairs that fit into that category. Until now, she actually wasn't aware that he'd occupied so many places in her life. She called her voice mail and listened to the message.

"Emma, this is Joyce. I'm going to the house and wondered if you wanted to take me up on that lunch. If you want, come by and see the colors we picked out for the bedrooms."

She put her feet up on the table and rested her head on the back of the chair. The sun was hot and soothing on her face. Even after all the coffee she drank, she could have easily been put to sleep by the warmth of the sun. That is, if her stomach wasn't growling. She picked up her phone and called Joyce back.

• • •

When Emma parked in front of Joyce's soon-to-be new residence, the place was crawling with workers. She hadn't seen this much activity at one time during any of her previous visits. The job was supposed to be almost wrapped up. She walked around a man she hadn't seen there before who was unloading tools from a van. Stopping briefly at the side of the vehicle, she read the words *Hunt's Plumbing* painted on the side.

Halfway up the driveway, she saw Joyce standing in the open garage talking to another man. He nodded his head at Joyce and then walked with urgency toward the house. Joyce had both of her hands clasped tight on top of her head.

"Joyce, what happened?" she asked.

"Emma, you wouldn't believe it if I told you." She turned and headed to the house. "Come see what I walked into this afternoon."

Emma followed her through the small hallway that led to the kitchen, and had to step around a man who was sopping up water with a mop. When she turned the corner, she saw what had happened. Frank and Paul were standing against the far wall watching a man on a ladder in front of the kitchen sink, taking down the light fixture. Water leaked freely through the hole. Another section of the ceiling in the middle of the room was buckling and already dripping water. Paul and Frank spoke in whispers to each other while the plumber evaluated the situation. Another man came to the kitchen and said he found the problem in the upstairs bathroom.

Sal came in through the kitchen door. He joined the men at the far side of the room. Another man rushed in with a shop vacuum, plugged it in, and immediately began sucking up the water. Emma recognized him as the man who was at her place that morning. Paul told Sal to pick up a few sheets of drywall and reassured Joyce that he would take care of everything.

"It could have been worse," said Joyce. "At least it happened during the day when someone was here."

"I am so sorry," Emma mumbled, taking in the whole scene.

"Well, there's not much I can do about this," she said to Emma. Joyce looked at the mess that was her new kitchen. "Well, how 'bout that lunch?"

• • •

The waiter took their order and went to get their second drink. De Luca's was the Italian restaurant owned by Allison's parents. It was a simple-looking place that appeared more like a diner but had the best Italian food in the area. The tables were covered with red-and-white-checkered table-cloths. Brightly colored paintings depicting scenes of the countryside and vineyards of Italy hung on the walls. The smell of simmering sauces and pastries was thick in the air. Emma insisted on ordering a couple of pizzas for the guys who were trying to save her new friend's kitchen. She liked Joyce. She was unassuming and kept things light and superficial.

"I learned a long time ago to go with the flow, not to sweat the small stuff, and all that happy horseshit," said Joyce after finishing her first glass of merlot.

Emma listened to Joyce put the kitchen incident into perspective. "I'd be on my third drink by now, if it was me."

"I may just get there," Joyce said.

Emma looked up when she heard a familiar voice behind her. Turning, she recognized Mrs. De Luca, Allison's mother, and she stood up and hugged her. The older woman was small but strong-looking with hair as black and brilliant as Allison's.

The woman held her tight before leaning back and taking both of Emma's hands in hers. "Honey, it's been a long time," she said with a slight Italian accent. Her smile faded, and her voice became a whisper. "I heard about your friend David. I am so sorry. Allison tells me you've been going through some...things."

"Well, at least David's awake," said Emma. She didn't want to discuss her trip up north, so she turned back to the table and introduced Joyce to Mrs. De Luca.

"I love the food here," said Joyce. "My husband and I order takeout at least once a week."

The woman smiled. "Thank you so much. I thought you looked familiar."

When she turned back to Emma, concern was painted on her face. "Hang in there, honey. Call if you need anything. Enjoy your lunch, ladies." She headed off to the far end of the room and disappeared through a single-panel swinging door.

Emma sat back down. "She was good to me after my mother died. I've been friends with her daughter since high school. I forgot you know. You read my book. Everything in that chapter was real."

Joyce reached across the table and put her hand on Emma's. "She seems like a very nice lady."

"Hey," Emma said, changing the subject. "You didn't show me the colors you picked for the bedrooms."

Joyce took two color samples out of her purse. One was a neutral color called "whole wheat," and the other was a purplish color called "amethyst."

"Let me guess which one's for Missy's room," teased Emma.

"Oh, it goes so well with pinks and darker purples, and my little darling picked it out herself."

"I have time today if you want some help painting," said Emma.

"I won't tell you no, so we better stop at two drinks."

They ate lunch and laughed about insignificant stuff. It took her mind off David, even though she'd been here several times with him. Joyce bought lunch, and Emma paid for the pizzas.

By the time they returned to the house, most of the mess had been cleaned up, and Sal was making headway on removing the saturated drywall. The plumbers had diagnosed the problem and were well on their way to replacing some of the pipes. Emma put slices of pizza on paper plates, and Joyce handed them out.

Paul walked over to Emma and took a slice of pizza out of the box and began devouring it. "Thanks," he said with a full mouth. "This counts as my breakfast and lunch."

He started on his second piece before Emma asked, "So how's David?"

"Stronger—doesn't get out of breath so easily."

"That's good," she said, without looking at him.

"He's been asking a lot of questions about what happened to him," said Paul.

"What does he know?"

Paul finished chewing and wiped his mouth with a napkin. "He knows about the accident, but he still doesn't remember it or why he was there."

Luke threw his plate away in a garbage can behind Emma. "I couldn't help overhearing, but your brother's coming around?" he asked Paul.

"He's doing better."

"Is he getting out of the hospital soon?" asked Luke.

Paul shook his head. "Hopefully, but then he'll be going to a rehab faculty."

"Glad to hear he's better," said Luke.

Emma had the urge to make herself busy. "We should get started."

"I'll go get the paint," Joyce said.

Emma followed her, glad to be away from talk of David.

● ● ●

Later that evening, Luke put the plate of chicken and beans on the tray. He'd left the dress for her that morning before he went to work. He wrote instructions on paper and left it with the food when she was asleep. She was to wash up using the buckets of water he lined up in her room. Using the peephole in the door, he looked in, not knowing what he'd find. Pleased with what he saw, he unlocked her door and, balancing the tray partially on his hip, went into the room.

Gwen sat on the bed, staring at him, looking somewhat subdued. The plate of food from this morning sat on the floor, and he could see that she'd eaten some of it. The drugs should be almost out of her system by now. He couldn't be sure she'd cooperate, but it was a good sign that she was wearing the dress, and the towels were on the floor next to the buckets. He took a few steps into the room, bent down, and put the tray on the floor within her reach.

"OK, I did what you asked," she said. "What do you want from me?"

He looked at her. "Eat."

"I'm not hungry."

His expression was flat. He took the buckets out of the room and set them down just outside the doorway. When he came back in, he picked up the breakfast tray and turned to leave. "I'll be back after you eat," he said over his shoulder.

Gwen watched him close the door and listened for the sound of the lock. She let out a long breath and sat on the bed for a minute before making a move toward the tray.

"Son of a bitch," she said as she stretched her arm to reach it. Some fried chicken and baked beans with a bottle of apple juice. The bottle of juice had already been opened, but she'd expected that to be the case. With nothing but time to weigh her options, she'd chosen to eat some of the food that morning even though she knew it was drugged—or poisoned, for that matter. Without food, she wouldn't have the strength to fight if the chance arose. One thing she knew for sure was that he wanted her alive, at least for the time being.

Cooperate, or pretend to, anyway. No one was coming to save her. No one knew she was missing. If she'd had a job, someone might have wondered where she was by now. She regretted being irresponsible about returning phone calls. If anyone called her, they wouldn't think it strange if she didn't call them back. Basically, she was on her own now.

Gwen put the tray on the bed, and with her back to the door, ripped off pieces of the chicken and tucked them into the underside of the pillowcase. Then she grabbed the bottle of juice and poured half of it into the bucket. Good thing it was the color of pee. She put a little of the toilet paper on top of it. No way was she going to be put to sleep again. He said he'd come back after she ate. She'd be ready for him.

• • •

Time moves slowly when you have nothing to measure it by. Gwen guessed it had to have been at least two hours since he'd left. She was hungry, but to eat now meant to give up. And that wasn't an option. Finally, she heard the dead bolt being slid open. Her heart rate quickened. She sat up a little straighter, keeping her eyes fixed on the door. She watched as her cell door opened, and he stepped in, smiling, as if he was nothing more than an old friend. He carried a notebook and held it in front of him. He stood just inside the room and began flipping through the pages, appearing to be in deep thought. She sat very still, watching his every move. He looked up from the notebook, noticing the half-eaten food and empty bottle of juice.

He finally looked in her direction, his expression not even vaguely hinting at his intentions. He put the notebook down on the table next to the bed, bent over, and looked directly into her eyes. His gaze was heavy and seemed to slice right through her, but she forced herself not to look away. Gwen let her eyelids droop slightly, trying to mimic someone who'd been drugged.

"I want you to stand up and take a step toward the wall behind the bed," he said.

Like an obedient puppy, she stood and did what he asked.

He took two steps in the other direction and stopped just past the foot of the bed. He lifted his shirt and slipped a knife out from a sheath that was attached to his belt.

Gwen's eyes widened. She held up her hand as if to shield herself and yelled, "Wait!"

He showed no sign that he'd heard her and calmly went down on one knee and began cutting away on the other end of her tether. He wrapped it around the palm of his hand several times and stood up. She tried to slow her breathing, to calm herself so she could think clearly. Maybe conversation would work.

"What do you want me to do?" she asked as if he'd hired her for a job.

He looked her over, as if assessing the dress. "We're going upstairs, you and me."

She nodded her head. "All right," she whispered, wanting to appear cooperative.

He pointed to the door and, holding on to the tether, motioned for her to start walking. She took a mental snapshot of her surroundings, hoping to find a makeshift weapon as they left the room. The staircase was straight ahead, and another door was just to the right of it. It was wide open. Making her way hesitantly to the stairs, she caught a glimpse of the inside of the other room. In it were a bed and a small bedside table. A carbon copy of the one he'd kept her in. She could feel his hand on her lower back as she stood at the foot of the stairs. He gave her a firm shove and said, "Up."

She pretended to rest after every couple of steps, as if she lacked the energy to tackle the climb. Once she made it to the top, she bent over, grabbed the railing, and faked the need to catch her breath. When she looked up, she saw a kitchen. She scanned the room for an escape route. The shade on the kitchen window and the curtain on the door were closed tight. She looked around for anything that could be used to inflict blunt force.

Once again he placed his hand on her back, directing her to a kitchen chair. When she sat down, he took the knife from its sheath again. This time she didn't flinch as he bent down and cut the rest of the tether off her ankle. He handed her the notebook, already opened to the first page. She looked at it. It was a written exchange between two people. A play? A story? She looked up questioningly at her captor.

"Read. Start at the top of the page. Only the lines that are underlined."

"What is this?" she asked.

He wasn't looking at her. He was staring off to her left, his eyes squinted as if listening intently. She cautiously turned in that direction, but nothing was there.

His head jerked back to her, and he yelled, "Read!"

The sudden outburst made Gwen jump. With a quivering voice, she immediately started reading her lines. He closed his eyes and listened. When she finished the page, she stopped and looked up. He stood silent, as if in a trance. She could do nothing but wait for his next command.

There was nothing warm and fuzzy about this room, except for a kitchen clock in the shape of an apple and something that looked like a frog statue. Whatever it was, it looked out of place here. He noticed her gaze land on the decoration, and walked over to it. He caressed the frog as if it was a prized possession. With both hands he picked it up, exercising extreme care, and brought it to her.

"Do you like it?" he asked.

She shook her head up and down several times. "Yes," she managed to say in a barely audible whisper.

He held it out toward her, and she raised her hands to accept it. Holding it with care, she pretended to admire it. He looked off to the left again at something that wasn't there. For a brief moment, his focus was elsewhere. She slowly raised the frog while trying to steady her hands and held her breath, afraid that the slightest sound would bring his attention back to her.

With the strength that embodied her will to live, she propelled the frog forward as she stood up, closing the distance between them. The object crashed into the side of his head, connecting with his left temple. He screamed out as he fell backward and landed on the ground. She flew out of the chair and made a beeline for the kitchen door. Her hands fumbled with the doorknob, but she managed to turn the lock and flung the door wide open. Afraid of wasting even a second to look back, she ran straight ahead and leaped off the porch. She winced in pain, feeling gravel and stones pound the bottom of her bare feet. She made a left and sprinted around the side of the house, cutting through the front yard. After making it to the road, she went right and ran along the tree line for cover. She didn't know that if she had made a left, she would have run right into the only neighbor, who was outside unloading groceries from his car.

The wind was gusting, and a storm was moving in, making it nearly impossible to hear anything else. Her long hair whipped her face and stuck to the dampness caused by the tears now streaking down her cheeks. She slowed her pace just long enough to scan the darkness behind her before deciding which way to go. Lightning lit the sky just long enough for her to see movement against the trees behind her. The threat sent her spinning around, unsure which direction she should take. Rounding the next group of trees, she made the decision to backtrack slightly in hopes of throwing him off her trail.

She searched for a house or a busy road, someplace where he wouldn't be able to grab her and drag her away. She had no idea where she was, but even in the dark, she was able to make out a cornfield on her right. Reaching down to brush something off her foot, she felt something wet and had no doubt it was her own blood. The pain in her feet was excruciating. If only she'd had shoes on, she was sure she'd be a mile away by now. Every step felt like walking on hot coals, but she refused to let that slow her down. The storm was getting closer, and soon lightning would fill the sky again and possibly pinpoint her location.

Running at a slow jog and favoring her right leg, she made her way across yet another road. She desperately needed to put space between herself and...him. The rain, now coming down in sheets, made visibility nearly impossible. It occurred to her that she could run right into him and not see him until it was too late. Up ahead, she could make out some kind of structure and veered off in that direction.

An old barn. Cautiously, she entered through a side door, feeling her way around in the dark. Using her hands, she followed an inside wall to a corner. She lowered herself to the ground, keeping her back against the wall. Gwen closed her eyes and listened. Exhaustion and the sound of the rain almost lulled her to sleep.

Then she heard the sound of metal hitting metal. Her eyes scanned the darkness for any hint that it was more than just the wind. *Lightning? A flashlight?*

"I know you're in here," the familiar voice stated confidently. Then silence.

She held both hands tightly over her mouth, afraid her fear would give her away. Her body shook not only with fear but from the thin, now-soaked dress that clung to her body. For a moment, her instinct to run almost got the best of her. Without the benefit of shoes, he'd be on her in a second. She felt around for something to defend herself with. Directly in front of her, she felt a long metal object. It was heavy, but she could lift it with one hand. She pulled it toward her and, holding it tight, she waited.

The beam of a flashlight swept the opposite side of the barn. He was facing the far wall with his back to her. He was methodically searching under and behind the junk that filled the area. She pulled her legs up so they were underneath her without letting go of her weapon. Standing up as slowly as she could, she looked toward the only exit between them. Inching along, using the wall as a guide, she headed toward it. It was no more than ten feet away.

Keeping parallel with the wall of the barn, she felt her way along in the darkness. Her left foot bumped something small and sent it skittering a few feet before it made contact with another object, causing a ping sound. The light beam turned and hit her square in the face. Within a few seconds, he was in front of her, blocking her escape. She took the metal rod in both hands and swung it like a baseball bat. It hit him in the ribs, catching him by surprise. He went down. Gwen took another swing but swung too high and hit the barn wall. The force knocked the rod out of her hands.

She jumped over him, landing on what felt like metal fencing. She rolled on her side and crawled out the door.

On nothing but raw determination, she was up and running again in the rain. Up ahead in the distance, through a line of trees, she saw headlights coming around a bend in the road, and began limping toward it.

The vehicle was fast approaching. She half turned to look behind her. And there he was. She limped a few more feet and then looked back again. He was gone. Gwen leaped out into the road with the last bit of energy she had. Waving her arms high over her head, she watched the approaching headlights come round the bend and realized too late that the driver couldn't see her.

• • •

"David wants to see you." That was what Paul said when he called earlier that evening. Hope sprang and then quickly subsided when he told her it wasn't because he remembered her. Paul only told him they were friends. She stood in front of her closet, hoping the right outfit would magically appear. Nothing grabbed her attention, so she rifled through her dresser one more time. Half her clothes were strewn around the room, and she hadn't found the winner yet. She should have borrowed something from Kate. Fashion wasn't something she was interested in. Comfort was. She took a white blouse and some jeans from her closet and decided it would have to be good enough for her visit with David tomorrow. She threw on some sweats and went back to her office. She needed to make changes to her story. The main character was too whiny, too wimpy to be doing all the things she needed her to do. Her love interest needed to be more of a free spirit, a risk taker.

A loud clap of thunder kicked her out of her thought. The rain pounded hard on her office window. The thin curtain did little to block the lightning that flashed every couple of seconds now that the storm was right overhead. She loved this weather, always had. As a child, she'd sit on the porch with her mother and watch the clouds roll in. The sky would get darker as the ominous presence crept up, and its wind would take control of everything in its path, making the trees come alive. The lightning was the real showstopper, though. Sometimes, if it was close enough, you could feel the electricity prick your skin. Her mother said it was a kiss from God. Then, in the aftermath, there was always a distinct smell in the air, fresh, earthy.

She pictured her mother and wondered how a person could get so weighted down by life that they couldn't fight their way back. Maybe what she told Kate on that beach wasn't all bullshit. Maybe their mother *was* doing her best, doing what *she* knew. By judging her mom on some distorted scale of toughness, she was able to ignore the real issue. She was mad. Just plain mad. Mad about all the responsibility she was left with when she died. Mad that she blamed herself. Mad because she fought with her mother the last time she saw her. One big mad mess. It happened, and she couldn't change it. She sat down, pushed it out of her head, and decided to give Allison a call before opening up her laptop and diving into a make-believe world.

• • •

The water went from hot to lukewarm and now teetered on the cool side. He reached down and turned the shower off. He had no idea how long he'd been standing there, letting the water soothe him. With a towel, he dried his hair, being careful not to touch the large cut on the side of his head. Pain coursed through his left side when he lifted his leg to step out of the shower. He wiped the steam off the mirror and wrapped the towel around his waist. It was hard to look at his reflection, knowing it was his fault. If only he had been able to get her back to the house, *it* wouldn't have happened.

Now that he had washed away all the blood and mud from his romp in the rain, he needed to stop the swelling on his side. He threw on some loose-fitting jeans and a tank top, and went to the kitchen. After swallowing a pill with the rest of the rum, he opened the freezer. There was no ice, so he pulled out a frozen chunk of meat. The storm outside was nothing compared to the one that was going on inside him.

Once in the living room, he gingerly eased himself down onto the couch. When he touched the frozen roast to his side, he thought he might pass out. After the initial shock, he found the pain comforting. At least he knew it was real. He swam in the pain, soaking it up, letting it ground him. Pain kept the whispers in the background.

He lay on the couch, thinking back to what seemed like a lifetime ago. He thought about his mother. He'd give anything to see her again, even take the bad with the good. When she was feeling good, the world was theirs. When she was sad, everything was dark. She'd go days without getting out of bed or taking a shower. He could hear her crying in her locked room and would sit on the floor, his back up against her bedroom door, waiting for things to turn around. When she felt happy again, they would spend the better part of a week doing nothing but playing and having fun. And shopping—she loved shopping. If the weather was nice, she'd take the top off the old convertible, and they'd drive around with the radio blaring.

Then they'd make her take her medicine, and everything went dull. She would get quiet again and didn't want to be bothered by anyone. His father would come by, yell at her, and tell her to snap out of it. Then he would leave again, and Luke would be alone until she came out of her room. Sometimes it would be days. He would try to make her eat, usually cheese and crackers because it was the only thing he knew how to make. He was five. He drifted off to sleep listening to the rain, wishing it could wash away all the bad memories. Instead, the dreams came.

● ● ●

He rested his arm on top of the glass display case and moved it slowly until it was next to the perfume bottle. To a ten-year-old, it was by far the best birthday present, and he knew his mother would love it. The woman behind the counter was busy helping a customer decide on a fragrance. In one swift move, he managed to conceal the bottle between the crook of his arm and his body. He turned and walked over to a rack of watches at the next display case. An arm came out of nowhere and landed firmly on his shoulder. He squirmed to get free, but the security guard wasn't letting go. He was escorted to a back room where he was told to wait. A little while later, he heard his dad's voice coming through the door of the small room he was detained in. The door opened, his father walked in, and without looking at him said, "Let's go." He knew what was coming, and he knew it would take place behind closed doors. His father told the guard it wouldn't happen again and led him out, holding him by the back of his jacket. He watched as his skateboard was thrown in the trunk haphazardly before they sped away from the store. They stopped at the market at the end of the street, where his father came out with the usual brown paper bag. When they got to his father's apartment, he went to the room he used when staying there and waited. He heard nothing but the radio for a while before the ranting started. He heard his name a few times and then watched as the door flew open. Then the other person came in. The one his dad sometimes turned into.

• • •

He sat up and wildly searched the room and then relaxed, forcing himself to breathe. Dreaming and being awake were blending together again. He leaned back on the couch and pulled his legs up to his chest, as if trying to protect himself from some unseen threat. The dreams were getting harder and harder to shake off, and sometimes they followed him, haunting him all day. The whispers were there, always in the background, making his head ache, always mocking. His new life was going to make all the bad fade away into the background.

Half an hour later, he went outside and breathed in the dewy smell that was left like an afterthought by the storm. Nightmares fought to occupy his mind while he let the cooling air fill his lungs. The sounds of the night soothed him as creatures came out of their hiding places, assured that the weather disruption had passed.

In the still air, the sound of crickets was hypnotizing. His trance was broken by a tune from the nineties coming from his cell phone. He stepped back into the house and found his phone under a pillow. It was her.

"How are you, Allison?" he asked.

"Good. Look, I hope you don't mind me calling you so soon, but would you like to come over for dinner tomorrow night?"

"Tomorrow?" Luke sat up straighter, causing the pain to radiate from his side. He bit his lip, trying not to moan out loud. "Sure."

"Call me sometime in the afternoon, and let me know what's good for you."

Luke squirmed, trying to find a more comfortable position on the couch. "I will."

"Great. Talk to you then," she said, and hung up.

Wondering if it was a good idea to get tangled up with Emma's friend but wanting to get closer to the situation, he reevaluated his decision to befriend Allison. On one hand, it seemed harmless enough, but on the other, it could be dangerous and complicate things. It was Allison who'd approached him first at the coffee shop. She'd noticed him watching her and struck up a conversation. That wasn't the plan. He just wanted to *watch*. Now he was going to have dinner at her house. He'd accepted the invite and planned to follow through. If she told Emma about meeting him, it would look like a coincidence. Small towns were good for that. He pulled his wavy brown hair down over the angry, swollen cut on the side of his head. His hair was thick enough to cover it up. Now all he needed to do was get some rest.

He fell asleep and was seventeen again. It was summer, and he was listening to the radio after working a late shift at the bowling alley. He'd worked there for only three months and already had his first savings account. It was easy to stash money away because he rarely had anything to spend it on, although it did help with the groceries. Kids from school came in on a regular basis. Some said hi, and others just looked away. Sometimes one of them, usually a girl, would tell him about a local party. He made it to a couple of them and would stay a little while, if the music was loud enough. That way he didn't have to talk to anyone. He could walk around or just sit and listen to music. And watch. Once in a while, a girl from the neighborhood would take a liking to him, but it never lasted long. He didn't know how to act around girls or crowds or people. The whole idea made him sweaty.

His mom had a new job, her third one in seven months, at a bar one town over. She said the tips were good and she'd made more friends. Great. More friends. When she wasn't at work, she was out. Wherever that was. Her friends were all much younger than she was, but she seemed to have no trouble keeping up with them.

Headlights shone through the living room curtain, and he jumped up to hide the empty beer bottle. It had become a habit to sneak one or two from work every night. He went out to the porch in time to see his mom being helped out of the car by one of her new friends. It was Colleen, another waitress from the bar. She'd driven her home every night this week because their car wasn't running again.

It took both of them to get her into the house. Colleen tripped on something in the bedroom, and they barely made it to the bed before they dropped her. They pulled her to the middle of the bed, and Luke slipped her shoes off. He knew the drill.

Colleen giggled and kissed his mom's cheek, grabbed Luke's hand, and pulled him to the kitchen. She took him by the shoulders. "She'll be OK."

He was finally getting a better look at Colleen, now that she was standing so close to him. She was a lot younger than his mom. Her hair was short and framed her round face. He noticed the way she looked at him. And the way her shirt hung open when she bent forward.

She saw him looking and gave him a crooked smile. He immediately looked away. She lit up a cigarette and offered him one.

"No, thanks." His face was warm and tingly, so he went out to the front porch and sat down.

Colleen followed and stepped off the porch. She took a few steps down the sidewalk before she spun around to face him. "Why aren't you out tonight?"

"I just got home from work." He thought it sounded good.

She pulled something out of her pocket and held it out. "Do you mind?"

He shook his head. He'd seen people smoke weed before. He was happy with a beer.

She lit it and took a few pulls, and then offered it to him. He hesitated but then put it to his lips and breathed it in. He started coughing almost immediately.

Colleen laughed and took it from him. "Watch." She slowly breathed it in and held it in her lungs before slowly pushing it out.

He finally got the hang of it and managed to inhale without coughing out a lung.

"I'm hungry. Come on." She just about skipped to the car.

He remembered their fridge was empty. "Wait." He ran in, got his key, and locked the front door behind him.

They drove to town and saw nothing but a dark street.

She slowed the car in front of a bar. "Just how old are you?" Colleen asked, eyeing him up and down.

"Not twenty-one," he said.

"Hey, there's a gas station up ahead that might still be open. Interested?" she asked.

Fifteen minutes later, he looked at the clock in her car. It was one in the morning. She came out of the store carrying a bag and a six-pack.

"Hope you like gas-station sandwiches." She tossed the bag in his lap.

Luke reached into it and pulled out a bag of chips. Salt and vinegar. She cracked a beer.

"These chips are awesome," he said, devouring them.

She was laughing again. "You have the munchies." She handed him her beer and put both hands on the wheel. "I shouldn't even be driving. My apartment isn't far."

"Let's go." He downed half the beer, trying to wash the chips down.

"Keep the bottle down, or I'll get pulled over." She turned up the music and put her hand on his thigh.

He wasn't nervous at all. The next morning, she drove him home, early. He asked if he could see her again. She wouldn't look at him when she said no.

That was all right with him. She'd just end up thinking he was weird. They all did. And he would have to get used to it.

CHAPTER 8

• • •

THE ONLY REMINDER OF THE storm were the puddles that were well on their way to drying up in the late morning sun. Emma took the long way to the hospital so she could stop at the flower shop first. During their conversation the previous night, Allison told her to come by and said she'd made a flower arrangement for her to give to David. It wasn't in Emma's nature to think of something like that on her own, so she was grateful she had a friend to do it for her.

When she walked into the shop, it was clear that Allison had her hands full. Two women were arguing about the type of flowers that should be used in the centerpieces for a wedding. They reminded her of two Chihuahuas fighting. Allison was between them, playing referee and blurting out ideas.

Emma strolled around the shop, happy as hell that she didn't have to work there. There was no way she'd be able to put up with that. Who cared about all that fluffy wedding crap anyway? It was nothing but a waste of money, one day in your life. She was basking in her righteousness when she rounded the corner, and on a shelf near the register was the most beautifully simple bouquet. It had large white flowers surrounded by tiny white bell-shaped ones and plum-colored rosebuds that were on the verge of blooming. The whole bouquet had a casual, thrown-together look about it. She reached out to touch it but yanked her hand back when she heard Allison's voice.

"Lovely, isn't it?"

"This? I guess." She turned her back to it. "How 'bout I come back another time? You have fights to break up."

Allison put her hand under Emma's elbow. "Nonsense," she said, and whisked her away to the back room. "Just another day for me."

The room had a long table in it with glass coolers lining the back wall. On the left side was a shelving unit full of pots and baskets. Stems and other pieces of greenery littered the table and floor.

Allison opened one of the coolers and pulled out a burgundy wicker basket with some dark-green ferns in it, dotted with small white-and-yellow flowers. "This should break the ice."

Emma took the basket by the handle. "Thanks. What do I owe you?"

"Nothing. Well, could you maybe watch Merlin for me on the weekend?"

"Why not? I've got nothing else to do," said Emma. "Where are you going?"

"I'm not sure I'm going anywhere yet. My friend from the coffee shop mentioned that maybe we could take a drive up north somewhere."

"You are bad," said Emma, pointing a finger at her. Then worry crept in. "You hardly know him."

"Not true. I've seen him enough. He's coming over tonight."

Emma shook her head. "I hope you know what you're doing."

"Don't I always?" She kissed Emma's cheek. "Got to go. Hope things go well with David."

• • •

Lena was waiting for Emma in the lobby when she arrived. She was talking on her phone while balancing her laptop on her knees and looking through a folder. Emma waited for her to finish. When she stood up, Emma saw that look on her face. The pity look. She pretended she didn't see it. "How is he?"

"He's doing better. His sense of humor is back," said Lena. "Do you want me to go in with you?"

Emma looked past her. "That's not necessary. I'm going to make it a short visit. Just say hi."

"OK, he knows you're coming. Don't be nervous. He's still the same guy. See you later." Lena touched Emma's shoulder and walked away.

Emma watched her leave before getting on the elevator. When she made it to his room, she knocked lightly on the door. David was reading the newspaper and stopped when he saw her.

"Come on in," he said.

She stepped into his room and nervously smiled back. "I brought this for you," she said, holding the plant straight out in front of her.

"Thanks. Can you put it on the windowsill?"

She put it down and then stood at the foot of the bed. "How are you feeling?"

David nodded his head. "Better. Have a seat."

She had rehearsed a few things to talk about on the ride over but now couldn't remember any of them. She sat down in the chair and looked at this man who saw her as just a stranger. An awkwardness filled the space between them, and they looked at each other, waiting for the other to speak.

"Paul says we're friends," David finally said.

"Yes, we were." Emma nodded her head and stammered, "I mean, we are."

He studied her. "I'm going to be honest with you. I can't remember the last couple years of my life, and it seems that no one wants to tell me the truth." He paused. "Me and you, we were more than just friends, weren't we?"

Her mouth was half-open, but nothing came out. She wanted to tell him the truth, but not for selfish reasons. "Oh, because I threw myself at you the last time I was here. What did Paul tell you?"

"Nothing. He'd make an awesome politician the way he so artfully changes the subject."

She watched the way his lips formed his words and knew she could watch them all day. They always had such an effect on her. She stood and walked around the bed, stopping in front of the window before turning to face him. "Yes, more than friends." His eye contact sucked at her soul. She let her eyes fall to the floor.

He sighed and looked up at the ceiling. "Thanks."

She looked up, not getting it. "For what?"

"For being the only one who's been honest with me."

She had the urge to grab him and kiss that mouth, but she didn't.

It was a few more moments before he looked at her again. He seemed more relaxed, more like the David she knew.

"I'm sorry," he said.

"For what?"

"For not remembering you."

She took two quick steps and was at the side of the bed. "It's not your fault, David."

He reached out to her, and she gave him her hand.

"I want to remember. I've tried."

"You don't remember anything about the accident?" she asked.

"No. Not even why I was there in the first place." His eyes locked on hers. "Do you know?"

She pulled her hand away from his. "Maybe I could bring some pictures to you. It might help."

"I'd like that."

"I should get going. You need your rest," Emma said.

"So...you'll come back then?"

"I'll come back."

• • •

Allison got home later than she'd planned and had less than an hour before her dinner guest arrived. Merlin hadn't been outside since early that morning, so he ran past her as soon as she opened the door. She went back on the porch, waiting for the dog to find the perfect spot to relieve himself. As soon as he finished, he came bounding toward her and dove to get the tennis ball that was on the porch. He dropped it at her feet and gave her that beaming canine smile he always sported when he wanted to play. She reached down and patted his head. "Not now, boy. Momma's got to get ready."

After coaxing him back into the house, she decided it might be a nice night to sit outside, so she grabbed the cushions for the porch swing. When she came back in the house, the phone was ringing.

"Hi, Luke. Not a problem, I'm running behind, too. All right, see you then."

She tried to remember where he said he lived. He said something about being half an hour away. Now she had an hour and a half. She took an avocado out of the refrigerator, gathered the rest of the ingredients for the dip, and started chopping. The steaks were marinating, and the salad was made, so there wasn't much more to do. She poured herself a small glass of wine, lit a few candles, and went upstairs to take a bath.

Forty-five minutes later, she was sitting on the porch throwing the ball around for Merlin. She called Emma to see how her visit with David went. They'd been on the phone for twenty minutes before the truck pulled into her driveway.

"Got to let you go, Em. He's here."

She watched him bend down on one knee to rub Merlin's head before continuing to the porch. "He likes you," she said.

"He must remember me."

"I told you he was a smart dog."

The three of them went into the house together.

• • •

After talking to Allison, Emma tossed her phone on the desk and got comfortable in her chair. She was glad she let David buy it for her when she bought the new desk. He said he wanted her to be comfortable, and he insisted on this one. And it was perfect. She missed him, them, the way they were. Enough of that. She opened her laptop.

While she waited for her program to start, her mind continued to wander. She laughed out loud when she thought about Allison and how excited she was about her new…friend. In the end, he would be nothing more than a memory. Even in high school, Allison had a new beau every couple months. Last month, Jason. This month…well, it didn't matter what his name was because next month it would probably be somebody else. Allison would make a perfect character for her story. And that's how it always happened. She decided to kick one of her main characters to the curb and add in one more like Allison.

Then another thought intruded. She needed to call her agent. She really liked Millie and couldn't have found a better agent, but sometimes she offered—and that was putting it more than mildly—advice where she shouldn't. She hated to admit it, but Millie had kept her in line more than a few times. That's why she dreaded calling her now. Her new story wasn't anything like the ones she'd written in the past, and she was sure Millie would give her flak. She was thinking about how she hated avoiding the woman, when her phone rang. She stared at the phone, mumbled under her breath, and then answered it.

"Hello, Millie," Emma said, channeling a fake smile through the phone.

"Listen, doll, I've been trying to get a hold of you."

"I know. I've been meaning to call."

"Are you all right, doll? Did something else happen? Why haven't you answered my texts?"

"Millie, I'm fine. I've been writing," said Emma, hoping to stop the questioning.

"Good, good, that's my girl. Tell me about it."

Emma fidgeted with a sticky note on her desk while deciding what to say. Millie started babbling about something, and Emma couldn't think, so she just spit it out. "It's about a woman who wins the lottery and buys a boat and travels around until she witnesses a murder." When she finished, there was nothing but silence at the other end of the line. "Millie?"

"No, really, what's it about?" Millie asked.

Emma rolled her eyes and let her head fall back on the chair. "Trust me, Millie."

"Of course I trust you, doll. Just reel it in a bit, and do what you do. Look, I've got another call. Don't be a stranger. Bye."

"Wow," Emma said. That was easy. Straight to the point. But that was Millie. Now she could go back to dodging her for a couple more weeks. She turned the phone off this time before putting it down. Done. She settled back in her chair and went to work researching boats.

• • •

The dishes were in the sink, and the leftovers were put away, so Allison poured them each another glass of wine to take out to the front porch. Luke was watching the news and didn't hear her when she called his name. She sat down next to him on the couch in time to catch the tail end of a news story. The anchorman was talking about the woman who was hit by a semi north of Allison's store. They showed a police sketch and asked viewers to call if anyone recognized her.

"That sucks. By now you'd think somebody would be looking for her," said Allison.

Luke took the glass Allison held out to him, reached for the remote, and pushed the off button.

When Allison led him outside, the breeze was starting to pick up, moving the wind chimes just enough to lure the melodic music from them. The crickets' song was thicker than it usually was this early in June.

Allison was on her third glass of wine when she realized why she liked this man. Besides the fact that he was looking yummier by the minute, he didn't talk about himself or about all the things he'd done, or even about his plans for the future. It was just now, with no pressure. She swirled the wine in her glass and allowed herself to be taken over by a giddiness from the evening and the spicy zinfandel. She inched closer to him. He was staring off into the distance and didn't seem to notice, so she kicked it up a notch. With the ability to recognize her own strength being more than slightly numbed, she scooted toward him and knocked her hip hard on his. He turned his head toward her with a dull, vacant look in his eyes.

She stood up and playfully tugged at his hand, pulling him up from the swing and through the front door. Just inside the foyer, she turned and stepped close to him, touching her body to his. She put her arms around his neck, their mouths now only inches apart. She pressed her lips to his. His body responded and aggressively molded to her form, pushing her back against the wall, forcing her up on her toes. There was an urgency, a neediness in his kiss, mixed with a rawness that made her want more. He roughly pulled her leg up to the side of his hip. He kissed her deeply. It was sweet and hot and then...it was over.

He slipped to his right, ripping himself from her arms. It took a moment for his sudden move to register with her. Even in the dark foyer, lit only by the moonlight coming through the front door, she could see him shrink away. It was a few seconds before she reacted.

She put her hand to her mouth. "I'm so sorry if...I didn't mean to..."

"It's all right," he said, looking everywhere except at her.

The moment was definitely over. They stood, facing each other, both trying to catch their breath.

He straightened his posture. "It's late. I should go." He thanked her for dinner and was out the door.

With her feet planted in the same spot, she heard the screen door close and wondered what had just happened.

● ● ●

At nine the next morning, Dr. Richard Novak looked over the paperwork Kate had faxed him just minutes before. "Everything seems to be in order," he said into the phone. "What can I do for you, Dr. Nelson?"

"Well, I've been seeing him for about six months now. It took me this long to convince him to sign the release of information document. He's rather vague about his past. I was hoping you could shed some light on his history, maybe diagnosis, response to treatment...anything you think could help me treat him."

"Luke. It's been a long time, but I remember him. A very bright boy," said Dr. Novak. "He was shy, guarded, took quite a while to come out of his shell. He was hospitalized here a few times. His first admission at this facility was when he was eighteen. He was withdrawn, with minimal interaction with peers. He was always visible in the milieu, would sit off to the side by himself but always seemed to know what was going on around him. Basically a loner."

"He seems to function appropriately," said Kate. "He works, mainly odd jobs. He does have difficulty forming relationships. Doesn't seem to have any friends. Well, maybe one. He works with another patient of mine."

Dr. Novak flipped through the paperwork he'd retrieved the day before after getting the voice mail from Kate. "He suffered from a thought disorder. Psychotic Disorder was my diagnosis. The first time I saw him was after he was picked up for shoplifting. It seems he'd had a problem with that in the past. The petition says he resisted arrest and was agitated. His verbalizations were loose with a paranoid flavor. He was brought in by the police and petitioned for treatment by a friend of his mother's. After a few days of antipsychotic medication, his thoughts became clearer, more reality based. He verbalized some remorse for his behavior."

"Yes," said Kate. "He does seem to have insight into his illness and need for medication."

"I wonder if his prognosis would have been better if he'd had treatment in his earlier years or a more appropriate support system," Dr. Novak added.

"What about family history?" Kate asked.

"If you can bear with me while I try to read my own handwriting...ah, here it is. It looks as if both parents battled depression. They were divorced when he was young. His mother had a thought disorder, possibly with periods of mania. Most of the information was provided by a family friend.

The last time he was here, again on an involuntary basis, his mother died. He wasn't stable enough to attend the funeral. He went into a deep depression and became severely withdrawn and preoccupied. Admitted to auditory hallucinations, said the voices were telling him to do things but refused to say what. He was very paranoid. Took weeks for him to come around after that episode."

"It makes sense to me now," said Kate. "He did say his mother died. Said it was cancer. Doesn't like to discuss his father. Says he wasn't around very much."

"He experienced abuse," said Dr. Novak. "Mainly verbal, but I suspect physical abuse as well. He said his father was always mad. He would see him sometimes on weekends. I do know his mother's friend tried to help him, but Luke wouldn't let him in, didn't know how. Too many trust issues."

"He says he doesn't know where his father is or if he's still alive," said Kate.

"Look, hope I've been some help, but I've got an appointment in a few minutes. Can I send you copies of his file?"

"Sure, no rush. At your earliest convenience," said Kate. "Thanks for your time. You've been a big help."

• • •

"I'm so sorry." That was all Emma could say when Allison called her at 11:00 a.m.

"No, you're not. Don't think I can't hear that snicker in your voice," Allison said.

"I'm not laughing at you, really. But I've seen what wine does to you."

"I just about attacked him," Allison whined into the phone. Then, as if a sickening realization came over her, she shrieked, "Em? What's wrong with me?"

"What?"

"He *ran* away from me. He actually *ran!*"

"Maybe he's just shy," Emma suggested.

"Or maybe he found me repulsive!"

"I doubt that. How much do you know about him, anyway?"

It took Allison more than a few seconds to think. "Not very much, actually."

"You're sure he's single?"

"Yes. No. I mean, he said he lives alone."

"I hate to say it," Emma said, laughing out loud this time, "but maybe you scared him."

"It's not funny. I've never been turned down like that before," said Allison.

"Poor baby."

"Come on, Em, what should I do?"

"I'm probably not the one you should go to for advice. What's his name, anyway?"

"Luke."

"Luke what?" asked Emma.

Again silence. "I don't know," Allison said in a high-pitched voice.

"Where does he live?"

"I'm not sure. He said about thirty minutes away."

"You really need to stop bringing home strange men."

Obviously ignoring Emma's last comment, Allison continued. "It was really weird. Everything was going along fine. Better than fine. We ate, drank wine. Sat on the porch."

"Maybe he'll call. Give him time."

"Hope you're right," Allison said. "A customer just walked in. I'll talk to you later."

• • •

Luke was still in bed at noon. When he rolled over, the pain in his side was the same as it had been last night. He shouldn't have accepted Allison's dinner invitation. He almost screamed in pain when Allison grabbed him.

If he'd kept seeing her only at the coffee shop, he wouldn't be in this predicament now. He couldn't tell her he'd chased a woman through the rain the other night and that she'd smashed a metal rod into his side before running head-on into a truck. He'd have to make something up. Or better yet, just stay away.

It was time to get up and start moving. He had the day off, but Paul asked if he and Phil could pick up some supplies for another job. The plumbers were almost done on Nolan Street, and he'd have to help repair the ceiling the following morning. He cringed at the thought of having to lift those heavy sheets of drywall above his head.

Finding another *guest* was out of the question. He was in no condition to handle anyone right now. Unless it was someone smaller. As he contemplated the idea, he was distracted by a sound. He listened for a minute more before that unnerving feeling settled in. The feeling of *being watched*. He sat up and carefully pulled on a pair of shorts and sat on the edge of the bed, keeping his eyes on the door. He told himself it was impossible, that all the doors were locked. He'd checked them and rechecked them, as always. The war within began. He crept into the hallway and peeked down the staircase. At a snail's pace, he made his way down the stairs, stopping every few steps to listen. He checked the back door and found it was still locked, and went to the living room. He checked that door. It, too, was locked.

He went back upstairs to get dressed and jumped when his cell phone rang in the next room. He followed the sound to a pair of jeans he'd left on the bathroom floor. Thinking it was Allison, he decided to wait and listen to the message. It was Sal. He sounded angry.

"Where the hell are you? I called Phil, but his phone was turned off again. I don't remember giving you the day off! Call me."

That man was a pain in the ass. Paul was the real boss, and he said the Nolan Street cleanup wouldn't be done till Thursday. Sal was a bully. He hated bullies. He took the jeans off the floor and slipped them on, anger marinating in his gut. It was fine with him. Any feeling was better than no feeling. Soon he'd be free of Sal.

He opened the pill bottle and swallowed a pill, then grabbed his keys off the kitchen counter and went outside. School was out for summer, and he was taking the long way to work. There was somewhere in particular he wanted to go, *needed to go*. It would make him feel better. With his mood on the mend, he picked up his pace and headed to the barn.

CHAPTER 9

• • •

HE WAS ALMOST THERE. JEREMY pedaled as fast as he could. The apple tree that marked the top of the hill on the road was in clear sight. Just a little more and he would be there. He pumped the pedals with every bit of strength he could muster, feeling the burn on the top of his thighs. He pushed past the pain, knowing he could rest on the way down. When he reached the top, he checked to make sure the road was clear. No cars. Smiling from ear to ear, he stopped pedaling and let gravity take over. The wind whipped his face as he hunkered down low to the bike to cut through the wind. His heart pounded so fast, he was sure it would beat him down the hill. It was over so fast.

He wished he had more time so he could turn around and do it again. His mom would be mad if she knew he'd ridden his bike this far. It was probably a mile away from his house, but he told himself he was big enough. And besides, he knew his way around the neighborhood. Part of the thrill was doing something he knew he wasn't allowed to do. It felt dangerous.

His mom was coming home from work early, and he couldn't let her see him this far from home. He found the path that cut through a field and some empty wooded lots. It was a shortcut he'd found the last time he went exploring. The path was more for walking, because several areas were too rough for a bike to coast over. At times, he had to get off his bike and walk it around the bumpy spots.

Within a few minutes, he could see the main road up ahead and decided to ride the rest of the way. He weaved around some deep ruts, as if on an obstacle course. Right before the path ended, his front tire grabbed and twisted sideways into a narrow rut. The bike came to a screeching halt, and Jeremy flew over the handlebars, landing face-first into a small bush.

After brushing himself off, he picked up the bike and pushed it the rest of the way to the gravel road. That's when he noticed the chain hanging down off its track. Jeremy leaned the bike against a tree and tried to put the chain back on. He'd seen his dad do it once before, but now he couldn't get it to stay on. The only thing he had managed to do was get grease all over his hands. After trying several times, he began to panic. Now he was really in trouble. He'd been gone too long, and his dad would be looking for him any minute.

Jeremy was frantic. He tried desperately to get the bike chain back on. It was no use. He wasn't going to be able to fix it. His eyes began to well up, and he wondered how he was going to get home. He was so absorbed in the task that he didn't hear the vehicle pull up alongside him.

"Do you need some help?"

Jeremy turned and saw a man sitting in a truck right behind him. He had been given the speech plenty of times about not talking to strangers and was a little leery of this man who appeared out of nowhere. He stared without answering. The man got out of his truck and walked over as Jeremy backed away from the bike. He watched the man turn the bike upside down before going to work on the chain.

The man glanced over and smiled. "I should have you back on the road in just a minute." After securing the chain, he turned the bike back over and put the kickstand down. "There. Good as new."

The two of them stared at each other while Jeremy sized him up. Since his mom taught him to be polite, he said, "Thank you."

The man bent slightly at the waist. "You're welcome, young man."

"I have to go before I get in trouble." Jeremy looked around. "I'm not supposed to be here."

The man's smile got wider. "I won't tell, if you won't tell."

Jeremy decided that there was no way this man could be a bad guy. After all, he fixed the bike, and a bad guy wouldn't do that.

The man turned around just before he reached the truck, stopped, and looked back. "You should head home now, Jeremy."

Jeremy put the kickstand up and stood, holding on to the handlebars. "How'd you know my name?"

The man took a step toward him. "Because I'm a friend of your aunt Emma's. I want to surprise her, so don't tell her you saw me, and I won't tell her I saw you. Deal?"

"Deal," said Jeremy. He watched the man get into his car and drive away. He wasn't going to tell anyone about this. No one would ever know that he rode to the hill alone.

● ● ●

Twenty minutes later, Luke was parked in the lot of the River Bend Park. It was a two-acre parcel that was next to the Clare River. It was the only local park within walking distance from two elementary schools and a middle school. Kids flocked to its banks in the hotter weather to swim in the shallow fork of the river. Groups of kids, friends, enjoying the start of what was predicted to be one of the hottest summers in recent history.

Luke remembered having a friend, even if only briefly, near the end of eighth grade. His teacher asked the class to team up with a classmate to work on a project. He looked around the classroom and watched everyone pair up with a friend. That's when he spotted Joel, the new kid, looking around just like he was. He'd been at the school for only about a month and kept a low profile like Luke did. He glanced in Luke's direction more than once, probably because he caught Luke stealing looks at him. Joel raised his shoulders and arms in a questioning, what-the-hell gesture, motioning toward Luke. Luke picked up his books and reluctantly took the empty seat behind his new partner.

"Hi, I'm Joel."

Luke slumped forward in the chair. "Yeah, I know who you are."

"Want me to come to your house?"

Luke sat mute, his stomach tightened.

"Or you can come to mine," Joel offered. "Either way, we have to do this. It's a huge part of our grade."

Luke didn't want anyone coming to his house. His mother had been in hyper mode again, and that was putting it mildly. "I'll come to your house."

"OK," said Joel. The boy wrote his number down on the back of Luke's notebook. "Come over tomorrow. Just call me first." The third-hour bell rang, and Joel collected his books, jumped up, and left.

After school that day, Luke found his mother singing and sipping on something in one of their good glasses. He followed her to her room and saw the mess. Clothes were all over the bed and floor, and the music was blaring. He tripped over a shoe box on his way to her dresser and turned the radio off.

His mother swung around and jumped on the bed, landed on her knees, and held up a hanger with a silky white shirt on it. "Turn that back on, sweetie. I need to hear music! Don't you ever feel that way, like you have to hear music?"

He noticed she was talking really fast again, her eyes were painted a dark shade of green, and her lips were bright red. She held the shirt in front of her and jumped off the bed.

"How do I look?" She danced around the room, turning and posing. "Oh, never mind. I think the paisley one looks better." She threw the white one on the floor and took a more colorful one off the hook on the back of the door.

"Mom, I have to work on a project with this kid from school."

Her smile drooped. "Today's Friday. Don't worry about school today." She dropped the shirt on the bed and came to him, grabbing both of his hands. "Let's go out tonight, maybe to the skating rink or the movies! Yes, the movies! No, dancing! We should go dancing!" She took him by the shoulders. "Go get ready, angel!"

"Ma, I can't go dancing. I'm thirteen."

"Of course you can. Lou at the Raven will let you in if you're with me."

Luke sat on the bed. "I'm not going to that place." He'd been there a few times when she'd made him go. It smelled bad, and the tables were always greasy, and she'd leave him sitting alone while she talked to her friends. And she had a lot of them. One time, she dropped him off at home and left with someone she'd just met. A guy. She didn't come home for two days that time. Then she was sad. That time it lasted a week.

She plopped down next to him and put her arms around him. "What do you want to do?"

He pulled away. Her perfume was so strong it stung his nose, and he could feel it in the back of his throat. "I want to go to that kid's house tomorrow."

She hopped off the bed and went back to her closet. "Sure, anything you want." She grabbed a red dress off the floor, took her drink, and turned the radio back on.

"Can you drive me?" Luke yelled over the music. He spun around, trying to keep up with her as she danced around the room.

"Sure, sure," she said.

Later that evening, he was watching TV when he heard the radio go off. His mom came out of her room wearing a black dress that seemed to float when she walked. She spun around and then danced over to the couch. He thought she looked like a ballerina.

"Bye, baby. I'm going out now." She bent down and kissed him. "There should be something to eat in the kitchen."

Luke waited until he heard the screen door close before he ran to the kitchen window. A silver car was parked at the curb, and a man he'd never seen before was leaning against it. He watched the man open the car door for her. She laughed and jumped in. The tires squealed as the car took off down the street. He stood looking out the window until he remembered that he was going to Joel's house the next day, so he checked his backpack to make sure he had what he needed for the project. He was curious about this boy who picked him, even if there were just a few kids left to choose from.

Luke remembered hardly sleeping that night, not just because he was excited, but because of the spring storm that was waging war on the old house. Every time he was about to doze off, he'd hear the branches of the monstrous willow tree whipping at his bedroom window. He got up to get a drink of water and heard a noise coming from the bathroom. The door was slightly open, and the light was on. He knocked on the door, and his mother yelled for him to go back to bed. He thought she was coughing or maybe crying, so he pushed the door open and found her leaning over the toilet, throwing up. Even though he was barely a teenager, he knew she'd drunk too much.

The next morning, he covered his mom up with a blanket. It wasn't the first time he'd found her asleep on the bathroom floor. He called Joel and found out he lived one street away from school. If he walked, he could make it there in twenty minutes. He grabbed his backpack and headed out.

Luke and Joel spread their notes out on the kitchen table. The house was alive with activity. It was distracting but also pleasant to hear Joel's parents and two sisters laughing in the next room. Joel's little sister came into the kitchen, asking if she could help them with what they were doing. His father hurried in to get her and told her not to interrupt them, calling their project "important." It wasn't like that at his house. His mom never even asked about his schoolwork.

Joel's mom asked Luke if he wanted to stay for dinner. When he called to ask his mom, she didn't answer the phone. He lied and said that it was fine with her. Luke watched Joel's mom make mashed potatoes while chicken cooked on the stove. Joel set the table as if it was the most natural thing in the world for him to do. His dad poured milk while his older sister served up bowls of salad. He was hypnotized by the whole surreal scene, like something in a movie or commercial. Dinnertime at his house wasn't anything like this. There was usually food, but it was mostly self-serve. They rarely even used their kitchen table.

After dinner, the boys packed up their papers and graphs and put the final touches on their poster before rehearsing their oral presentation.

Secretly, Luke wished they hadn't finished it in just one day. He gathered up his things and put his shoes on. Joel's mother insisted on driving him home.

When they arrived at his house, the front door was open and all the lights were on. He could see his mother through the kitchen window. When she saw the car in front of the house, she came running out. Luke got out of the car, and so did Joel's mom. His mom's face was bright red, and she was yelling obscenities before she reached them. His friend's mom took a step back, and the irate woman started accusing her of stealing her baby. Luke wanted to disappear. Then Peter came running out behind her, grabbed her arms, and held her back and at the same time apologized to Joel's mother. Peter pulled at her, finally getting her to turn around and walk back to the house. A few neighbors had come outside to see what all the noise was about.

Luke stood with his hands in his front pockets, looking at Joel as the car pulled away from the curb. It usually went something like that, and sometimes it was even uglier. He got an A on the project, but he knew he'd never go to Joel's house again and eat mashed potatoes and chicken. He didn't belong there, anyway. He'd always known that. The *whispers* told him so.

Luke snapped back to the present, and looked up. The pain was still fresh, as though it just happened. He shook it off and focused his attention on a birthday party that occupied the picnic area. Next to it, groups of children played on the swings and monkey bars. One particular group of boys caught Luke's eye. A boy of about twelve was playing Frisbee with three younger boys. The older boy had no problem catching the Frisbee. The younger boys consistently missed it, chasing it to the river's edge.

Luke cut through a patch of trees and strolled casually to the water and sat down with his back to the boys. He'd been listening to their game for five minutes when he heard squealing behind him. The younger boy with the full head of auburn hair came running toward the river, jumped into the air trying to catch the flying disk, missed it, and landed in the water. His friends started laughing. The boy waded through the waist-deep water, retrieved the Frisbee, and threw it back to the group. They immediately started playing again, ignoring their fallen friend.

"Good try," said Luke. He looked behind him and saw the other boys walking off toward the swings.

The boy climbed out of the river, sat down, and took off his shoes. "Great," he said, as he squeezed the water from his socks.

"I have a towel in my truck if you'd like to use it," Luke said.

"I guess I should dry my shoes off. They're new."

"I can go get it," offered Luke, pointing toward the tree line.

"Thanks." The boy stood up, holding the wet shoes in front of him, and started following Luke.

"Should you tell your mom first?" asked Luke.

"She's not here."

"You're welcome to walk with me to the parking lot. It's closer to the swings where your friends are."

"Yeah, I should get dried off," said the boy. He continued to follow Luke toward the parking lot.

They cut through the trees and were only twenty feet from the truck when the older boy ran past, yelling, "Sam, your sister's looking for you!"

The boy stopped and then started walking backward. "Thanks, anyway, mister."

"Sure," said Luke. He watched the boy disappear back through the trees before getting into his truck.

• • •

Emma was sitting on her back patio when she heard someone knocking on her front door. She closed her laptop and walked around the side of the condo and saw Lena standing on her porch.

"Lena, hi."

"I should have called, but I was running some errands out this way and wanted to see how your visit with David went."

"It was good. Do you have time to visit? I can get you something to drink."

"Sure, I'm ahead of schedule," she said, and followed Emma back to the patio and sat down.

When Emma returned with the lemonade, Lena was on the phone.

"Really," Lena said, smiling at Emma. After a few minutes, she said, "Love you, too," and hung up. "That was Paul. He said David remembered something. About you."

Emma refused to get her hopes up. "What?"

"He wouldn't tell Paul. Said he would rather wait and see you."

Emma didn't want to rush right over to find out that it was really nothing. "Maybe I could call him."

"It's up to you. So your visit was good?"

"I didn't want to tell him anything he wasn't ready to hear, but I did answer his questions. Well, some, anyway."

"Personally, I think we should lay it out on the line for him. He's not ten," said Lena.

"What about his parents?" Emma asked.

"He's a big boy. He does what he wants. They really have no say."

"I know, but they're close. I don't want to change that."

"You're perfect for David, so screw them," said Lena.

"I've accepted that they don't like me."

"That's because they don't know you," said Lena.

"I'll go see him. I told him I'd bring some pictures. And changing the subject, Sal's guy, Luke. What's his last name?"

"Stone. Why?"

"Allison's seeing a guy named Luke."

"Is it him?"

"Don't know. I love Allison, but she doesn't always ask the right questions. Sometimes her judgment when it comes to guys is a little off."

"Don't know much about him," said Lena. "He's not from around here. I think he told one of the guys that he's from up north somewhere."

Emma laughed. "Sounds as if you know more about him than Allison does."

Lena pointed at the laptop. "You're writing again?"

"I am."

"That's good to hear. Listen, Paul's having some of the guys over Saturday night, just a small get-together. Why don't you come by?"

"Thanks, I'll think about it."

CHAPTER 10

• • •

Thursday morning, Sal was standing in the driveway smoking a cigar and wearing his usual sour expression when Luke and Phil got out of the car.

"Hey, Sal," Luke said, trying to sound amiable. "Paul said he didn't need us till this morning."

Sal's face turned red. "You work for me, not Paul."

Phil put his hands in his pockets and looked at the ground.

It was clear Luke was on his own. He stepped forward. "Didn't mean any disrespect."

Sal took a step closer to Luke and exhaled smoke into his face. "Your kind doesn't even know what the word means!"

Luke swallowed hard. "Back away or…"

"Or what?" said Sal in his gravelly voice.

Luke bit his lower lip, looked down, and took half a step backward.

"That's what I thought!" said Sal. He pointed to the truck in the drive-way. "The drywall isn't going to unload itself." Sal turned and walked away, mumbling under his breath.

Phil finally spoke up. "You gonna let him talk to you that way?"

Luke watched Sal disappear into the house before walking over to the truck.

• • •

After a full day of dirty looks from his boss, Luke dropped Phil off in front of his apartment and then stopped at the corner market. A few minutes later, he was sitting in his truck sipping on a half pint of whiskey, stewing over the confrontation with Sal. It was just a matter of time before the bastard fired him, and he couldn't let that happen. He'd have to set Sal straight.

After soaking up courage from the whiskey, he drove back toward Nolan Street, cruising slowly as he got closer to the house. Paul's truck was gone, and Frank was backing out of the driveway. He waited down the street, his car idling, until Frank drove off in the other direction. Perfect. He would talk to Sal alone this time. He drove past the house, turned around, and parked on the opposite side of the street. He went around to the back of the house, quietly opened the door, and stepped into the kitchen. Sal had his back to him, packing up supplies.

Luke cleared his throat.

Sal must have thought Frank had come back for something. He turned, opened his mouth to say something, but stopped when he saw Luke. At first, surprise registered on his face but then quickly changed. His eyes narrowed, and he looked as if he had just tasted something bitter. Luke had seen that look before. On his father's face.

Sal turned away and continued with his work. "What the hell do you want?" he said, as if thoroughly disgusted.

"Thought we should clear the air."

Sal went about his work, ignoring Luke's attempt to talk.

Luke heard the whispers and tried not to listen. His stomach muscles tightened. He shook his head and tried to shake free from the unwanted distraction. The *whoosh, whoosh* echoed, coming from every direction, and within seconds, he was so absorbed that he didn't notice Sal standing directly in front of him. He looked off to his left.

Sal looked in the same direction. "What are you looking at, you freak?" he yelled.

The insult tore through him. He directed his gaze back at Sal. The whispers changed to laughter. He clamped his hands over his ears. The instinct to protect himself collided with the disrespect that Sal threw at him. The voices were loud, taunting, filling his head to the breaking point. Adrenaline pumped through his chest as he obeyed the urge to flee. He tried to back away but was stopped by the kitchen counter. His elbow slammed into a toolbox.

Sal advanced toward him.

His brain, flooded by too much stimuli, tried to make sense of the situation. He saw Sal's lips moving, but the noise in his head made it impossible to hear anything else.

Luke slid along the granite countertop to the right, his hand making contact with something. Metal and rubber. He grasped the object tightly and swung it high in the air. His hand swooped down, and the hammer stopped dead as it punctured Sal's left temple. The sickening, crunching sound silenced the voices. Blood shot sideways as if it, too, wanted to flee. In the stillness before Sal's body hit the floor, he found irony in the look of total disbelief on the face of the man who always seemed so sure of himself. Luke stood motionless, as if the slightest movement would make it real. The deafening silence was almost louder than the noise that was in his head only moments ago.

He dropped the hammer and looked down at his hands. *So much blood.* His shirt was spattered with red. A small chunk of flesh was stuck to his jeans above his left knee. He shook his leg frantically to free himself from the bloody blob. *Think, think, think.*

Luke looked at the gory scene. He knelt down and rolled the dead man over, reached into his back pocket, and pulled out his wallet. *A robbery.* Now, all he had to do was get to his car without being seen. *The hammer.* After slipping off his shirt, he wrapped the hammer in it and then stuck his head out the back door. A woman next door was in her yard putting something on a barbecue grill. He quickly closed the door and went back through the house to check the side entrance that led to the garage. It was clear. He walked outside and around the garage to the back of the yard. He scanned the area and then hopped over the fence into the park that bordered a few of the backyards. He looked between the houses as he moved through the park until he could see his truck on the street. He hopped back over the fence and made his way to his truck, using a clump of bushes on one side and a garage on the other for cover.

The street looked clear, but he couldn't be sure that someone who happened to look out a window wouldn't notice a man with bloody jeans running to his truck. Casually, he strolled across the street, as though he had a right to be there. Once safely in the truck, he scanned the area. A man about five houses away was cutting his grass, and another neighbor was getting the mail out of her mailbox. He started the truck, backed up into a driveway, and headed the other way down the street. He put the hammer, wrapped in his shirt, along with the wallet under his passenger seat. His side was throbbing from all the physical activity. He would go home, get some rest, and make sure he wasn't the first one at the job in the morning.

• • •

The girl from food service was collecting David's dinner tray when Emma walked into the room. This time, he was sitting up in the chair next to the bed, looking stronger than the last time she'd visited. He immediately smiled when he saw her. She stood in the doorway, unsure of the proper etiquette when visiting someone who didn't know you.

David must have seen the uncertainty in her face. "Are you going to come in?"

Emma walked into the room with the gracefulness of an awkward teenager. "I wasn't sure if I should have called or..."

"It's not as if I was going anywhere," David joked, obviously trying to put her at ease.

Emma pulled the other chair closer to him and sat down. "So how are you feeling?"

"Better. I'm glad you came," he said. "I've been thinking about you."

Emma tried to hide her smile. "When are you getting out of here?"

"Soon. I saw the doctor this morning. Looks as if I'm going to a rehab facility for a little while."

"That's progress," Emma said.

"I wanted to ask you something," he said. "I was looking through a magazine yesterday, and I saw some pictures of a small town somewhere, I can't remember where, but they showed pictures of people riding horses. I thought I remembered horseback riding on a beach with you."

"What else do you remember?"

"That's it." He watched her face. "So was it a real memory?"

Emma nodded her head. "We did go horseback riding last year. On a beach—so yes, it was real."

David gave her a thumbs-up.

When he smiled at her, for a brief moment she could see something in his eyes that was familiar. The part of him she knew. It was there, floating near the surface. And then it was gone. The lost look returned, and that spark of knowing vanished from his eyes. She couldn't bear seeing that recognition being ripped away, so she turned her head.

He noticed the rapid change in her expression. "Am I making you uncomfortable?"

"You're not," she said without hesitation. "It's just the situation. I don't know what to say or what not to say."

He turned his body to face her. "Nothing you say is going to freak me out. I'm past that. I mean, I've lost my memory." Anger tinged his face. "What I need is for everyone—Paul, Lena, my parents, and you—to be honest with me and stop avoiding my questions."

Emma stood and paced across the room and then spun around to face him. "OK," she said loudly, using an authoritative tone. "We have been seeing each other for a year. Sometimes I stay at your place, and sometimes you stay at mine. So I'd say we're intimate. I am a writer, self-taught, and I enjoy it. My mother is dead, probably a suicide. My father is dead, probably a murder. My sister is a psychiatrist who likes to tell everyone what to do. I've worked at your renovation properties on and off. And oh yeah, your parents hate me." She stood with her arms crossed, eyebrows raised, staring at him. "How's that?"

"Wow," he said. "That was great! Why can't everyone be like that?"

Emma starting laughing and plopped back down in her chair. "Now did that make you uncomfortable?"

"Not at all. One more question. How could my parents possibly hate you?"

"That's a long story. How about we leave it for another day?"

"Some other day, huh?" A sly smile rested comfortably on his lips. "So I didn't scare you away?"

"I don't scare easily."

"Good."

"What else can you tell me about us?" David asked.

Emma swung her legs over one side of the chair and leaned toward him. "How much time do you have?"

"All night," he said.

Emma started from the beginning. She was glad he was so interested in...their story.

• • •

The street was brimming with people when Phil and Luke arrived at the Nolan Street job Friday morning. Two police cars were parked in front of the house. Frank and Paul were talking to an officer on the sidewalk that led to the front door. Neighbors were gathered in the street, whispering to one another, as more people joined the group of onlookers. Luke walked up the driveway but was stopped by another officer who had just come from the side of the house.

"I'm sorry, but you can't go any further. This is a crime scene," said the young officer.

Phil caught up to Luke. "What's going on?" he asked.

The question went unanswered, and the officer told them to stay back by the street.

Paul saw them and immediately came over to them. "It's Sal. He's dead."

"Dead?" Phil said loudly. "What are you talking about?"

Paul looked back over his shoulder before he continued. "Someone killed him. Frank got here and saw his truck. Sal wasn't supposed to be here till later. He went in and found him in the kitchen. The police think it was a robbery."

"A robbery?" asked Luke.

"Yeah," said Paul. "The police want to talk to everyone who was here yesterday, so don't go too far." He turned and went back to Frank.

Luke and Phil went back to the street and leaned against the truck.

"Murdered?" Phil mumbled. "In this neighborhood?"

Luke went around the truck and started to get in the driver's seat. "Well, looks as if we just got the day off."

Phil opened the passenger door and stuck his head in. "Paul said we can't leave. The police want to talk to us."

"Calm down. I'm not going anywhere." His side was throbbing again, and he needed to sit down. He looked at the hectic scene in front of him, wondering what they knew.

Phil got in and closed the door. "It's terrible about Sal and all, but I can't afford to be off work. My rent was due last week."

Luke didn't respond. He watched Paul and Frank go into the house as Phil rambled on about his bills.

"So can I work with you on that job?" Phil asked.

Luke shot Phil a distracted look. "What?"

"That job. The old lady? At the farmhouse?"

Phil finally had Luke's full attention. "There's no work there. It's done."

"Already, huh? I thought maybe that's where you've been staying since you left my place."

"Didn't think I needed to check in with you."

"I got you this job...thought maybe you'd help me out," said Phil.

"I said, 'The job's done,'" Luke said, with an iciness in his voice.

"OK, OK." Phil stopped talking and looked out the window. "Where are you staying, then?"

"With a friend. Why?"

"Just curious, is all," said Phil.

Luke turned the radio on. The last thing he needed was more chatter from Phil.

• • •

After Emma got out of the shower, she listened to the frantic message from Joyce. She threw on her clothes, slipped on some shoes, and flew out the door, combing her wet hair on the way to Joyce's new house.

The usually quiet neighborhood was crowded with police cars and more neighbors than the street had residents. She parked her car in the first spot she found and walked the rest of the way.

A Channel Six news truck was parked directly across the street from Joyce's house. A female reporter was pointing at the house while a man with a camera panned the area. Emma weaved through the crowd and finally spotted Joyce, who was standing with a man Emma didn't know.

"I got your message. How did it happen?"

"Oh, Emma. Frank found him when he got here. They think he was robbed."

The man standing next to Joyce offered Emma his hand. "I'm Joyce's husband, Jim."

"Nice to meet you," she said quietly, taking in the whole scene. "Sorry it had to be here."

"I can't believe something like this happened," Jim said.

"Does his family know?" asked Emma.

"Frank said he has a son in another state," Joyce said. "Paul said he'll call him."

Luke came out of nowhere. "Do they know anything yet?" he said as he joined the group.

Emma shrugged. Just then, Paul and Frank emerged from the house. Joyce and Jim met them on the sidewalk. Emma stayed back with Luke.

"How awful," said Emma. "I guess this sort of thing can happen anywhere."

"Guess so," said Luke.

"Were you here last night?" she asked.

Luke shook his head. "Me and Phil left around five thirty. Frank and Sal were still here."

Paul made his way to Emma, while Jim and Joyce continued to talk to the police.

"Hi, Paul," said Emma. "Joyce called and told me what happened."

"We're all shocked. I tried to call Sal last night—left a message around eight. Figured he was tired and went to bed."

"They haven't removed him?" asked Emma.

"Not yet. He was hit on the head with something. It's bad."

"If I can do anything, let me know," she said.

"Thanks. Heard you saw David."

"Yes, he remembered something we did together."

"That's what he said," said Paul.

"What did he remember?" asked Luke.

Emma smiled. "Horseback riding."

"It's something," said Luke.

"Yes, it is." Emma rested her hand on Paul's arm. "Tell Joyce to call me if she wants." Emma nodded at Luke and Paul and then slipped away into the crowd.

●　●　●

Luke threw the wrappers from the burgers he ate for dinner in the trash, put the bank information back in the drawer, and then sat down at the kitchen table to finish his beer. The old lady had her bills directly deducted from her retirement fund, so at least that was one less worry. The stress headache was lessening now that he'd put something in his stomach. He'd expected to be questioned by the police but by Phil, too? He never should have let the guy help him with the work he'd done in the beginning, but Phil should have been long gone by now. He was supposed to move to Ohio to live with his brother, but that was before his car broke down. Now Luke was stuck with him till he bought a new one. Maybe he could give Phil some of the money he'd tucked away and call it a loan. Then he'd be free from him. He didn't need him anymore. He went to the living room, closed the drapes, and eased himself down on the couch. He practiced the breathing exercises Kate had taught him, even though they caused pain in his side. Then, with the beer gone and his anxiety eased, he fell asleep sitting up.

The arguing was getting louder. He held his hands tightly over his ears, careful not to touch the spot above his eye where the belt buckle had sliced. The shoulder that was knocked into the wall earlier throbbed. His mother's friend opened the bedroom door. His father jumped in front of him, telling the man to leave. The man shoved his father aside, stepped into the room, smiled at him, and told him to put his jacket on. Peter lifted him up, stepped over his crying father, carried him to the car, and drove him home to his mother.

Luke woke up with tears streaming down his face. The pain. It never left but hid, only to emerge when dreams poked at it. It scratched and clawed its way to the surface whenever it wanted. He couldn't control it. Keeping it at arm's length had become a constant struggle. A painful, lonely one.

There was new pain now. Peter's words. A betrayal that cut deep, one he didn't see coming. He closed his eyes. He could see that hateful look on Peter's face and hear his voice when he called him unstable and ordered him to stay away from the girls. Peter talked about them all the time. All those pictures and so much talk about visiting them on the holidays. Peter told him that he had a lot in common with Emma—said they were both rebels. He only wanted to talk to him, but the old man wouldn't listen. He kept insisting that he had to tell Emma about him so she could protect herself and Kate. He should have run from Peter, but he didn't.

He opened his eyes. The familiar pressure in his head was building. Then the *whoosh, whoosh.* The whispers, still faint but drifting closer. Calling him. Always calling him. Getting louder. Blaming. Laughing. *No!* He put his hands over his ears and screamed, "No, no, no! I didn't mean to do it!" He ran through the house to escape. Once upstairs, he opened the bedroom closet and ducked in, closing the door behind him. In the dark, he sat with his back to the corner, his knees pulled up to his chest, and his arms wrapped tight around his legs. He fervently rocked back and forth, sweat now racking his body. He was transformed, a little boy again, hiding from an adult who said he loved him.

• • •

After rehashing the murder that happened ten minutes from Allison's front door, Emma listened to the ridiculous ranting her friend did from time to time. She listened because she knew Allison wouldn't stop until she got it out of her system. At one point she even put the phone down to change clothes.

"Emma?" Allison barked into the phone.

"I'm listening," Emma said, still pulling a tank top over her head.

"So he hasn't called me yet, and it's been three days."

"Have you tried to call him?" Emma said, trying to sound invested in the conversation.

"No. Should I?"

"I don't see what it could hurt. Do you even have his number?"

"I do, right here. Oh, by the way, his last name is Stone."

Emma froze. "Did you say Stone?"

"Yes, why?"

"He works for David and Paul."

"Oh my God. Sal is his boss?" asked Allison.

"Was. Now Paul is."

"What a coincidence."

"Small world," stated Emma.

"I hate to talk bad about the dead," said Allison, "but I can't imagine working for him. He did some work for me when I bought my first shop, and he managed to scare some customers off with his foul language."

"The first time I met him, he was tearing into Luke and another guy," said Emma. "Oh, Lena invited me over…well, that was before what happened to Sal, but if it's still on, I may see Luke there tomorrow."

"Tell him you know me. See what he says."

"Just like in high school. Should I pass him a note, too?"

"Funny. Really, Em, see what he has to say about me."

"Will do. Look, I should get to work. My laptop's calling me."

After they hung up, Emma thought about what a small world it was. Allison really liked this guy. He was attractive, with all that wavy brown hair, but she couldn't see Allison dating him. He was too quiet, but what did she know? People tend to hide their real selves. Maybe he was just being professional. After all, she'd really only seen him when he was working. If Lena was still having a get-together tomorrow, she intended to go. She was curious about this guy Allison was so taken with.

CHAPTER 11

• • •

IT WAS SEVEN FIFTEEN ON Saturday evening when Emma finally looked at the clock. The time had slipped away. She'd been working all day and had a headache, so she closed her laptop. The calendar on her desk said it was already the middle of June, and she'd spent way too many nights sitting home since David's accident. Lena called earlier to say they were still having some people over. Paul and the guys were going to talk about having a memorial service for Sal when Sal's son came to town the following week. Emma promised Lena she'd be there by eight, and now she was going to be late. She took a couple aspirins, checked herself in the mirror, threw on some jeans and a jacket, and left for the party.

Paul and Lena's house was a large log home that sat on twenty acres, most of which were wooded. When she got there, Paul and a few guys were in the yard unloading wood from the back of a pickup truck and piling it next to the fire pit. People were standing around in front of the pole barn, and others were going into the house. She found Lena in the kitchen stirring something on the stove. Lena saw Emma and immediately grabbed a red plastic cup, scooped something from a large glass punch bowl, and handed it to her.

"You've got to try this." She took her own cup and tipped it to touch Emma's. "I'm really glad you came."

"A small get-together?"

"Well, word travels."

"I think it's nice that Paul's arranging the memorial. Any word from the police?"

"No," said Lena. "Paul says it was just a robbery gone bad. He feels responsible. Thinks that if he'd stayed longer that night, it might not have happened."

"I know how he feels," said Emma. "I keep thinking if I'd picked David up that night or if I'd done something different, his accident wouldn't have happened."

"You're both ridiculous," Lena said while unplugging a slow cooker.

The kitchen was spacious, and it opened up to a large living room. People lingered everywhere. Emma scanned the area but saw no sign of Luke.

"Here." Lena threw two hot pads toward Emma. "Carry that out for me," she said, pointing to a roasting pan on top of the stove.

Emma followed her across the yard to the barn. A table was set up buffet-style with a number of dishes already on it. "Sorry I didn't bring anything."

Lena stepped back, surveying the table. "I think we'll have plenty. Let's go back to the house and get some more punch."

The fire was roaring when Lena and Emma came out of the house. The flames shot straight up, and smoke rose high into the air. Car headlights illuminated the yard as more people arrived, turning the lawn into a parking lot. Lena greeted a man who asked about David and another man who said he used to work for Sal. Emma slipped away and walked around the fire to where Paul was.

"Emma, glad you made it," said Paul.

"How are you doing?"

"All right. Did Lena tell you about the memorial service?"

Emma nodded. "Just that you're planning one."

"It won't be for a week or so. His son's having him cremated."

The air chilled as the sun set. Emma pulled her jean jacket a little tighter around her. "It's not your fault, you know."

"Feels like it," he said, staring into the flames.

"I struggled with the same thing, about David."

Paul cocked his head and then turned to face her. "How's that your fault?"

"Exactly." Emma started laughing, maybe from Lena's punch or maybe from taking a step back and realizing how ridiculous it really was.

Paul didn't laugh but was smiling. He put his arm around her. "Well, we're quite a pair, aren't we?"

They stood that way for almost a minute before a man approached Paul. They shook hands and started talking about an addition Paul had put on their house. Emma watched an ember float up and over the fire before it burned itself out. When she brought her eyes back down, they landed on a familiar face. Straight across from her was Luke. He was staring at her. She waved. He hesitated but then smiled back. With Paul otherwise occupied and Lena nowhere in sight, she headed over to him.

"Nice to see a familiar face," she said.

He jammed his hands into his front jean pockets. "I don't know many people here, either."

"Sorry again about Sal."

"Yeah, it's awful," he said quickly. "How's your book coming?"

"Good, thanks," said Emma, remembering the difficulty she'd had the day he replaced her door. "I found out we have a mutual friend."

"We do?"

"Allison."

Luke seemed to physically withdraw at the mention of her. Emma was sure it wasn't a good sign.

"She's...nice," he said.

He wasn't forthcoming with any other information, and she wasn't satisfied with leaving it at that. "How'd you meet? I don't think Allison said," she lied to keep the subject alive.

He hesitated before answering. "At a coffee shop."

"She likes her coffee," said Emma, unable to think of anything more intelligent to say.

"So what's your book about?" he asked.

"Well, adventure…there's some—"

Lena came up behind them. "Come get something to eat." She grabbed Emma's hand and pulled her away toward the barn.

Emma turned back to say something to Luke, but he was gone.

• • •

He turned the key, and a few seconds later, he was standing in Emma's living room. The lamp on the end table provided just enough light for him to find his way around. As Luke took in the room, the corners of his mouth curled up. He took a few steps toward the kitchen, his fingers touching the furniture as he moved along. He stopped briefly to pick up a blanket that was lying in a heap on a chair. He held it up to his face and breathed it in. After making sure he put it down the way he found it, he moved on to the kitchen. He needed to see what she was writing about. The light over the sink was on, so he took a look around. The notebook and laptop weren't there.

It was time to take a look upstairs. He turned on the hall light and went up. The first room on the left was her bedroom. He hesitated in the doorway but then forced himself to cross the threshold. While passing the open closet, he ran his hands over her clothes, taking his time to soak up the textures. He made his way around the bed, stepping over a pile of clothes on the floor. On top of her dresser was a framed picture. When he got closer, he took a good look and then swallowed hard. It was a picture of her with David. He retreated to the hallway, passed a bathroom, and found another room with a large desk in the middle. He approached it and switched on the lamp that sat on top of it. No notebook or computer in sight, just an empty bag of cookies and a coffee cup. He tried two drawers, but both were locked.

He remembered the last time he'd been there. She was upset, ripping pages out of the notebook, balling them up, and whipping them at a garbage can. He moved quickly and found one on the other side of her desk. He dumped out its contents and found several crumpled-up pieces of paper. He picked out a few and put them on her desk. He unfolded the first one, scanned the page, and read the names in the second paragraph. Earl and Anna. Who the hell were they? He skimmed the rest of the page. Nothing was familiar. He balled up the paper and threw it back into the basket. He opened the next one. Still no names he recognized. He tossed it down and frantically unfolded more paper, reading, skimming, and crumpling. His hands worked faster, until he finally put it all together. His lips closed to a straight line as his fist squeezed the wadded-up paper. *She was making it all up.* The story, the characters, everything. None of it was real. How could she write him into this crap?

He stood, spun around, and knocked the garbage can over. Queasiness twisted his stomach. He paced the room with the ferocity of a wounded animal. Regroup. Think, think, think! He closed his eyes, hoping an answer would come. It's not going to be this way! She not going to do this! He bent down, righted the garbage can, and scooped up the scattered paper. It had to be written with him in it, and then it would be *real*. He deserved to be a part of it. They were all connected. *Control. I need to be in control.* He turned off the lamp and went downstairs.

On his way to the front door, he passed a grouping of pictures on the living room wall. He ran his finger over a picture of Kate and Emma. Longing replaced the anger. He started to back away from the wall but stopped when he saw a picture of Jeremy standing next to his bike. A large bow was tied to the handlebars. He backed up a little more and took in all the smiling faces. Pieces of a life, not his. There was no place in this world where he'd find pictures in pretty frames with his face in them. It hit him like a personal attack. His face was warm, and his eyes stung as they filled and then overflowed. He opened the door and slipped out—a nobody, unnoticed—into the night.

• • •

Lena was putting the leftovers away while reciting her pasta salad recipe to a neighbor who was writing it down on a napkin. Emma poured herself more punch and slipped out to the yard, hoping to find something, *any-thing*, more interesting to do. The party was starting to thin, and the remaining guests were gathered around the fire. Rock 'n' roll drifted from the open door of Paul's truck.

Emma knew her walk was less than graceful as she crossed the yard. It amused her that she was having so much trouble keeping the punch in her cup. She staggered a bit as she reached the fire and tripped over a small cooler. An arm reached out to steady her. Her eyes followed the arm up to its owner. Luke.

"Thanks." She took a sip from what little was left in her cup. "Now that was an entrance," she declared, her words somewhat slurred.

"I wouldn't want you to fall into the fire," Luke said, while still holding on to her arm.

"Me, either," she said, tipping her cup over. "Looks like I need more punch."

Luke reached down, grabbed a beer from the cooler, and opened it. "Here."

She took it from him and brought it to her lips. "Thought you left."

"Not yet. Where's Lena?"

"Doing dishes." Emma leaned toward him. "I snuck out," she whispered.

Paul came over and started talking about a drywall job that was scheduled for Monday, and then he introduced Luke to another man. She stared deep into the fire, watching as the bright purple color on the bottom shimmered and then rose into golden flames, and then her mind jumped to David. Maybe he wouldn't get his memory back. It was hard to think about, and it made her stomach hurt. Or maybe that was from mixing alcohol. While she breathed in the heavy, comforting smell of the burning wood, she managed to come up with a good argument for why he'd be better off if he didn't remember her: his family ties and the family business. She had ties, too, on a much smaller scale, but she wasn't *responsible* for them. So many people counted on him. She wasn't good with the whole family thing. Anyway, he wanted to be married. And have kids. Maybe his mother was right. Maybe he'd be better off with what's her name.

Emma looked around and wondered what she was doing there, anyway. She brought the can of beer to her mouth but decided she'd had enough and put it down on top of the cooler. Sleep—she needed sleep. She walked away, hoping no one would notice.

The night air was crisp as Luke got farther from the fire. He put his hood up and followed her to her car.

Emma dug into her pocket, pulled out her car keys, and dropped them. She almost fell over when she bent down to pick them up. She cursed while searching for them in the long grass.

"Let me help you," Luke said, and scooped them up.

She reached out to take them.

He pulled them out of her reach. "How 'bout I give you a lift?"

"I can drive, really," she said, her words running together. She put her hand out, palm side up.

"I'm sure you can," he said, and then moved his face closer to hers. "But I'd hate to see something happen to you." He took a step back when he heard Paul's voice.

"Emma? Where you going?" Paul asked.

"Home. I had fun. Tell Lena bye for me." She turned to face Luke. "Now, if you'll give me my keys."

"Lena said you were staying. Anyway, you shouldn't drive," said Paul.

"I told her I'd drive her home," said Luke. "I'm going right past her place."

Emma raised her hands in the air. "All right, drive me home."

Paul watched Luke help her into his truck and then headed back to the party. Luke listened to her ramble on about how ridiculous it was for her to leave her car there. Halfway home, she fell asleep.

He found it difficult to concentrate with *her* sitting so close. All those old photos came to mind. The girl with the light eyes smiling back at him.

Now here she was, asleep in his truck. He remembered that large envelope that came in the mail for Peter. School pictures of the two sisters, and more pictures of the skinny teenager and her younger sister. He planned to give them to Peter the next time he showed up, but so much time passed before he saw him again. At the time, he'd felt guilty about keeping them, but now he felt justified. Peter was a liar. He made up all the stories about the things they would do together. His jaw tightened as he thought about that place Peter sent him to. It wasn't a hospital. It was his prison. He was angry for ever trusting that man. His breathing quickened. Then with anger came the *whispers*. Intruding, laughing, mocking. Luke lowered his window just enough for the sound of the wind to drown them out.

Five minutes later, he sat in her driveway with the truck running. He focused on the hum of the engine while he struggled to pull himself together. When his breathing was steadier, he woke her up. She said she was dizzy and had to throw up. He got her out of the truck just in time. After she threw up in the bushes, he walked her into the house.

"I'm sorry," she said, and went straight to the couch and asked for a drink of water.

By the time he made it back from the kitchen, she was asleep. He put the glass down on the end table. His eyes washed over her. His hand involuntarily rose and inched toward her face, but he regained control and yanked it back. He couldn't touch her. Her breathing became ragged, and she mumbled something. He moved his ear in closer to listen.

"Can't, can't. I'm not good. For you." With her eyes still closed, she reached up and rested her hand on his thigh.

He wanted to touch her, to feel her hair. "Emma, you're—"

"I'm sorry. Sorry, David."

Luke jerked away and stepped back. The words stung like a slap across his face. His expression went slack, his fists hit the sides of his legs, and he stood in a defensive stance, as though ready to pounce. The voice in his head hissed and squawked and then laughed at him, gaining more space in his brain. He backed farther away for fear he'd hurt her. With his hands clamped over his ears, he knelt on the floor. His brain screamed, *Stop, stop,*

stop! She couldn't see him like this. *Breathe.* He looked up at the couch, hoping she wasn't watching. She hadn't moved. Minutes passed before he was calm enough and could trust himself. He got up and went back to her. His features softened as warmth flowed back to his limbs. She affected him in a way no one else ever had. He pulled the blanket off the chair and unfolded it over her and left, and this time he was careful not to look at the pictures on her wall on the way out.

• • •

The knocking on the door was getting louder. When Emma opened it, she was hit in the face by the bright, early morning sun. She shielded her eyes and looked at her friend. "Do you know what time it is?" Emma asked.

Allison didn't even try to answer as she barged in. "Good morning, sunshine," she said, and handed Emma a large coffee. She had a white paper bag in her hand and went straight to the kitchen. "Hungry?" she yelled over her shoulder.

Emma reluctantly followed. "I don't usually eat in the middle of the night." Her head hurt, and she wanted to lie down.

Allison set the bag down on the table and took two plates from the cupboard. "Didn't you notice the sun shining or the birds singing on this beautiful Sunday morning?"

"No. Only morning people do," Emma said, and took a sip of her coffee.

"Up late last night?"

Emma looked at Allison over the rim of her cup. "Is this about Luke?"

Allison's face lit up. "So what did he say?"

"You are unbelievable. What is it about this guy, anyway?" Emma watched her open the wrapper and take a big bite of a biscuit sandwich. Even with a hangover, the light went on in her head. "Oh," Emma said slowly. "I get it now. A guy doesn't happily jump into bed with you, and you freak out." Emma pointed at her and laughed. "You. Can't. Handle it!" Even the sound of her own voice made her head pound.

"That's not it at all," protested Allison.

"OK. Tell me what's so special about him, then."

"He's..." She threw her napkin at Emma. "I just want to know why."

"Move on. He can't be worth all this."

"Did you talk to him last night or not?" Allison asked.

"I did. I told him we had a mutual friend. He said you were nice."

"Nice?" she yelled. "What the hell does that even mean? The old man next door is nice. The girl at the drugstore's nice."

"Please lower your voice." Emma lifted the greasy wrapper and took a peek at her breakfast. Her stomach did a backflip. "He drove me home last night," she said with the still-sour look on her face.

Allison exaggeratedly let her jaw drop.

Emma did a head roll. "Come on, I needed a ride home. Well, Paul and Luke said I did, anyway."

Allison took a closer look at her. "You do look pretty rough. I can drive you to your car if you want."

"That would be great."

"Em, what would you do if you were me?"

"You don't want to know what I'd do." Emma pushed her breakfast to the side. "Just call him."

"I did. He never called me back."

"Then give it up," said Emma.

"I don't give up. Just wait." Allison's eyes narrowed. "I will find out what happened."

"I think you're wasting your time."

"Why's that?" asked Allison.

"Because by the time you do find out, it won't matter. You'll be on to someone else, anyway."

Allison gave Emma her best you-hurt-my-feelings look. "Wanna hang out today?"

"Don't tempt me. I have to work, and then I think I'll swing by and visit David. Lena said his parents have a graduation party to go to tonight, so I won't run into them."

"And you think I'm being silly?" said Allison. "You're the one hiding from your boyfriend's parents."

"I am, aren't I? Maybe I'll get there a little earlier and see what happens."

CHAPTER 12

• • •

THE HOSPITAL PARKING LOT WAS full, and Emma had to circle around a couple of times before finding an open spot. The gift shop was packed as well, but she waited in line to buy David some licorice. On their first date, they went to see a movie, and he smuggled in a one-pound bag of multicolored licorice, which he said was his favorite candy. She had eaten so much of it, she felt sick by the end of the movie. It was some time before she could even look at licorice again.

She could hear his father's voice before she reached his room. She stopped just short of the door, straightened her posture, and knocked.

"Emma, come in," said David, smiling.

His mother half turned and then quickly looked away. David's father said hello.

Emma held her head high and stepped into the room. "Nice to see you," she said, looking at his father and then his mother. She approached David and asked how he was feeling.

He swung his leg off the bed and then, using both hands, lifted his other leg, cast and all, off the bed and stood up.

Emma put her arms forward to steady him. He looked directly in her eyes, leaned in, and kissed her on the lips.

Shocked by his sudden show of affection and unsure what to do next, she said, "I brought you licorice."

He took the candy from her without taking his eyes off hers. "Thanks."

She looked at the floor and tucked her hair behind her ears. "You like licorice."

"Yes, I know. It was thoughtful," he said.

David's mother stood up. "Ted, we should go." She kissed her son, gave Emma a forced, closed-mouth smile, and left the room. David's father politely nodded his head and obediently followed his wife into the hall.

"You didn't have to do that," Emma said softly.

"I know. I wanted to. Please, have a seat." He eased himself back onto the bed. Strain from the physical exertion hung on his face, but so did satisfaction. He stared at Emma. "Lena told me the reason behind my parents' rude behavior."

"They're just trying to—"

"There's no excuse. It's rude, and I won't have it."

Emma heard that strength and confidence in his voice she knew so well, and her mind wandered. It was so sexy. She had to snap her thoughts back to where they should be. "So, how long have you been able to stand up like that?"

"This was the first time," he said.

Emma started laughing and just shook her head.

He opened up the package of licorice and held it out to her. "Want to share some candy with me?"

She pulled an orange piece out of the bag. "I can't think of anything I'd like to do more."

• • •

Kate was going to be late for her Monday morning meeting. The traffic was thick, and it seemed no one was in a hurry except her. St. Catherine's Hospital was a forty-five-minute drive from her house. She was running late because she got a call from Phil, who was one of her clients from the clinic. He asked if she could see him later that afternoon. His voice was pressured, but he wouldn't discuss what was bothering him. She told him she wouldn't be able to see him until six that evening, after she did her rounds at the hospital. She agreed to swing by the clinic on her way home from work.

There was a lot on her mind. Derrick's family reunion was on Saturday, and she had to pick up extra hours at the clinic, due to an associate having to leave town unexpectedly for a family emergency. She was always able to handle family and work but wasn't exactly feeling at the top of her game the past few weeks. She was listening to some classical music, trying to get into a better frame of mind, when her phone rang. While feeling around for her phone, she managed to dump her purse out on the passenger seat, and some of its contents rolled onto the floor before she found the phone. It was Emma.

"Hi, Emma," she said in a clipped tone.

"Did I catch you at a bad time?"

"No," Kate lied.

Emma rushed right into the subject. "I had an amazing visit with David yesterday."

"That's great. Does he remember anything else?"

"Just the horseback riding. Oh, and he remembers he likes licorice."

"Licorice?"

"That's a long story," said Emma. "I won't keep you if you're busy."

"I've got a minute. Any word about Sal's murder?"

"Not that I've heard."

"Hey," said Kate, "hate to change the subject, but that landlady left a message for me to call her back. I've got a pretty full day ahead of me. Could you call her and see what she wants?"

Emma hesitated. "Sure, don't worry about it."

"Thanks. Gotta go. I'm at the hospital now."

● ● ●

The coffeepot beeped, signaling the liquid gold was ready for consumption. Emma immediately walked over, as if obeying the machine's command, and poured her first of the many cups she'd consume that day. She was on her way upstairs to her office when she remembered her promise. She scrolled through her contacts on the phone, wishing she hadn't agreed to make the call, and found Lorraine Moore's number. She let it ring several times and was getting ready to hang up when Lorraine answered it.

"Hi, this is Emma Simms. Kate said you called. If you're having a problem with the man I hired to clean out Peter's place..."

"No, he's done a fine job. It's empty, and I've already found another renter. I'm calling because that lady friend I told you about, the one who used to visit your father, called, looking for him. Anyway, she was quite sad about the news. I told her about you and your sister coming by. She left her number and was hoping you'd give her a call. I didn't think it was right for me to give out your number."

Emma rolled her eyes. Now what? "Did she say what she wanted?"

"No, but she didn't seem as surprised as I was when I found out he had two daughters."

Emma didn't want any fallout from the whole miserable situation, but she took down the number the woman had left. When they hung up, Emma looked at the number in her hand. She didn't want anything ruining her mood, so she put the phone number aside and sat down at her desk. Maybe she'd call this Connie Fulton later.

● ● ●

The traffic was horrendous, and Kate was running late again. She hadn't been able to find anyone willing to pick up a couple hours tonight at the clinic. Since she was already seeing Phil anyway, what were a couple more hours going to hurt? She needed to hammer out another contract with the other doctors. The one they had wasn't working. It seemed she was always picking up the extra time that no one wanted. Kate was mindlessly walking through the clinic's parking lot when Phil cut her off just before the sidewalk. She plowed right into him.

"I'm so sorry!" she said after she bounced off him.

"It was my fault," stammered Phil, avoiding eye contact.

Kate went around him. "Let's go talk," she said, expecting him to follow her.

Phil stood in the same spot, staring at the ground.

She turned and pointed toward the building. "If you come with me, we can talk about it now."

"I'm not sure I should say anything."

Kate, sensing Phil's struggle, slowly walked back to him. She gave him an empathetic look, waiting for him to continue.

"A friend of mine didn't like this guy. I didn't like him, either. Well, no one really did. Anyway, he's dead."

"And you feel guilty about it?" she asked.

He looked up, finally making eye contact with her. "Not really, but if he died and someone had a fight with him the same day..."

Kate felt concern now. "Did you fight with this person, Phil?" she asked quietly.

"No, no!" he said, jumping back, his eyes round and wild.

She put her hand out to him. "Let's calm down. I'm just concerned for you, Phil."

"It's not me who argued with him all the time—it's my friend, the one I work with."

Kate thought for a minute. "Luke?"

Phil looked more frantic than before. "Don't tell him I told you!"

"Are you afraid of him, Phil?" she asked.

"No," he said more quietly. "But I've seen him get mad before. I don't want him getting mad at me."

She tried to reassure him. "I can't tell anyone anything you tell me." His bottom lip quivered, and she thought he might cry. "Can we go to the office and talk some more?"

"I shouldn't have come here," he said, smacking himself on the side of his head with the palm of his hand. He backed away, still looking at her, then turned, ran around the building, and was gone.

Kate stood facing the direction he ran, wondering what she should do, could do, since she had to honor doctor-patient confidentiality.

• • •

Emma stood and stretched. Her back felt tight from sitting so long, so she took a break and decided to call the woman Lorraine Moore said was her father's friend. What kind of friend was she? She didn't even know he was sick. Probably just some nosy woman looking for all the sordid details of his demise. She looked at the phone number, wondering what the woman could possibly have to say. Lorraine said that this Connie person didn't seem surprised that Peter had children. Maybe she knew about her and Kate. So what if she did? Curiosity was a powerful thing, after all, and what could it hurt? She picked up the phone, tapping it on her bottom lip. She made her decision and punched the numbers into her phone. It was answered on the third ring.

"Hello."

"I'm looking for Connie Fulton," said Emma.

"This is Connie."

"My name is Emma Simms. Lorraine Moore gave me your number."

"I have been looking forward to hearing from you or your sister. I was a friend of your father's."

"Yes," said Emma. "That's what she said."

"I am sorry for what happened to him. We've been out of touch awhile. He was a good man."

Emma was beginning to rethink her decision to call. "I wouldn't know about that. I haven't seen him since I was very young."

"Yes, I know. He used to talk about you and your sister quite a bit," she offered in a softer tone.

Wanting to get the call over with, Emma got to the point. "What can I do for you, Miss Fulton?" she said, trying hard to hide her irritation.

"I have some of his belongings. He's lived in several different places and asked if I would keep a few boxes for him. I am going to live with my daughter soon, and I was wondering, could I mail his things to you?"

"I'm not sure that's a good—"

"Please, Miss Simms, I don't want to throw them away, and I can't take them with me."

Emma looked up at the ceiling and ran her hand through her hair. "Sure."

"Oh, thank you. I'll be mailing them out in the morning."

She gave the woman her address, regretting having made the call.

"Miss Simms, your father was a good man. He regretted leaving you and your sister. He had...difficulty with life. He helped others when he could. He tried to help my sister's son who was always in some kind of trouble, maybe a way to make amends...I don't know."

Not wanting to sound rude or take something out on a stranger, Emma simply said good-bye.

$$\bullet \quad \bullet \quad \bullet$$

Kate paced the length of her office while she waited for Luke. He was already half an hour late for his appointment. He had never been late before. She tried to call Phil last night, after he ran from her office, but his phone had been shut off again, and she was worried about him. She knew he worked odd jobs but had no idea how to find him, other than to go to the address in his paperwork. She did know that Luke worked with him, and she planned on finding out more. She opened the office door, planning to ask the secretary if he'd called, when he walked into the clinic.

He looked at the secretary and then at her. "Sorry I'm late. I got stuck behind an accident," he said as he signed the log book at the front desk.

Kate smoothed the front of her skirt with her hands. "No problem. We'll just have a shorter visit today," she said, trying to appear calm. She didn't know exactly what Phil was so worried about, but she wanted to see what she could learn from Luke. "Let's get started then."

After they were seated and covered the usual issues, Kate asked him how work was going. She immediately noticed a change in his demeanor.

He stopped, his usually friendly dark eyes turned a little colder, and he sat up straighter in his chair.

Luke looked at her for a few seconds and relaxed some before answering. "I had a horrible week. My boss was killed."

Kate wanted to know more. "Were you there? Did you get hurt?"

This time he answered quickly. "No, I wasn't. I had left for the day. He was robbed. He was alone."

Kate froze. She wondered if...no, it couldn't be David and Paul's co-worker. That would be too much of a coincidence. "I'm sorry," she said, her voice slightly quivering. "Was your boss from around here?"

Again he seemed to hesitate before answering. "Yes, I guess he was."

"I heard about a robbery-murder. What was his name?"

His gaze was piercing. "Sal. His name was Sal."

Kate abruptly looked away. "I'm sorry about your boss."

"Thanks."

After a brief, uncomfortable silence, Kate regained her composure and asked if it would affect his job.

"No. I'm working directly for the builder now."

"That's good." She opened his chart and changed the direction of the conversation to his medication. After writing another script for him, she asked about his new friend, the one he mentioned to her on his last visit.

He looked down at his hands. "It didn't work out."

"That's too bad. Hope you aren't giving up on relationships."

His eyes brightened. "Oh, I'm not. I'm just looking for the real thing."

Kate smiled and flipped through a few more pages. "I talked to Dr. Novak."

The statement made Luke flinch.

"You signed the paper that gave me your permission, do you remember?"

"Yes, I do. I forgot."

"He told me a little about your family. About your mother and her—"

"I would have told you about her," Luke interjected. "I don't see what that has to do with anything."

"It helps me understand your past so I can better help you."

"What else did he tell you?" Luke asked.

"We discussed diagnosis."

Luke said nothing.

"Basically we agree. You have trouble with your thought process at times. You do seem to be at baseline now. Do you know what that means?"

"That I am doing good?"

Kate nodded her head. "Yes. You're not hearing voices anymore, are you?"

"No. Not for a long time," he lied.

"Good." She looked at the clock on the wall. "We're running out of time for today. Anything else you'd like to discuss?"

"No."

Kate stood up, indicating their session was over. "It was nice seeing you, Luke. Make your next appointment before you leave."

After Luke left, Kate sat down behind the desk. She rubbed her hands together, noticing they were clammy. This whole coincidence about Luke working for Sal wasn't sitting well with her. It occurred to her that he must know Emma, too. Due to the recent events, it would be helpful if she could talk to Emma about Phil and Luke, but that was definitely off limits. As both men's psychiatrist, she couldn't even admit that she knew either of them. If she didn't hear from Phil soon, she'd drive by his residence to make sure he was all right.

• • •

Emma took the first bite of her submarine sandwich before she swung the door open and walked into the clinic. Amy had the day off, and the part-time receptionist stood up as Emma approached the front desk.

"I'm sorry," she said, looking at Emma and pointing to the sign that said No Food or Drinks. "That's not allowed in here."

Emma looked at the stylish woman in her early twenties who stood there using the tone of voice you'd use when scolding a toddler. "Sorry," said Emma, putting the sandwich back in the bag. "I'm here to see Kate—I mean Dr. Nelson."

The woman continued in her stern voice. "You'll have to sign in on the log." She hastily ran a magic marker over the last name on the list before handing Emma the clipboard with a pen connected to it.

"No, I don't have an appointment..."

"Ma'am, please sign the log."

Emma decided to humor her and picked up the pen and signed her name on the next available line. The name above hers was barely concealed under the marker, and caught her eye. Luke Stone. Kate was professionally seeing Luke. The world was getting smaller all the time.

She sat down with her back to the receptionist and took another bite of her sandwich, wondering what Luke was seeing her sister for. Kate came out of the office and grabbed a folder from the secretary.

"Emma?" asked Kate.

The receptionist stood up, noticing that Emma continued to be non-compliant with the office rules. "Doctor, I'm sorry, but I've already asked her to refrain from eating in here."

"That's all right, Shelly. She's my sister, and she doesn't like rules."

Shelley said nothing else and sat down, her face taking on a reddish hue.

"This is a pleasant surprise," said Kate. "Come, I have a little time before my next client."

Emma followed her into the office, noticing the way it always smelled. Not bad, but it reminded her a little of that smell that hit you in the face when you walked into a motel room. She sat down in the same chair Luke had sat in less than an hour before.

"Well, I talked to Derrick, and he said you'd be here late. I brought you dinner," she said, pulling another sandwich out of the bag.

"Thanks." Kate grabbed it and immediately started opening it. "I'm so hungry; I had to skip lunch."

Emma took out two cans of soda and started opening one. "Your girl Friday out there made me sign in on the log book. I couldn't help but notice you're seeing one of Paul's recently acquired workers."

"Emma! That's confidential. You shouldn't have seen that."

"Couldn't help it," she said while chewing. "His name wasn't covered up very well."

Kate stared at Emma and shook her head but kept eating.

"He didn't look crazy when he fixed my door," said Emma.

"You're horrible!"

"Come on. You know what I mean."

Kate pointed her finger at Emma. "You're not going to trick me into discussing anything about anyone on that log. So don't even try."

"I know who he's dating—or was, anyway," said Emma.

Kate stopped chewing. "Who?" She quickly caught herself and raised her hand. "Stop. I know what you're trying to do." She leveled her eyes with Emma's. "I can't talk about anything with you."

"Well, you can't, but I can," said Emma. "Your client was seeing Allison until very recently."

"Really," Kate stated flatly, and went back to eating.

Emma's eyes drifted out the window and then back at Kate. "It's kind of weird."

"What is?"

"Luke. He keeps turning up. Everywhere."

"It's a small town," said Kate.

"I guess. Did David or Paul refer him to you?"

"Emma," Kate snapped, now visibly irritated with the conversation. "Again, I can't discuss anything with you," she said slowly, carefully pronouncing each word.

"All right! I get it. Sorry."

Kate's eyes narrowed a little. "Any word about Sal's death?"

"No."

"Were there lots of people working there that day?"

"Paul, Frank, a few other workers."

"Was he having problems with anyone?"

Emma cocked her head sideways. "What's with all the questions?"

"Nothing. Just making conversation. How's your friend, the one who owns the house?"

"Upset. Someone died in her kitchen." Emma stood up. "I should go, get to work."

"How's the book?"

"It's coming along. It feels good to write about something different, lighter than what I'm used to writing."

When they stepped into the lobby, the next client had just arrived.

Emma walked past the front desk and smiled at Shelly on her way to the door. The young woman, looking a little sheepish, told her to have a good evening.

• • •

"Damn!" Luke slammed his fist down hard on the hood of his truck. Why didn't Phil answer the door? Was he hiding something? He was more than pissed off at himself for signing that paper Kate asked him to. He tried to imagine what the old doc might have told her. Even though he was smarter now, he couldn't erase all the stupid things he probably had said back then. At least he had more sense now not to talk about the things in his head. Nothing good came out of being truthful, except being locked up. He remembered being told what to do, when to eat, when to shower, when to take his medicine, and when to go to bed. They said they were trying to help him. His mother swore she wouldn't let them put him in a place like that. Then she got sick.

His mind raced back to Kate. She asked him about work. Why was she so interested in that? What did she know? She forced him to tell her about working for Sal. She knew something, but what, exactly? Phil. What a traitor. He finally decides to think for himself, and this is what he picks. What did he tell her, and what would Kate tell Emma? Then it dawned on him. He smiled when he remembered what she said. Whatever he told her couldn't be repeated to anyone unless he gave her his written consent. He was safe. He turned back toward Phil's apartment. There was one place he might find him.

• • •

Phil sat in his usual seat at the Twisted Tavern, eating from the free bowl of popcorn. The bar was within walking distance of his apartment. Besides the corner market, it was the only other place he went to since his old car finally broke down for the last time. Now he had to save up for another vehicle so he could move to Ohio to work with his brother. Hopefully Paul would give him enough work until he could afford one. He'd had his anxiety under control, but now with everything that had happened, it was flaring up. He blamed it on all the arguing he'd been forced to endure between Sal and Luke. Now he wondered what part Luke may have had in Sal's death. Just as he started struggling with regret about telling his doctor about Luke, he heard the familiar voice behind him.

"Hey, Phil."

Phil turned and said hello to his coworker. "Didn't expect to see you here."

Luke took the stool next to Phil. "I was hungry and in the neighborhood, so here I am." He signaled the barmaid to bring two more beers.

Phil would be the first one to admit that a greasy bar burger hit the spot sometimes, but even so, this place wasn't known for its food. His pulse jumped up a notch, wondering what Luke was really doing there. He finished his beer and waited for Luke to kick-start the conversation.

When the next round arrived, Luke lifted his bottle to Phil. "To friendship."

To Phil, the whole situation seemed off. They weren't drinking buddies—hell, they weren't even friends. No, Luke wanted something. Phil remembered sitting in the same spot when he first met Luke, two months after he started working for Sal. At the time, he seemed nice enough, just a guy down on his luck. Phil knew all about that. Luke was so thankful when he got him the job with Sal. He also hooked him up at the clinic.

"Have you seen Dr. Nelson lately?" Luke asked.

The hairs on the back of Phil's neck stood straight up. He took a long drink of his beer in hopes of buying some time to come up with the right answer. He figured Luke must know something and lying about it wasn't the best choice. "I have."

Luke said nothing for a full minute and finished his beer in three swigs. "What did you two talk about?"

Phil fought the urge to squirm in his chair. "The usual, I guess."

"Which is…"

"My nerves."

Luke took a long, exaggerated look at Phil. "I'd say you look pretty nervous right now."

Phil wished he'd never gone to see the doctor. He tried to remember exactly what he'd told her. It seemed as if someone cranked up the heat. He pulled at the front of his shirt, desperate to let some air in. "I am nervous. It seems like you're mad at me."

Luke let out a fake laugh. "Why would I be mad? Did you do something I should know about?"

"No, no. I…I didn't do anything," he said, swallowing hard. "Look, I have to go. See you in the morning." He got up and made his way to the door as if the place was on fire, almost knocking down an elderly man who was coming out of the restroom.

• • •

Wednesday morning, Kate was glad she'd beat the traffic and got to the hospital early. She had errands to run for the reunion, now only three days away, but first had to attend a family meeting scheduled with one of her new patient's parents. By early afternoon she should be on her way home and have plenty of time to get everything done. She shared an office with Marlene, who wouldn't be in for a couple of hours yet. It would give her enough time to finish the paperwork she'd been putting off before her talkative colleague arrived. While sorting through her mail, she came across an envelope from Dr. Novak.

She opened it and was pleased he'd sent copies of all three admissions Luke had had to the facility. She skimmed the legal petitions for treatment and saw that they told the story she had expected. Noncompliance with medication and follow-up treatment when he was discharged. The daily charting by hospital staff reflected paranoid thoughts, diminished capacity to care for self along with periods of agitation, usually followed by an increase in auditory hallucinations. She was glad Luke had finally gained enough insight to stay clear of the hospital. She'd been a psychiatrist for two years but worked in the field for eight and had seen that maturity sometimes played a role in helping one manage their illness. She was also aware that some could mask symptoms and hide them in fear of being sent back to an institution. He took his medication as prescribed and never missed an appointment with her. With no family support, he seemed to have come a long way on his own. She placed the papers on top of the envelope and pushed it to the side of her desk, bumping her coffee cup on the way. Coffee splattered on the desk and across the pages. She reached for a tissue box, pulled out a wad of tissues, and wiped at the mess.

One of the petitions for treatment grabbed her attention. Her mouth dropped open, and she blinked several times to make sure she was seeing it right. The person who filed the petition was Peter Simms. Granted, it was somewhat of a common name, but it was the handwriting that sent a dull stab deep into her chest. She would recognize his penmanship anywhere. Her father knew Luke. Emma's voice rang through her head. *It's a small world.* She gathered up the papers and sorted through each hospitalization, looking for the other two petitions. Each one was signed by Peter Simms. The paperwork spanned a time period of a year and a half. He'd been in Luke's life in some capacity for at least that amount of time. Kate picked up the phone to call Emma but quickly put it back down on her desk. She was alone with this information. She couldn't tell anyone, not even her sister.

She was wrestling with her dilemma when the phone rang. "Emma," she said in a pinched tone. "You're up early."

"I've got some research to do for the book. I have an interview with— oh, never mind. I'm calling because I have time today if you need help organizing the picnic, or just need me to pick up anything."

"Maybe. Let me get my thoughts together, and I'll let you know," said Kate.

"Everything all right?"

"Yes, why?" Kate said a little too quickly.

"You sound distracted."

"You know me, got a million things up in the air."

"All right then. Just let me know."

"I will. Talk to you later."

Kate stared at the paper her father had signed when she herself was just a freshman in high school and wondered how he fit into Luke's life. She felt compelled to find out more as she put the papers back in the envelope and tucked it into her briefcase. Right now, she needed to get a few things done, so she checked the time and went to work on the stack of papers on her desk.

• • •

Emma's interview at the local fire department went better than she had expected. All of her questions about fire investigating and probable cause were answered. She was confident that she took enough notes and had enough information to finish a scene in her book. By later today, she hoped to make major headway with that part of her story. With that put to bed, she walked into the Third Street Deli with a sense of accomplishment and an appetite.

The place was busy with the lunch rush, and people were standing in line to pick up carryout orders. She took a look at the dessert counter and was tempted to skip lunch and go right for the sweets. Allison sat at a small table in the corner, laughing about something with a cute waiter who looked to be in his mid-twenties. Sizing him up, Emma decided he was probably waiting tables to pay for college or for his share of an apartment payment. Or both. He was light-years away from being with a woman like Allison. Even though Luke was older, it was basically the same category she put him in.

"Here's my friend now. Hi, Em," she said, waving Emma over to the chair next to hers. She looked back at the waiter. "Told you my lunch date wasn't a guy," she said in her flirty voice.

As soon as the waiter moved to another table, Emma shook her head. "Did you used to babysit him or something?"

"He's a cutie," Allison said, leaning slightly to her left as she continued to check him out.

"Didn't I say you'd be moving on to someone else?"

"Him? No, just having a little fun. Still haven't heard from Luke, but I swear I'm going to find out what happened."

"I don't doubt that," said Emma.

"Oh, by the way," Allison said, reaching into her purse. "I'm still leaving Saturday for the conference, but I'm not sure what time. Can I drop off Merlin on my way out of town?" She handed Emma a card from the hotel.

"Sure. If I'm not there, just let yourself in. I'm sure Merlin will make himself at home."

Allison smiled big when the young waiter came back to take their order.

• • •

Luke was relieved the job at the new renovation house had taken up only a couple hours of his day. He was glad to be rid of Phil, who acted like a scared rabbit, all anxious and jumpy whenever he talked to him. There was something Phil wasn't telling him, and it made him uncomfortable. Right now, he needed a little space. He turned his truck down the dirt road where he had fixed Jeremy's bike chain. It had become a habit to cruise this neighborhood. It was fate that made their paths cross that day when he found the boy, about to cry, trying to fix his bike. Sometimes he'd find himself driving down this road without even remembering how he got there. Some invisible force, much stronger than himself, drew him here. That's how he knew if things were meant to be or not. It was even stronger with Emma. He knew her. Peter had shared so much about her.

With his car still running, he sat in the spot where he'd helped Jeremy that day. He was daydreaming when he caught a flash of orange in his peripheral vision. He snapped back to the present and saw a couple of kids on bikes turn on the next road. He drove to the corner and saw the source of the bright orange color. It was the shirt of a blond boy, and next to him was another boy with dark hair. He couldn't be sure, but it looked like Jeremy. He turned the corner and drove slowly, following far enough behind them. The boy in the orange shirt turned right while the other boy continued down the road alone. Luke increased his speed, and within a minute, his whole day magically turned around.

Jeremy slowed his bike and drove as close to the side of the road as possible without falling into the culvert. Luke lowered the passenger-side window and pulled up alongside him.

"Good afternoon," he yelled, and waved at the somewhat startled boy.

Jeremy stopped riding and put one leg down to balance the bike. His face went from suspicion to recognition. "Hi, mister."

"I thought that was you. I didn't want to be rude and not say hello. Did you make it home in time the other day?" Luke asked.

Jeremy smiled. "Yeah, I didn't get in trouble or anything."

"I'm glad. Did you tell anyone you saw me?"

Jeremy shook his head from side to side. "Heck, no."

"Do you need a lift?" Luke asked.

Jeremy hesitated before answering. "I'd better not."

"I'm still working on that surprise for your aunt."

"You should bring it to the picnic on Saturday. She'll be there," said Jeremy.

"Oh, the picnic. Where is it again?"

"At the Clare Park, silly. There's going to be an archery contest and everything." Jeremy became animated, jumped off his bike, put the kickstand down, and walked over to the car. "I practice every day. Dad says I have a good chance to win."

"Well, I'll be rooting for you."

"Thanks, mister," said Jeremy. He tilted his head. "What's your name?"

"Luke."

"I better get home." He got back on his bike. "See you on Saturday, Luke." He waved and rode away.

Luke watched Jeremy until he went over a hill and disappeared. Even the muffled whispers couldn't bring Luke down now. He reached into the backseat and took the half bottle of whiskey from the brown bag. He held it up and toasted himself. Maybe he didn't need medicine after all. Maybe he just needed…them.

• • •

Emma leaned in and scooped all the bags out of her backseat at once, determined to make only one trip into her sister's house. She stood up straight with the bags draped over her arms, trying to get the kink out of her back. If she'd bought that SUV David told her about, loading and unloading her vehicle wouldn't be an issue, but she had to prove her independence by buying something completely the opposite. How infantile. She couldn't help but laugh out loud at herself.

Kate came up behind her and took some of the bags from her. "What are you laughing about?"

"Nothing, just remembered something."

"Thanks for picking up all this stuff. You saved me from another trip to town."

Emma looked around as soon as they set the bags down in the kitchen. "Where's Jeremy?"

"He's upstairs drawing a picture for you. Jeremy," she yelled down the hallway. "Aunt Emma's here."

"Aunt Emma!" Jeremy called as he ran down the stairs. "You're coming on Saturday, right?"

"Wouldn't miss it," Emma said.

"Good. You're gonna get a surprise," Jeremy said.

"I love surprises." Emma looked questioningly at Kate.

Kate shrugged her shoulders.

"Here," said Jeremy, pulling a piece of paper from behind his back. "I made you a picture for your refrigerator."

"Thank you," Emma said. "My refrigerator will love it."

Jeremy smiled. "It's a picture of me at the archery contest on Saturday."

"Wow, look at all the people. I better get there early to get a good seat."

"Mom, can I practice shooting my bow? I only have three more days!"

Kate shook her head. "Wait till Dad gets home."

"OK, can I have something to eat?" asked Jeremy.

Kate rolled her eyes. "You just had a snack when your friend was here."

"Please?" he begged.

Kate was sorting through the bags and checking the items off on a list. "In a minute. Let me finish this first, and I'll get you some fruit."

"I'll get it," said Emma. She put some grapes in a bowl and handed it to Jeremy.

"He's been a handful today," Kate said after he ran outside.

"I wouldn't mind one like him," said Emma, watching her nephew through the window.

Kate distractedly looked up. "Thought you didn't want any kids."

"I don't, or didn't."

"Well, no one said you couldn't change your mind." Kate slapped the list down. "There. The only thing left to do is pick up the chicken Saturday morning and throw the beans in the slow cooker."

"I should get home. I've got lots of notes to sort through for the book," Emma said. "Call if you need me to pick up anything else."

Emma went out through the side door, said good-bye to Jeremy, and gave him an extra-long hug.

CHAPTER 13

• • •

THURSDAY AFTERNOON, THE PHYSICAL THERAPIST positioned the wheelchair at an angle next to the bed. David stood and pivoted to his right with determination visibly stamped on his face, completed a half turn with assistance, and then finally eased himself down on the bed. The therapist, a rather small-framed woman in her late forties, was able to maneuver him around with the greatest of ease, even though he outweighed her by at least sixty pounds. She said he was coming along "just fine." He didn't feel fine—no, he felt wiped out. Not that he was in pain, but this last session kicked his butt and didn't do anything helpful for his attitude. After she gave him the usual directions to practice his exercises after dinner, she left the room, and he was left alone to lick his wounds.

He stared at the ceiling and tried to focus on something else. Emma. It seemed to be the go-to thought for the day quite a bit lately. He smiled when he thought about the way she moved when she walked and how they laughed at stupid stuff when they were together. Those eyes. They gave a glimpse of something deeper, wiser. And the way she smelled like oranges, but spicier, made him warm. He trusted her more than he trusted anyone else right now, because she was honest with him, and that was what he wanted. With the past two years absent from his memory banks, he imagined he must have grown up some. The old David would have been intimidated by this woman that he couldn't get off his mind. Her visits were the only thing that kept him from giving up. Was this the way he felt when they met the first time? He relaxed into the bed, his mind finally unwinding. He closed his eyes and let the tension of the past hour drift out of his spent body.

Emma's face, smiling, hair blowing in the wind. Something in the corner of his mind, pushing his thoughts deeper. Looking down in his hand, something shiny catching the light. Feeling euphoric, excited. Wanting to get to her. Stepping off the curb, the squealing of tires! Coming fast! A face. Wait!

His eyes sprung open and darted around, searching, as his lungs sucked in the stale air of the hospital room. The car. The vehicle seemed to aim at him like a dart arching for its target. He pushed the blanket off his body and felt the need to jump out of the way. Some unseen fear combined with confusion cloaked him like a second skin. A memory? A nightmare? Reality continued to guard its hand. He closed his eyes, trying to see the face, but was jolted from his thoughts by another presence. Someone cleared their throat. He turned toward the source of the sound—a man, standing there, his hand raised, knocking on the door.

"Is this a bad time?" the man asked, but continued to walk into the room.

David looked at him. "No. I mean, I was sleeping."

The man closed the door. "You looked upset," he said as he got closer.

"Just...a dream."

"How are you?" the man said, his voice deep, monotone.

The voice was familiar, somehow, but not the face. "I'm sorry, but I don't recognize you."

"I'm Luke. I worked for Sal."

David shook his head apologetically.

Luke smiled. "It doesn't matter, really. Just wanted to see for myself how you were."

There was something about the man. David took a harder look at him. No, it was nothing. He didn't know him. He tried to be polite, because as far as he knew, this man could be his best friend. "How long have we known each other?"

"Not long." He stepped closer.

David had a few other visits from people he didn't remember, but this one was the most awkward. He guessed he'd have to get used to it.

A nurse came in and signed her name on the information board on the wall. "Hi, David, I'm Dena. I'll be here till eleven thirty tonight. If you need anything, let me know." She went back into the hall and left the door open.

"You look tired," said Luke. "You should get some rest. See you soon."

David watched the man go, leaving him feeling like an intruder in his own life again.

• • •

"Shit!" Emma yelled as she inspected the cut she'd inflicted upon herself while cutting through the packing tape. She agreed to have the boxes shipped to her, but actually seeing them in the middle of her kitchen was something else entirely. She watched as the cut on her finger started to show the first faint sign of red, and then slowly the liquid rose and began to seep out of the perfectly sliced skin. She put her finger in her mouth and sucked up the blood. When it showed no sign of stopping, she went to the first-floor bathroom and got a bandage.

A few minutes later, she sipped a beer while staring at the boxes. It wasn't too late to put them at the curb on garbage day. Kate didn't know about them or about their father's friend. Emma outright lied when she told Kate the landlady called to complain about the man she'd hired to clean out his place. It was what it was. Lies. To protect Kate. Or maybe herself. From what, she didn't know. More than twenty years later, these boxes threatened to reopen old wounds and toss a little salt into them.

Being this indecisive was new to her. So many things were new to her lately. She surprised herself when she reached for the half-opened box and tore it open the rest of the way with her hands. It looked like mostly papers, a few pictures, and some letters. She flipped through the envelopes before she realized they were all returned to sender. Peter Simms. They were addressed to Miss Emma Simms. Even though she couldn't remember the exact address, she remembered the street. Bluebird Lane. It was the house they all lived in together. The third letter had a different address on it. She remembered an old, run-down apartment with sun-bleached curtains and squeaky furniture. It was managed by an old man who always smelled like evergreen trees and flirted with her mother every time they saw him. It wasn't till years later that she equated the strong smell with gin.

So many letters. Either they'd moved away before the letters arrived, or her mother had sent them back. The latter seemed more probable. Her mother never mentioned them to her. The only letters she knew about were the ones she'd received when she was older, maybe because she'd pulled them out of the mailbox herself. She tore open the first letter and saw the familiar handwriting. In the third sentence, he asked if she liked the present. A few lines down, he wrote about why he picked the green bike with the yellow-and-green sparkles instead of the pink or purple one. He said he remembered that she hated pink. She tossed the letter aside and ripped into the next one. He talked about wanting to see her at Christmas. He told her to enjoy the new boots, and he mentioned sledding. The third letter talked about going fishing on spring vacation. Even though they were returned, he kept sending them.

Emma put the letter down and thought about the green bike and the boots. She remembered how protective her mother was. Like looking into a mirror, she saw herself, guarded and protective. Always reinforcing the walls around herself and her sister. Her stomach churned. She was doing the same thing her mother had done. Lying to Kate and lying to herself. Doing what she knew how to do. Tuck it away, nice and neat, and then pretend it's not there. Only it was there. She'd put so much energy and effort into pushing people away, and now she didn't know how to stop. It was an ingrained habit forged out of fear. Fear of getting too close, of getting hurt, and of needing someone. *We all just do what we know how to do.* The tears were falling, and she didn't try to stop them. She backed away from the boxes and cried for her mother, her father, for Kate, and then for herself.

• • •

Kate had been on call twice this week without actually having to go in. Friday morning, she hung up the phone and jumped in the shower. The doctor she shared an office with had called in sick. Any other day she wouldn't have minded, but her sitter was out of town till Tuesday. She'd have to find somewhere for Jeremy to go for a few hours. Derrick couldn't leave work. He had a meeting with a new client, and then he was picking up some relatives from the airport.

She dried off, grabbed her phone, and went to the kitchen. After pouring herself a glass of orange juice, she called Emma, who agreed to watch Jeremy. She opened her briefcase and rummaged through a folder till she found what she was looking for. Phil's address. She still hadn't heard anything else from him and didn't want to wait till his appointment next week to see how he was. She would stop at his apartment after she dropped off Jeremy.

● ● ●

Luke pulled into the parking lot and drove around the apartment building to the usual spot at the curb where he always picked up Phil. There wasn't much work this week, but Paul said if they wanted to put in a few hours, they could clean up a new property the company had just purchased. The Dumpster had been dropped off last night, and an old shed needed to be torn down.

After waiting five minutes, he figured Phil had overslept. Luke opened the truck door, but before he got out, he saw Kate standing at the intercom box of Phil's building. He watched her push the button, saw her talk into the speaker, and then stared in disbelief as she reached for the door and went in. He jumped out of the truck but then thought better of it, got back in, and decided to wait. Five minutes later, she came out, walked down the sidewalk, and got in her car. There was one Dumpster that wasn't going to get filled today. Phil was going to ruin everything. He waited until she pulled out of the complex and followed her, staying a safe distance behind.

She got on the freeway and headed east. He merged into traffic, keeping a few vehicles between them.

Twenty-five minutes later, she exited and turned right. He knew where she was going. Her day job. He had followed her before and was certain that this was the way to St. Catherine's Hospital. She parked in the small side lot that was reserved for doctors and entered through a breezeway that he knew housed the psychiatric unit.

Luke parked in the back of the outpatient surgery lot and walked toward the hospital. Using the same door Kate had, he went in, turned left, and took the elevator to the third floor. He checked both ways before turning down the hall that led to the office. His thoughts ran wild, crashing around in his head, making noise only he could hear.

A man in scrubs and a lab coat came around the corner, holding a folder in his hand, looked through the thin horizontal window of her office door, smiled, and went in. Luke made a quick left and turned the next corner. He waited there until the man came out. He heard him thank her and say he'd fill out the petition. A minute later, Luke was standing at her door. He knocked.

She was looking at a computer monitor, and without looking up she said, "Come on in."

He stepped in, closed the door, and waited for her to finish what she was doing.

She looked up, confusion dawning on her face. "Luke?" Kate stood up. "What are you doing here?"

The look on her face told him he wasn't welcomed there. "I had to talk to you."

"Did you call the clinic?" she asked.

He took a few steps and was in front of the desk. "Why were you at Phil's?"

"Did you follow me?"

"I want you to understand," he said through clenched teeth.

She took a step backward and bumped into her chair. "Understand?"

His face contorted. He looked at her as if she was stupid. "What I'm trying to do."

She smiled, but her lips trembled. "And what's that?"

His face went blank. "I counted on you." He turned and walked out of the office.

• • •

Shortly after one o'clock, Allison dropped off the flowers at the Sampson Banquet Center for a retirement party. She had to make two trips with her car because the delivery van had been acting up again, and she didn't want to drive it until she had it looked at. She hated putting the Closed sign in her store window in the middle of a workday, but she had no choice because Rachel wasn't feeling well and had gone home early. Hopefully her employee would feel better by morning because she needed her to cover the weekend. Allison's usually good mood had taken a hit with all the unexpected problems she had to deal with the day before she was scheduled to go out of town. She sat at a red light scrolling through her contacts on her phone, looking for the number of another employee who might want extra hours if Rachel couldn't work in the morning. The light turned green before she found it.

She started to accelerate and then saw the red pickup coming through the light, heading in the opposite direction. Her eyes landed on the driver's face. Luke. She beeped and waved, but he didn't respond. He must not have seen her. Or maybe he did. She yanked the steering wheel and turned left into a used-car dealership, made a U-turn in the driveway, and managed to make it through the light as it turned yellow. The speed limit was twenty-five and was enforced because of the close proximity to an elementary school. Determined to catch up with him, she increased her speed to twenty over the limit. Up ahead, she saw the pickup turn right. A patrol car was sitting in a gas-station parking lot, so she let up on the gas and slowed down. After stopping at the four-way stop, she turned right and looked for the pickup, but it was nowhere in sight.

Her cell phone rang. She reached for it while carefully scanning side streets as she passed them. "Hello."

"Hey," Emma said. "Where are you?"

"Right now I'm driving through town, why?"

"I'm at the Creamery with Jeremy, and I thought if you were around, you might want to take a break and meet us here."

"Wish I could. I'm down an employee at the shop, and I just got done with a delivery," Allison said, checking every parking lot she passed. "I'm taking a different route in the morning. Could you pick up Merlin tomorrow?"

"Sure. What time?"

"In the evening would be fine. He'll be all right till then." Allison spotted the truck parked in front Monroe's Pizza.

"Gotcha!" she said.

"What?" Emma asked.

"I saw Luke driving through town, so I turned around and followed him."

"They call that stalking."

"Call it whatever you want. I've had a hell of a day, and this is one thing I want to put to bed. No pun intended."

"Hope you know what you're doing," said Emma.

Allison pulled into the parking lot and parked next to Luke who was still in the truck. "Thanks again for watching Merlin, Em. I'll call you Sunday night. Have fun at the reunion."

She opened her car door, got out, and knocked on his passenger-side window. He looked up, reached for the button, and unlocked her door. She pulled it open and got in.

"First, let me say that I don't usually make a habit of tracking down men I see on the road. I just want to say I'm sorry if I offended you that night at my house."

"You didn't. Look, let me run in and pick up a pizza. And then we'll talk," Luke said.

"Sure," Allison said.

She watched him go into the restaurant and was relieved that he didn't blow her off, but now she felt like an idiot. Allison looked down at the floor, trying to remember why she thought this was a good idea, when she noticed a wallet. She picked it up, intending to run it in to Luke, but stopped when it fell open in her hand. The driver's license picture wasn't of Luke. It was an older man, familiar looking. She read the name. Sal Wagner.

Allison dropped the wallet on the floor. Luke had a dead man's wallet. She got out of the truck just as he came out of the building. Their eyes met.

"I...I have to go," she said, pointing at her car. "We can talk another time."

Without looking his way again, she pulled into the street, trying to sort out what she just saw. With her hands shaking, she reached for her phone and almost swerved into the next lane. She hoped the cop car was still in the gas-station parking lot. When she got closer, she saw the spot was empty. The flower shop was only a few minutes away. She'd call the police from there. Luke was somehow involved in Sal's death. There was no other reason he would have his wallet.

She parked behind her shop and used the back entrance. She flipped the Closed sign to Open, unlocked the door, and went to the phone. She heard the buzzer on the front door go off as someone walked in. "I'll be right with you," she said, and continued to punch the police station's number into the phone.

Allison dropped the phone before she completed the call and reached up with both hands to free herself from the strong arms that restrained her. She struggled as something was held over her face, but her strength and will to fight were sucked away as her body went limp.

•   •   •

Jeremy licked away at his double-scoop vanilla ice cream in a waffle cone with sprinkles as Emma stirred her mocha-flavored iced coffee. Business was booming, now that the local schools were out for the summer. The noise level was at an all-time high as mothers and children stood in line waiting to place their orders. Normally Emma would be annoyed by all the noise and squealing children, but today, sitting with her nephew, it seemed different. Her perspective on a lot of things seemed to be different lately.

"My mom never lets me have ice cream for lunch," Jeremy said.

"Well, then you're lucky she's not here."

"I can't wait for tomorrow. There's gonna be games and prizes and a trophy for the winner of the archery contest."

"I'm sure it'll be fun," said Emma.

"And you get a surprise," added Jeremy.

Emma leaned in toward him and whispered, "What is it?"

"I can't tell you because I don't know."

Emma narrowed her eyes. "Are you fibbing?"

"Honest, I'm not. He didn't tell me." Jeremy put his hand over his mouth. "Oops."

Now Emma was confused. "He?"

"I'm not supposed to say anything."

Emma eyed him suspiciously but didn't push the subject. Instead, she'd ask Kate about it later.

• • •

Luke chewed his bottom lip, grasping the severity of this latest development. She was going to tell. He couldn't let her run to Emma, or worse. She had been following him. Maybe she even knew about the farmhouse. The whispers stirred, *buzzing* in his head, filling every ounce of space, taunting him, making it hard to think. It was dangerous befriending Allison, and he should have been smarter.

The back roads weaved through one city and then the next, taking him past farms and vacant land and only occasionally another vehicle. It was by no means a shortcut, but it offered some cover, so he wouldn't have to explain the woman in the back of his truck. She should have minded her own business. And Kate. She had betrayed him, all the while telling him he had the right to make a life for himself. Emma was different. She would understand, and soon everything would be as it should. She could write at the farmhouse. Write him into his new life. It would be on paper for all the world to see. It would be *real*.

He swung down the long driveway and pulled the truck up to the back porch of the farmhouse. Allison stirred a little when he pushed the blanket off her. He scooped her up and carried her over the creaky deck boards and into the house.

• • •

Kate hung up the phone with the nagging feeling that she should do more. The visit from Luke this morning had thrown her off kilter, and she was still feeling uneasy. She'd left word at the clinic for them to call her if he showed up or called. There was no answer at the only phone number she had for him. The voice mail was generic, but she'd left a message anyway, hoping it was still his number. The petitions with her father's name on them, and what Phil had told her about Luke fighting with Sal the day he died, added to the discomfort that hung over her. The screen door closed, and Emma called out her name.

"In the kitchen," Kate said.

Jeremy kicked off his shoes and ran to hug his mother. "I had fun today with Aunt Emma. We had ice cream and went to the park!"

"Good. Now go get cleaned up. We're having company over for dinner."

He hugged Emma and ran upstairs.

"Can you stay for dinner?" Kate asked. "Derrick's cousin and aunt should be here soon."

"Thanks, but I'm picking up some desserts for tomorrow, and I want to visit David."

Kate picked up her work folders and slid them into her briefcase. "I am officially done with work for the weekend," she said, not feeling totally convinced.

Emma looked toward the stairs before changing her voice to a whisper. "Jeremy talked about a surprise again. I asked what it was, and he said he didn't know. He said *he* didn't tell him what it was. Any idea what he's talking about?"

"No," she said, still preoccupied. "He's always coming up with...stuff."

"I'm sure it's nothing," Emma said, and then changed the subject. "There's something I should tell you. Remember when you asked me to call that landlady?"

"Yes," she said, sorting through some notes on the kitchen table.

Emma looked down at the floor and then blurted out, "I lied when I told you what it was about."

Kate looked up. "Lied?" she asked.

Emma continued. "She said she got a call from that lady who used to visit our father. She left a number and asked the landlady to give it to us. I called her, and she asked if she could mail me a few boxes that she was keeping for him."

"Did she?"

Emma nodded her head. "Yeah. She also told me that he was a nice man and that he tried to help her nephew who was always in trouble."

"Why didn't you tell me?"

"A lot of reasons, not any of them good ones. I opened one of the boxes. There were letters, unopened, addressed to me."

"Unopened?"

"They'd been returned to him, I'm guessing by Mom."

Kate let that statement sink in. "Well, did you read them?"

"I did. Kate, he was making plans to visit us. He sent gifts. My green bike was from him. Other stuff, too."

"Mom must have had her reasons."

Emma was quiet for a few moments. "I figured she thought she was protecting us. It's the same reason I didn't tell you. It's the same reason I've done so many things over the years. I'm sorry. I know you don't need protecting anymore."

Kate came to Emma and put her arms around her. "It's all right." She held Emma tight. "I know those years were hard on you, taking care of a bratty, ungrateful little sister. I gave you a lot of shit. I am who I am be-cause of you." Kate's voice cracked. "You did...good."

Emma pulled back. "Don't make excuses for me. I'm just like her. Or maybe I'm just like him, running away from everything."

Kate reached out and firmly grasped Emma's arms. "Aren't you the one who said we're not them?"

Emma jerked away from her. "I only said that to make you feel better."

"It worked. And it's true. We're not perfect. They weren't perfect."

"I want to be...better," Emma said. "I want to be honest with you and with myself."

"That's how it works. You just choose to be."

Emma's eyes welled up. "And you should know, Doctor."

The moment was interrupted by the sound of laughter. Derrick tripped into the foyer, a large suitcase in each hand. An older woman with fiery red hair trailed behind him laughing, and a younger man, who mirrored the same fair complexion Derrick had, carried another suitcase. Kate made it down the hall just in time to catch a piece of luggage before it crashed into the oak hall table.

Kate greeted them and gave Derrick a kiss. "Good to see you," she said to the newly arrived guests. "You remember my sister," she said, pointing to Emma.

The woman smiled at her, and the younger man said, "How could I forget the beautiful Emma?"

"Down, boy," Derrick said.

"Nice to see you again," said Emma. "I'd better scoot before the bak-ery closes. I'll see you all tomorrow." She slipped through the door and was gone.

• • •

The door was solid wood, and Allison felt every grain as she pounded on it with the bottom of both fists. "Let me out of here, you bastard!" she yelled, even though her voice had become hoarse from yelling for what seemed like hours. There was no way to tell just how long she'd been in this room. The high glass-block windows were just like the ones that were in the basement of her first shop. The way the light streamed almost sideways told her it was probably early evening. When she first woke up, she could hear him walking back and forth upstairs, but now there was only an occasional sound.

"I know you can hear me! Let me out of here!"

She leaned back against the door and slid down to the floor. Screaming and yelling had accomplished nothing but adding to her nausea. Her head was pounding, and her mouth was dry. Whatever he did to her had left a foul taste in her mouth. She sat on the floor, looked around the room, and saw something she hadn't noticed before. Something reddish was sticking out from underneath the bed. She pushed herself onto her knees and crawled over. It was a woman's jacket. She flipped it around and stuck her hand in an outside pocket. A tissue, a quarter, and a dime. The other pocket was empty. The inside pocket had a slip of paper in it. She unfolded it. A receipt from Greenfield Market. Not one she was familiar with. The signature was neat but hard to read because all the letters had a loopy look to them. It looked like G-U...no—Gwen. Gwen Singer. She looked up and said the name out loud. A customer, maybe, or someone from her parents' restaurant? Then she remembered. The name of the girl on the news. The one who was hit by a truck somewhere north of town. She dropped the jacket and turned to the door, listening. The lock was being turned. She stood and kicked the jacket back under the bed just in time. The door opened, and he walked in.

His movements were jerky as he paced back and forth in front of the open door, mumbling to himself. She barely even recognized this man. Everything about him was different.

Luke abruptly stopped pacing and cocked his head to one side. "What? Do what? Stop!" His chest heaved with each breath.

When she realized she'd been holding her breath, she exhaled quietly. The girl. Then she remembered Sal. She had to get out of there. Slowly she inched toward the open door. His head turned. His eyes landed on her.

She lunged toward the open door, but he was quicker. He grabbed her arm and shoved her against the wall, his nose almost touching her face.

"This is your fault," he said through clenched teeth. "I didn't want to hurt you."

"Just let me go," she pleaded.

His eyes narrowed, creases gathered tight on his forehead. "I'm not stupid. You'd tell her."

"No, I won't tell anyone," she said, her voice coming out hoarse.

He looked into her eyes. "You will. You're like the rest of them. You'll turn Emma against me, won't you?" he yelled.

Allison winced. "Emma?"

"She'll see things my way. That's how it's meant to be." He released his grip on her arm, calmly left the room, and locked the door behind him.

There was no reasoning her way out of this. Something was wrong with him, and he wasn't making sense. His mood went from calm to psycho in less than ten seconds. She pulled the bedside table on the bed and tried to balance it against the wall the best she could. She started to climb on top of it to get closer to the window. The wood door flew open, and in two steps he was next to the bed.

"Get down," he said, his voice monotone.

Allison climbed back down to the bed. The table tipped and crashed to the floor, missing Luke by only a couple feet. He had a bottle in his hand filled with something orange. He held it out to her.

"You can't keep me here," she said.

He shoved the bottle closer. "Drink."

She pushed the bottle back at him, her chin jutted forward, and defiance set on her face.

He leaned in. "Drink!" he shouted, his breath hot on her face.

She took the bottle from him.

"Open it," he said in a calm, casual tone.

Allison complied and raised it to her lips. Her throat was so dry, and the urge to guzzle it was strong. The amount she swallowed did little to quench her thirst. She took a few short drinks and looked him in the eye. "They'll be looking for me soon."

"More," he said.

She put it to her lips and tipped it back, allowing only a small amount into her mouth. He turned his head and stared into the corner on the right side of the door. She let the liquid drip out of her mouth and down her chin. He nodded several times, as if he was answering someone, and then walked out of the room again.

Allison ducked behind the bed and put her finger down her throat. A small amount came back up, and she hoped it was enough to stop it from getting into her system. She reached for the table again but realized one of the legs had buckled and cracked when it fell. There was no way she was going to be able to climb to freedom on a broken table. She was stuck there, wherever that was.

CHAPTER 14

• • •

CLARE PARK WAS SITUATED ACROSS the street from the Clare River. Its grassy hills stretched the length of the mile-long property and offered an unobstructed view of the half-mile-wide river. Four pavilions were scattered throughout the park, and each could accommodate a large group of people. Today the park was full, and all four pavilions were occupied. The smell of charcoal and barbecue richly saturated the air as people gathered in the shade of the pavilions.

The Nelson reunion was in full swing. There was a water-balloon toss going on next to a volleyball game, and at times the two games intermingled. A roar of laughter erupted every time a water balloon accidently flew into the volleyball game. The two groups of people finally became one and started another game, dodgeball with water balloons.

Children were forming lines to participate in a ring toss under an old elm tree next to their pavilion. A few of Derrick's uncles were finishing a game of horseshoes, while a group of teenagers headed off to the beach across the street. She watched how they joked and teased one another, as if it was the most natural thing in the world. They weren't strictly the fun-loving bunch they appeared to be today. No, there were some sticky layers to them that if peeled away would reveal a darker side.

The two older men sitting at the next picnic table were brothers. Kate told her about a fight they'd had years ago that left them estranged for almost eight years. Derrick said that neither of them could even remember what started it. Then there was the dispute between a few cousins about who paid for what at an aunt's funeral. The list went on and on, but here they were together, eating, drinking, and playing games in the sunshine on this Saturday in June. It used to seem pointless to Emma. Disagreements, arguments, betrayals, confrontations, then making up and watching the cycle start over again. It seemed like too much effort, this constant struggle to continue being a family. Once again, the common thread was always there. This group of people, whether behaving or not, were only doing what they knew how to do. They ran their lives the only way they knew how. From her view, even as an outsider, she could see it worked for them. Maybe it could work for her, too, someday, if she gave it a chance.

"Emma," Kate called for the second time.

"Sorry," Emma said, swinging her legs out from the picnic table. "Do you need some help?"

"Have you seen Jeremy?" Kate asked.

"He said something about watching the boys practice for the contest. He went off toward the baseball diamonds with Sandra's two boys."

"He has archery on the brain," joked Kate. "Could you check on him for me? Tell him not to wander too far."

"Sure, then I'm going to swing past Allison's and get Merlin. He could use some fresh air after being locked up all day."

• • •

He watched through an opening in the trees. Jeremy was with two boys, both a little older than him, who were playing catch next to a baseball diamond. Jeremy's focus wasn't on the boys; he was looking off into the distance. Luke followed his gaze to a group of people setting up targets and chairs.

"Put that thing down and play catch with us," the taller boy yelled at Jeremy.

"It's not a thing. It's a bow," Jeremy yelled back, while giving the boy the evil eye.

"Whatever," the boy said, and continued to play catch.

Jeremy intently watched the activity in the distance as the two boys joined a baseball game already in progress. Jeremy suddenly jumped backward and tucked his bow into some bushes. Luke took a few steps beyond the trees to get a better look but stopped and retreated when he heard her voice.

"Jeremy, there you are," Emma said. She walked over and stood next to him, both facing the baseball game.

After a few minutes, Emma patted him on the back and walked toward the picnic area. As soon as she was out of sight, Jeremy retrieved his bow, looked at the baseball game, turned, walked along the tree line, and was gone. Luke strolled casually in the same direction Jeremy had taken. The trees were thicker in this part of the park, which made it harder to catch a glimpse of the boy through the trees. The wood line curved to the right, and a path came into view. Luke checked behind him and then ducked under some low branches and followed the path for about fifty feet. It opened up into a field with a view of the river.

Jeremy stood facing a large tree stump. He pulled an arrow from his quiver and drew it back in his bow, taking careful aim at the stump. He released the arrow. It soared over the stump and cut through the brush. Jeremy stomped his foot into the ground.

"Good try," said Luke.

Jeremy spun around. "I'll never find it now, and my dad will know I was shooting."

"How are you supposed to get good at it if you don't shoot it?"

"He means not supervised."

Luke walked past Jeremy and headed to the stump. "Come on."

"Where?" asked Jeremy.

"To find that arrow."

Jeremy was on Luke's heels in an instant. The two of them, heads down, searched for the lost arrow, getting farther and farther from the picnic.

● ● ●

All the way to Allison's, Emma thought about the festive atmosphere at the park and the way Derrick's family got along. There were no guarantees when it came to family relationships, and that was if they stuck around. She didn't totally trust anyone except maybe Kate and Allison. It was safer. Period. Since David's accident, she'd been questioning everything. She'd used the fact that his parents didn't like her as a way to keep her distance. Actually, it didn't bother her. It was the piece that helped keep her dysfunctional plan working. The realization sickened her. She had the urge to turn the car around, drive to the hospital, and lay it all out for David. Then she remembered. He wouldn't even know what she was talking about, just like the day she charged into his hospital room when he first woke up. She hoped she'd never have to see that look in his eyes again. It was then that she knew she loved him.

She'd reached Allison's house and was in the driveway without even remembering actually getting there. "You thought you were so smart," she said into the rearview mirror. "Independent. Don't need anyone. You were wrong." She flipped the mirror up hard with her hand. She walked up the steps and turned the key, still mumbling to herself. "If I ever get the chance to tell David that I—" The smell assaulted her nostrils before the front door was fully opened. "Shit."

The dog came bounding down the hall, pushed his way past her, and was on the lawn with his leg up before the screen door closed. Emma waited on the porch until he finished relieving himself. They went back into the house, and Merlin, with his head hanging down, ran to the pantry where he knew his food was kept. He sat patiently while Emma cleaned up the mess he left her in the entryway.

"Well, at least it wasn't on the carpet," she said, glancing at Merlin, who seemed quite intent on not looking at her. "It's OK, boy." She knew it was out of character for him to make a mess in the house. Allison bragged, more than once, that he hadn't had an accident since he was a puppy.

She went to the pantry and took out the bag of food. Merlin jumped up, almost knocking it out of her hands. "All right, just a little." She poured some in his bowl and noticed his water bowl was dry, so she filled it halfway. He drank every last drop before inhaling the food. She grabbed his leash and said the magic words, "Want to go for a ride?"

With Merlin's head hanging out of the passenger-side window, they drove through town. When they approached Allison's shop, Rachel was in the process of closing up for the day. The girl was wheeling in a display cart when Emma noticed Allison's black sports car parked behind the building. She hadn't noticed it on her way to pick up Merlin, probably because she had been so preoccupied. She couldn't think of one good reason for the car to be parked there. She put her arm out in front of Merlin, hit the brakes, and made a U-turn.

"Rachel, is Allison here?" Emma asked as soon as she put the car in Park.

"No."

"How long has her car been here?" Emma asked.

"Since I opened this morning."

"That's strange. She didn't say she was catching a ride with anyone, did she?"

"Not to me."

"I'll give her a call and let you get back to work."

Emma searched her purse but couldn't find the card Allison gave her for the hotel. It must be at home. She couldn't even remember the name of the place. With a bad feeling taking root, she pulled out onto the street while Merlin went back to windsurfing out the passenger-side window.

• • •

Luke sat on the edge of the couch, watching Jeremy sleep. The boy should be awake by now. Luke was eighteen years old the first time they made him take the medicine. The memory still made him angry. He remembered how hard he fought that first time, even though he knew he couldn't win. In the end, he was restrained, his pants were pulled down, and they injected it into his backside.

He had given Jeremy only a quarter of what he gave Gwen. He shook the boy again. No response. He repositioned Jeremy's head on the pillow and watched his chest rise and fall. He covered him back up with the blanket and sat in the recliner, which he had moved closer to the couch. He leaned back and waited.

The silence didn't last long. A *swooshing* sound started somewhere behind him. He didn't turn around. He knew nothing would be there. *Shh... shh...shhh.* He swatted at the space around his head. The whispers swooped and then swarmed around his head. He squeezed his eyes closed tight, focusing with all his will to push *them* back where they came from. He hung his head and rocked back and forth. Jeremy would wake up, and everything would be all right. They would all be together, just as Peter always promised. Emma would explain it to Kate and make her understand. The book Emma would write would tell the story. Belonging somewhere was within his reach. He was tired of being alone.

When he closed his eyes, he could still see Peter's photos. The girl who was the same age he was. Her eyes pierced right through the glossy picture, as if she was looking straight at him. He saw it in her eyes even then. Hope outweighed all the sadness that they both had endured. Together, they'd put all that behind them. The emptiness that was at his core ached. Soon there would be a new story. One that he was a part of.

• • •

At home, Emma sat and stared at the hotel business card in one hand, while still holding the phone in the other. The words hadn't registered yet.

"She never checked in yesterday," the man said so casually through the phone.

"There's been a mistake. Please check again," she demanded, but the answer he gave her a few seconds later was the same.

She hung up and searched her memory for any remnant of information her friend may have given her regarding her travel plans. Maybe she wasn't listening to Allison again and missed something major that would explain why her car was at the shop and why she ditched her hotel reservation. With Allison being the free spirit she was, the answer could be something as simple as Allison meeting up with an old boyfriend and deciding to spend the weekend together. She remembered a few times that had actually happened, but that was a decade or so ago, and Allison was more responsible now.

Merlin was hungry again and had started wrestling with the bag of dog food, and was making considerable progress by the time Emma snapped out of it. She got up, patted him on the head, and poured food into his bowl. After filling his water bowl, she slid the stack of boxes over to make more room for him. The two boxes on top tipped and came crashing down behind the dog, sending him skittering across the kitchen.

"It's OK, boy. Look, it's just some old boxes." She bent down and reached for the box that had been in the middle of the stack, and a flap opened, spilling out some of its contents. On her knees, she gathered together what looked like some old pictures and magazines. One picture in particular grabbed her attention. It was of her father and some other people sitting outside on lawn chairs in front of an open garage. She picked it up and examined it more closely. Sitting next to him was a younger man, maybe seventeen or eighteen, with wavy, shoulder-length hair. Everyone was smiling except him. There was no doubt in her mind who he was. The young man was Luke. Her father and Luke, together. "Small world" echoed in her head. Luke kept turning up—everywhere.

Emma dropped the picture. Yesterday, Allison saw Luke on the road and said she was going to follow him. Did she catch up to him? She glanced over and watched Merlin scarf down his food. It seemed he couldn't get enough. And the accident in the house. Maybe it happened because he was left alone too long. Allison would never have done that on purpose. Emma jumped up and walked the length of the kitchen, stopping in front of the fridge. Mindlessly, she stared at the drawing Jeremy had made for her. The picnic. She'd forgotten about the picnic. In the drawing, Jeremy was aiming at a bright yellow-and-red target as others looked on. Something about the picture caught her eye. She stepped closer. Her eyes widened, and she inspected the figure standing directly next to her nephew. He was wearing a cap, but wavy brown hair flowed from beneath it. Something stirred deep in her being as the image dragged her in. Her face was so close now, she could almost smell the dried Magic Marker on the paper. Right next to the rim of the hat, over his eye, was a dark line. She wiped at it with her finger and then checked the placement of it, hoping she was wrong. It wasn't just a smudge. No, Jeremy had purposely placed it there. The scar. The one that Luke tried to hide from her that day at her house. Instantly, her legs seemed to lose all feeling. She backed up and sat in a kitchen chair. Her father knew Luke, and now, so did her nephew.

Her phone was in her hand. Her finger punched in 9-1, and before she punched in the final 1, she hung up. What would she say? That her friend's dog pooped in the house, or that she found a picture of her father from years ago and that a guy in the picture looked like someone she knew? Or she had a suspicious-looking picture an eight-year-old drew for her? The picture was eerie, but that didn't make it a crime.

The conversation with her father's lady friend came to mind. "Your father was a good man," she had said over the phone. "He tried to help my sister's son who was always in trouble." Was Luke the kid she was talking about? Emma decided that she needed to talk to Luke, and Lena would know how to get in touch with him.

• • •

Lena answered on the first ring. She gave Emma his phone number but said she wasn't sure where he lived. "Why the sudden interest in Luke? Is everything all right?"

"I hope so. Look, I'm in a hurry. You don't have an address for him?"

"No," Lena said. "I have to update our files now that he's working for Paul. He was living with another worker named Phil, but I don't think he's still there."

"Where does Phil live?" Emma said, trying not to sound so rushed.

"Tell me what's going on," Lena demanded.

"I may have left something in his truck the night he drove me home," she said, hoping Lena believed her.

• • •

Luke checked his phone. It was her again, for the third time. The second time she left a message: "Hi, Luke, this is Emma. Could you give me a call when you get this?" She left her number, but he already knew it. He would answer when he was ready. His energy was pulling her to him. It was happening. Fate. He sat back in the recliner and imagined the kind of future he would have.

• • •

"Damn!" Emma dropped her phone on the passenger seat. "Why won't he answer the phone?" she yelled.

Up ahead on the right was the apartment building. She used to pass this way on a regular basis but never paid much attention to the apartments. She drove around the back of the building and found the address. They were old, run-down, and in desperate need of a paint job. She walked up the steps and pushed the buzzer for number seven. Nothing—so she pushed it again. This time she heard a static-like noise and then a man's voice.

"What?"

Emma put her face closer to the intercom. "I'm looking for Phil."

Silence and then, "Who's asking?"

"My name is Emma. Emma Simms. I help Paul out sometimes."

Again silence and then a buzzing sound. She pulled open the door and went in. The inside didn't look any better than the outside. The walls were a drab gray color, if you could even call it a color, and the lighting was rather dim. It reminded her of an apartment she lived in briefly when she was a child. She went halfway down the hall before she found number seven. She knocked on the door and waited. A thin, light-complexioned man answered it. He was wearing shorts and an unbuttoned short-sleeve shirt and was holding a bottle of beer. She recognized him. He was the guy she saw with Luke at Nolan Street.

She held out her hand. "I'm Emma."

He opened the door wider but ignored her hand. "I know who you are." He took a drink from the bottle. "What can I do for you?"

"I'm looking for Luke."

"What do you want with him?"

"I really need to talk to him. Is he here?" she said, looking past him into the apartment.

"He doesn't stay here anymore."

"Any idea where he might be?"

"Yes. No. Hard to say. He lies." He turned and walked to the kitchen, which was just past the living room, took the last swig from the bottle, set it down, and went to the fridge.

Emma took a few steps into the room. "Lies about what?"

Phil took two bottles of beer out and held one out in her direction.

"No, thanks."

He opened one and set the other on the counter. "Everything, I think. About where he stays, about side jobs he has." His eyes narrowed, and his facial muscles tightened. "You'd think he'd help me out when he had extra work. After all, I'm the one who hooked him up with David and that Dr. Nelson. He owes me." He stared at her, a pained expression on his face.

Right now, she needed help from this rambling, half-drunken man. "Yes, he should help you," she said softly, taking a few more steps toward the kitchen. "How'd you meet him?"

"At a bar in town. Said he was looking for work, needed a place to stay. I let him rent my couch and got him his job. I think he—" Phil looked down, smiling. "Never mind."

"No, what?" she asked, trying to sound especially friendly.

"He has a thing for you."

Emma's mouth opened, closed, and opened again. "What?"

"Can't you see the way he looks at you? The way he…watches you?"

The night at the party came to mind. The way he was looking at her when she spotted him across the bonfire. She shook off the feeling. "All right, enough. You said you may know where he is?"

"He did—well, actually we did—work for a lady a few towns up Highway 28. She needed a handyman. I went there twice with him, and then he cut me out. Said there wasn't enough work for both of us."

"You think he's there?"

"Maybe. I asked him about it. He got real defensive-like."

"Could you tell me how to get there?" asked Emma.

"It's been a while. Don't remember the name of the road."

"If I drove you, could you find it?"

"Probably."

• • •

Kate walked back to the picnic area and found Derrick's cousin Sandra. "Did the boys come back yet?"

Sandra was mixing the dressing for her famous chopped salad. "They're over there," she said, pointing to a group of boys playing Frisbee. "Would you taste this? It's missing something," she said, holding up a large serving spoon.

Kate didn't waste any time. She ignored the woman's request and walked straight over to the boys. She'd already checked the baseball diamond and the area where the archery contest was going to be held, but there was no sign of her son.

"Have you seen Jeremy?" she asked the older of the two brothers.

"I saw him talking to his aunt and then he went down the path where all the blackberry bushes are," the boy said.

The smaller boy spoke up. "Maybe there's berries there now, cause I saw another guy go down the path right after Jeremy did." He grabbed the bottom of his older brother's shirt. "Can we go see if there's berries there?"

Another boy, who was about Jeremy's age, had walked over and was listening to the conversation. "I don't think they found any berries because they weren't carrying any when they came out."

"They?" asked Kate.

"Him and the man," he said.

"What man?" Kate asked. "Did you see him here, with our group?"

"I don't remember. He knew him, though. I heard him call him Larry or maybe Lou. No, he called him Luke."

• • •

Emma turned the car around for the fourth time since leaving Phil's. She made a left on yet another dirt road, and by now they all looked the same.

"Are you sure it's this way?" she asked, this time not even trying to hide her irritation.

"No, but it looks familiar. That house," he said, pointing to a newer brick ranch. "I think I remember seeing that house."

"How much farther? We've been driving almost forty-five minutes."

"I don't think we're too far."

They had just passed an old barn on the verge of collapsing when Phil blurted out, "Next road, take a right!"

Emma made the turn, hoping this time Phil knew what he was talking about. They'd driven about a quarter mile down the road when her cell phone rang. She looked at the number and let out a groan. "Kate, sorry, I meant to call you, but Allison—what?"

"Tell me Jeremy's with you!" Kate said again.

"Why would he be with me?" Emma took her foot off the gas.

"We can't find him! I know this sounds crazy, but I think he's with Luke."

The car had slowed even more, and Emma pulled over to the side. Everything seemed to be in slow motion. She was numb. Things that seemed random before now seemed connected. Small world...*he* kept turning up. Then, like a tidal wave, everything sped up. Through the sound of her heart beating loud in her ears, she heard Kate's voice.

"Emma? Emma!"

She snapped back. "I'm here. I think Allison's with him. What makes you think Jeremy is, too?"

"One of the kids saw them together, and now he's gone! There's things I should have told you. Dad knew Luke. Dad had him committed. Luke came to my office yesterday, real spacey, delusional. I should have done something!"

Emma's mind went on rewind. "The man on the tape up north. Could it have been Luke? The guy was about the same size. And the baseball cap." All the people who were somehow connected to her knew Luke. A sickening kind of knowing flooded her. Did Luke do it?

Kate was in panic mode. "I don't know what he's capable of. Of all people, I should have seen something. I have copies of his hospital records. They said he was delusional, paranoid, hears voices. He's trying to make a life, wants family, relationships. He's starved for it. Maybe that's why he took Jeremy. And all this time, I thought he was doing well."

"I think he sought you and Allison out," said Emma. "And David. It's just too much of a coincidence."

"Emma, it's possible he had something to do with Sal's death. I'm not sure how or why, but I do know they had an argument the day he died."

"He told you that?" asked Emma.

"No. Someone else did, but I can't talk about that."

Emma glanced over at Phil. "I think I know who." She resumed driving and coasted slowly down the road.

"What are we going to do?" asked Kate. "Derrick has everyone searching the park, but I don't think he's here."

Phil smacked his hands on the dashboard. "It's right up there!"

"Kate, I'm checking something out. I'll call you right back."

Phil slid closer to the door. "What do you think Luke did?"

Emma ignored him. "Is that it?" she said, pointing to the large house on the right.

Phil squirmed in his seat. "What do you think he'll do to us if he finds us snooping around?"

Emma pulled to the side of the road a short distance from the house and shut the car off. She scanned the property, looking for any movement. It was quiet, with no sign of its occupants. No cars in the driveway.

"Let's go," she said, getting out of the car.

"Oh," he said, frantically shaking his head, "I'm not going in there."

"Fine!" She was careful not to slam the door. She walked along the tree line, keeping her eyes on the side of the house. No movement, no sound. She kept a steady pace until she reached the far side of the barn, stopping just out of view from the house.

She leaned against the barn and wondered what the hell she was doing there. Fear wrestled with her. New plan. Go back to the car and backtrack a little and then call the police. But where was she, and what would she say? She didn't have to think about that for very long. The sound of a car's engine interrupted the thought. The car was in Reverse, disappearing down the road. Her car. Shit. For a split second, she thought about making a run for it. Maybe she could catch up with that worm if she cut across the cornfield. Well, she might have had a chance if she'd kept up the exercise routine she and David had in place before the accident. Before the accident. When everything was fine, or at least seemed fine. She was different. She'd changed in the past few weeks. She finally knew what she wanted in her life and wasn't scared anymore.

She checked the road and decided Phil wasn't coming back. The worm. He'd have to be dealt with later. Now she needed to find out what was going on, and if Allison was here, and where Jeremy was. There was no sign of a vehicle anywhere. He might not even be here. She walked back to the front of the barn and peeked around. A door with an iron bolt was only a few feet from her. She lifted it; the door was heavy and made a creaking sound as it opened.

She stepped in and waited for her eyes to adjust to the darkness. The place didn't look like a working farm, but the barn housed an array of farming equipment. She could make out old tractor implements, and toward the back she saw the outline of a tractor. The slits between the barn's boards let in just enough light to see that the space in the front of the barn was turned into what looked like a workshop. Phil said Luke was doing some work for the resident. The entire left side of the barn was empty. On the dusty barn floor were rows of tire tracks. Her eyes followed them to the back bumper of a car. Maybe someone was here. She approached the car. She could make out the word *Bonneville* imprinted on the back of it. Since coincidences seemed to dominate lately, she hesitantly walked to the front of the car. She strained her eyes but couldn't be sure, so she ran her fingers along the front near the hood. Nothing. She squeezed between the wall and the car, letting her hand glide across to the other side. Her fingers felt the contour of an uneven dent. Could it be? Was it the car that hit David? Things were lining up in a frightening manner. She made a run for the door. She pushed it open, stepped out, replaced the bolt, and ducked around the side of the structure. She fumbled for her phone and called Kate.

"Did you find Jeremy?"

"No, no one's seen him in hours. Where are you?"

"I'm at a farmhouse somewhere off Highway 28. Phil took my car."

"Did you say Phil?" asked Kate.

"Yeah. Listen, I think I saw the car that hit David. I think Luke did it. I think he has Allison. Maybe you're right and he has Jeremy, too."

"Hang up the phone, Emma," Luke said.

She looked up. He was standing near the front of the barn, smiling, and he wasn't alone. Jeremy stood directly in front of him. Luke rested his hands on the child's shoulders. Jeremy looked at her through sleepy eyes.

"Jeremy," she whispered.

"Hang up the phone," he said again.

She could hear Kate's voice as she hung up and held the phone in her hand.

"Throw it over here," he said.

She held it out and tossed it to him, the whole time smiling at Jeremy.

"Let him go."

Luke caressed the boy's head. "We've become pretty good friends, haven't we, Jeremy?"

"He helped me find my arrow so I wouldn't get in trouble," Jeremy said. He looked up at Luke. "We better get back to the picnic, or we'll miss the contest."

Emma swallowed hard when she saw Jeremy's confusion. He didn't know he was miles away from the park. She looked at Luke, forcing a smile to keep the situation from escalating.

"Yes, he's right. We should be getting back."

"Oh, there will be plenty of time for archery," he assured the boy. Luke let his hands fall to his side. "Go give your aunt a hug."

Emma dropped down on one knee, and Jeremy flew into her arms. She hugged him tight but kept her eyes on Luke.

"How'd you find me?" he asked, then tapped his hand to his head. "Phil. Should have known."

"I'm so tired," Jeremy whined.

"Let's go back into the house for a bit then," Luke said. "Come on. You heard the boy. He's tired." He grabbed her upper arm and pulled her toward the house.

She reluctantly let him guide her up the driveway with the lethargic child in tow. Her eyes searched the property as she tried to formulate an escape plan. Luke stopped abruptly about ten feet from the porch and released his grip on her arm. When she turned her attention to Jeremy, she heard Luke talking. She couldn't make out the words, but that didn't matter. He wasn't talking to them. He was looking at something straight ahead. Kate's words echoed in her head. Delusions…paranoia…hallucinations. She knew enough to know it wasn't a good combination. He was smart, though. He'd fooled Kate, which from her own experience, wasn't an easy feat.

With Luke preoccupied, she bent down and whispered to Jeremy, "Honey, this isn't right. Luke isn't right. Do you understand?"

Jeremy nodded.

"I want you to run and keep running until you find a neighbor. Can you do that for me?"

He nodded his head. "Are you sure?"

"Yes." She grabbed his shoulders and flipped him around, giving him a push. "Run."

He was almost to the road before she looked back at Luke. His face contorted with disbelief and then flared with anger. "What are you doing?" His eyes shot past her. "Jeremy!" He leaped forward, attempting to follow the fleeing boy.

Emma lunged at him. He tried to shove her out of the way, but she had a solid grip on his arm and caught him off balance. They both landed hard on the ground. Emma struggled to keep him down as gravel sprayed up around them. He tried to twist to break her grip, but she had no plan of letting go. He finally broke free and was almost on his feet. She spun around, landed hard on her knees, and grabbed his pant leg and pulled. He tripped and landed face down in the dirt. She let go and pushed herself up, jumped over him, and started running toward the road. He caught up to her within seconds, grabbed the back of her hair, and yanked her toward him. As her head jerked back, she reached over her head and scratched at him. Her nails tore into his cheek. He screamed, pulled her hair harder, and wrapped his arm around her neck. She gasped for air as he dragged her to the house, up the back steps, and through the door. He pushed her into the kitchen, and she landed prone on the floor. He slammed the door.

She struggled to breathe. Her knee was on fire, and pain shot through her shoulder. The fight was knocked out of her, but Jeremy got away. With her eyes closed, she tried to move, but everything hurt. She listened. Someone was crying. It was...him. As soon as she opened her eyes, she saw it. Something shiny just under the stove. It was yellow, and one side was jagged. Next to it was another chunk of something orange. A flower. She reached for the first piece and slid it closer to her. It was a bow tie. The area around the bow tie was green. She knew what it was. She'd seen it every day for years. Her breathing became shallow, and she rested her head on the kitchen floor. She pictured the smiling frog with the yellow bow tie and orange flower that had sat on the counter in her kitchen. She could almost hear Allison making fun of it as everything started to fade and then went black.

CHAPTER 15

• • •

"Emma, sweetie, wake up. Emma!"

Sinking, then floating, then rising to the surface only to be pulled back, weighted down again. Sound echoed, first distant and muted and then closer, clearer.

"Wake up!" yelled Allison.

She was being thrashed around. Like a rag doll, her head jerked forward and then backward. Emma struggled, slapping at the hands that held her.

"No, no!" She opened her eyes, flailing her arms defensively.

Allison pulled away. "Stop! Emma, stop. It's me!"

She squinted her eyes and then focused. "Allison." Then panic swooped back in, and she tried to get up. "Where's Jeremy?"

"Jeremy?"

"He was here. Luke took him. He took you." Emma spun around, taking in the room. "Where are we? Where's Luke?" She pushed herself to her feet and tried the door, then limped back to the bed and looked up at the window.

"Sit down before you fall," Allison said. "We can't get out. I already tried."

"I have to find Jeremy."

"When he brought you here, I didn't see Jeremy. Emma, I think he killed Sal. I followed him that day and found Sal's wallet in his car. I freaked out and went to my shop. He followed me, and then I woke up here." Allison dropped down to the floor and pulled the jacket out from under the bed. She held it up to Emma, her hand visibly shaking.

"There's a credit card receipt in the pocket with Gwen Singer's signature on it."

"Who?"

"That woman on the news, the one who was hit and killed by a truck a couple weeks ago," Allison said.

Emma shook her head. She didn't watch the news but vaguely remembered hearing something about it.

"Anyway, when the police found out who she was, they said it was suspicious. She wasn't from the area they found her in. I think she was here, in this room."

The common denominator was Luke. "There's an old Bonneville in the barn with a gash in it. I think he hit David, and I think he may have killed my father."

Their eyes locked. They were at ground zero.

"What are we gonna do?" asked Allison.

"We're going to get out of here—that's what we're going to do," said Emma. She walked the room, checking out each wall.

"There's more," said Allison. "All this has something to do with you. He accused me of wanting to turn you against him."

"My cookie jar," Emma mumbled.

"What?"

"He was the one who broke into my condo. My cookie jar is in his kitchen...well, pieces of it, anyway. And there's more—he knows Kate."

• • •

Luke left his truck parked between an abandoned oil well and a shed not far from the farmhouse. The plot of land sat behind a stand of trees that made it difficult to see from the road. He'd been having that feeling again, as if he was being watched, and he couldn't make it stop. Hiding his truck gave him a sense of security. He picked up his pace in hopes of crossing paths with Jeremy. Driving the roads hadn't panned out, so he'd try his luck on foot. It wasn't too late to fix things. Emma was confused right now, but if he could bring Jeremy back, he could make it right. After all, every family had fights.

In his mind's eye, he pictured the two of them burning that garbage of a book she was writing now—each page being engulfed in the flames before turning to ashes. They'd laugh about how stupid she'd been, and then she could start writing a new one. The real one. One that included him, Jeremy, Kate, and maybe even Allison. It would finally be real, written down for everyone to see, in the pages of a book. Something that would last.

Luke stopped. He sensed something was different. He stood in the road, listening. The crickets had stopped chirping. Then came the rustle of leaves and then crunching in the thick trees to his right. He waited. No more than twenty feet ahead, he saw a small figure emerge from the woods and sit down on the shoulder of the road. He walked almost on his tiptoes for a few feet before the boy looked straight at him.

"Jeremy, I've been looking everywhere for you," he said. He smiled, knowing everything was going to work out.

"Where are we?" Jeremy asked. He got to his feet. "Aunt Emma was right." He looked around. "I can't find the park." His voice became high-pitched. "Where's my aunt? Why do I feel sick?"

Luke stopped advancing toward him. "Take it easy," he said, trying to sound soothing. "Let's go see your aunt. We can all talk about it together."

Jeremy took a deep breath but didn't budge. His stance remained defensive.

"Remember the surprise I was talking about?" asked Luke.

The stiffness in Jeremy's shoulders visibly melted away. "It's here?" His voice had dropped a few decibels.

"Yeah, back at the house. Come on."

Jeremy stood his ground but looked down the road as if weighing his options. "OK."

• • •

David sat with his head in his hands. He'd had a splitting headache since he'd woken up that morning. He racked his brain trying to remember more details about the dream he had last night. He'd dreamed that he was looking at jewelry through a glass showcase. A man was talking to him. He felt so happy. Was it a memory or just a dream? All day, bits and pieces of things he couldn't place kept popping into his mind. Emma. A restaurant. Driving in a truck with her sitting next to him. Being in bed with her. Touching her. These thoughts would last a few seconds and then disappear. A job site—Paul and Frank were there. Snapshots. He could see it but not remember it.

"Are you ready for physical therapy?" asked the always too-peppy therapist. She looked up from her clipboard, sensing David's discomfort. "Are you OK? You look a little pale."

"I'm fine, just having those flashbacks again. It's frustrating."

"Don't try so hard. Try getting your mind on something else," she said. "I'm going to find an aid to help get you up. Be right back."

David wasn't in the mood to be pulled, pushed, lifted, or stretched today. He felt like someone's pet with all the "great job; good try; come on, you can do it" comments. They meant well with their over-the-top accolades, but he didn't feel like playing along today or being nice. He wanted to remember everything. He wanted his life back, but mostly he wanted Emma. When she was here, he felt motivated. Motivated to remember, motivated to get back on his feet. She didn't treat him as if he was fragile. She always told him the truth whether she thought he'd like it or not.

He reached for the crutches, even though he had orders not to get up without assistance. How could he get his life back if he couldn't even get to the bathroom by himself? He'd done it earlier and made it back to the chair before anyone noticed. As soon as he stood up, the room began to spin, and he had a prickly feeling on the top of his head. He sat back down, grabbed the arms of the chair, and waited for it to pass.

A buzzing sound filled his ears, and he thought he was about to pass out. He leaned back, hoping he wouldn't tumble to the ground. The room stopped spinning, and the awful buzzing noise stopped.

Then he saw it.

The street with his truck parked on the other side. He stepped off the curb and put the small box with the ring in it in his pocket. He heard the squeal of tires and looked up. He was about to wave...the man in the car looked right at him. Then pain.

David struggled to catch his breath and find his voice. He swallowed hard. "Nurse! Someone!" He reached for a crutch and used it to try to scoop the phone on the bedside table toward him. It slid across the small table and landed on the floor. "Nurse!"

The therapist and a stocky man came running into the room. David screamed for them to hand him the phone. The therapist tried to calm him down while the man picked up the phone and handed it to him.

David punched in three numbers and looked at the confused pair before him. "He tried to kill me! I remember!"

• • •

The leg from the broken table sat against the wall next to the door and would be hidden when the door opened. Emma went over the plan one more time with Allison before she sat down to rest. Allison was weak from not eating for twenty-four hours and fell asleep. Emma's knee throbbed, and her jaw was swollen. She needed to ignore the pain so they could get through this.

Ten minutes later, floorboards creaked. A muffled voice echoed somewhere above them. He was talking, hopefully to himself again. Emma tried to control her breathing and hoped that Jeremy was far from this place. She flew over to Allison when she heard him unlocking the door. She shook Allison and whispered, "Wake up. It's time."

Allison was groggy and looked like crap, which would make her act seem convincing. She curled up on her side and began to moan. Emma put her hand on her friend's back and rubbed it. The door opened wide, and he stood in the entrance.

"Luke, help me! Allison's sick."

He looked at the two women and glanced over at the broken table on the floor next to the bed. Without hesitation, he walked over and used his foot to push the pieces out of reach. "She'll be fine when it wears off." He crouched down next to Emma and rested his hand on her back. "I had to. She left me no choice."

Taking advantage of his "friendly" gesture, she said, "I understand. Please help her."

He touched the back of his hand to Allison's forehead. "I'll get her something to drink." He stood up and went back to the door. "Emma," he said without turning around. "I knew you'd understand." He left, but not without locking the door behind him.

Allison sat up. "What if this doesn't work?"

"It'll work. He's not ruining my life. Or yours. I finally know what I want, and I'm not going to die like this."

The door opened less than halfway. The table leg was in clear view. Luke walked to the bed and handed a glass of water to Allison. She took her time, taking small sips.

"Thank you," she said, just above a whisper.

Emma was already backing up by the time Allison raised the glass to her lips a second time. She was almost to the door. She'd reached behind her and was only inches from the table leg when Luke turned around. She stood straight up, hoping to block his view of her weapon. She smiled. "She's probably just hungry."

His stare was dark, piercing. She was sure he sensed her intention, and she was barely able to control her breathing.

He tilted his head, motioning toward Allison. "Get her up."

Emma thought about going for the table leg but needed the element of surprise on her side, and Allison was in no condition to help. She was close enough to the door, so she gave it the slightest nudge with her shoulder, hoping it opened enough to conceal what was behind it. She went to Allison and helped her stand up.

Allison took a few steps and then purposely stumbled and reached for Luke, forcing him to catch her.

Emma used the moment to take a step back and reach around the door. With her hand firmly around the table leg, she swung it sideways, landing it just under his arm on his side. He let go of Allison and doubled over.

Using both hands, she swung again, aiming for his head. He turned, and his arm reached up and easily deflected it.

She pulled it back again, but he charged at her and slammed her into the wall. The table leg flew across the room as she slid down to the floor. He stood above her, looking down, his face twisting in pain. Allison threw herself on his back and wrapped her arms tight around his neck.

He turned sharply to his right and smashed her head into the cement wall. She hit the ground a few feet away.

Luke turned his full attention back to Emma. His voice was controlled, but the veins in his neck bulged. "This was so unexpected." His wide, glassy eyes searched her face. "And after everything I went through!" He crouched down in front of her. "It was all for you. She doesn't surprise me," he said, jutting out his thumb toward Allison's too-still body. His mood flipped back to calm. "You're special." He reached out, and the back of his hand traced her check.

Emma sat motionless against the wall, even though every cell in her body told her to punch him. He sat down in front of her and leaned in, closing the distance. The stench of stale alcohol filled the small space between them.

She forced herself not to turn away as his hand moved toward her again.

He touched the side of her head, his hand gliding over her hair as if he were petting a puppy, and then the fire in his eyes burned hot again. "And David. You couldn't stay away from him. I didn't *want* to hurt him...I didn't *want* to hurt *any* of them!" His breath hit her in the face, moving her hair.

She saw true anguish ooze out of him as he waited for some kind of response.

"You can make it right," she managed to say. "Let us go, now, before anything else happens."

The hard lines on his face relaxed again. "I've waited for so long. We're connected, Emma. Tell me you can feel it."

"Connected," she stated flatly. "Yes."

"Like family, but better." Tenderness dripped from his lips. "Peter said I was like you, that we were the same. Said we were both strong. When your book came out, I knew it was time."

"Time?" she asked, making sure to keep the disgust out of her voice.

His eyes lit up, and he looked like an excited five-year-old. "Time to write the story, our story, one like your book, *Lost Days*. You, me, Jeremy, and Kate. A real story." His nostrils flared, and the simmering anger resurfaced. "Not the trash you're writing now. Yeah, I saw your notes in your office."

Emma looked past him. Allison hadn't moved. "We have to help her."

He ignored her plea and stared at the open door. Emma half expected to see someone standing in the doorway, but it was empty.

His gaze swung back on her. "The park—do you remember the park? The one with the footbridge over the river, next to the campground?"

Now Emma was more confused. What did a park have to do with anything? Then it hit her. "The Belamy Park?" she asked. She hadn't been to that place in years, even though it was less than an hour from town.

"Hide-and-seek. Remember, Emma?"

Her mother used to take her and Kate to that park. One summer her mother borrowed a tent, and they spent the weekend at the campground.

"I remember the park."

"You were hiding behind the gazebo in the bushes. I found you there, but I didn't tell."

His expression was so animated, childlike. He was less threatening than before, and she wanted to keep it that way. She smiled and nodded her head. "Yes, the gazebo," she said, even though she had no idea what he was talking about.

"Remember you asked me how I knew your name? Peter told me. He was there, too."

Her father had been watching her play with Luke. She vaguely remembered playing hide-and-seek. It was the end of summer, and so many other kids were there. No one in particular stuck out in her mind.

"I wondered how you knew my name," she lied. She consciously commanded her shoulders and neck muscles to relax and appear more at ease.

His face turned more serious, stern. "I sometimes think that I've always known you. Peter had so many pictures of you and your sister. He'd tell me stories," he said with a gentle reverence. "Then I met you that day in the park, and I knew it was true. That's where it started. That's where I first truly believed."

"Believed what?" she asked, using her sweetest voice.

"That you're part of me, the good part. You said I was good. You told me not to listen to them."

Emma wished that she could remember the day he was talking about. She couldn't have been more than eleven or twelve. Whatever he remembered must not have had quite the impact on her as it did on him. "Them?" she asked.

"They were calling me names, making fun of me. You had to have heard them, too," he insisted. "You said to ignore them. You remember, right?"

A mixture of pain and fear swirled in his eyes, and she felt sorry for that child he had once been. But it had gone too far, he had crossed so many lines, and she needed to get Allison out of there.

"Luke, help me get Allison upstairs."

He nodded his head in agreement and stood up.

Emma knelt at Allison's side and pushed the hair away from her face. "Allison, please wake up." She stuck her arm under the back of Allison's neck and lifted her head up off the floor.

"I didn't mean to hurt her, I swear!" he said.

She took an authoritative approach. "Help me get her up, then," she said and pointed, directing him to go around to Allison's left side.

He obediently followed her direction and went down on one knee, reached behind Allison's shoulders, and was about to lift her up when a voice called out from upstairs.

"Aunt Emma?"

Emma raised her head, her breath caught in her throat.

Luke pulled his arms away from Allison's limp body, and they fell to his sides. His face hardened.

They stared at each other, both afraid to move. Emma could feel the tides turning. The stillness and silence exploded, and all at once their bodies were in motion.

In one swift move, Emma was up and running for the door. Following immediately behind her, Luke reached out and grabbed the back of her tank top.

She twisted free, regained her footing, and made it to the stairs before he did. Halfway up the staircase, her legs were swept out from under her. She reached out and grabbed the handrail on the wall. It slowed her fall, but the rise on the step cut sharply across her thigh. She screamed.

With Luke's arms wrapped tight around her legs, they both slid down the stairs. Emma bounced on her backside, while Luke's ribs took the brunt of each step on the way down. He whimpered once when he reached the ground, his breath coming hard, but he was on his feet again within seconds. He made it halfway up the stairs before Emma could even get herself up.

"Jeremy!" she yelled. Her thigh throbbed, but she climbed the stairs on all fours. She stopped on the third step and looked up.

He was already near the top. "Stay down, Emma. I don't want to hurt you, too," he said over his shoulder. He took the last step and was gone.

"Luke, leave him alone! Luke!" she screamed, and kept climbing. When she made it to the top, she looked into the kitchen. "Luke! Jeremy!"

The room was empty and still. To her right, a light was on over the kitchen sink. She turned left, found herself in the dark, and followed along a wall with her hand. She saw stars when her thigh hit the corner of a table, but a few seconds later, her fingers found a lamp. She switched it on and saw that she was in a living room. The room was closed up tight, and the air was musty, just like the basement. No sign of a phone. She limped across the room to the window and held the heavy drapes open. It was dark outside, with no streetlights as far as she could see. Her gut told her they weren't in the house. It was too damn quiet. On her way to the front door, she passed a chair, and her foot hit something next to it, knocking it over. A bottle of beer poured out its warm contents just in time for her to step in it with her stocking feet.

The wind hit her in the face when she stepped outside. "Jeremy!" She hobbled toward the road. "Luke! Luke!"

Emma feared that even if they were within earshot, the sound of the wind would muffle her yells. To the left of the farmhouse, she saw a light and went toward it. The shoulder of the road was mostly loose stone, but a few larger rocks made each step difficult without the benefit of shoes. She picked up her pace when she realized that the light was coming from another house. She pounded on the front door, and when no one answered it immediately, she pounded harder. Within seconds, a man in a bathrobe came out to get a better look at the battered-looking woman on his porch.

"Help me! Please! Call the police!" Emma backed away, exhaustion took over, and she lowered herself down to her knees. "My friend needs an ambulance."

A minute later, a woman stepped out of the house and joined them on the porch. "I called and gave them our location," she said, "but they said the police were already on their way."

Even the wind couldn't cover the sound of sirens wailing in the distance.

• • •

The Norton Community Hospital was fifteen miles southwest of the farmhouse. Allison was in and out of consciousness since they'd arrived, and had been whisked away for another test. Emma sat on a gurney in the ER, wearing a flimsy hospital gown, and was beyond irritation, having just been questioned by the deputy for the third time.

"You have a description of his truck," she said, "so why in the hell are you still here talking to me? You need to be out there looking for him!"

A shrill voice traveled down the hall. "Where is she? Where is my Allison?"

Emma slid off the cart and met Mr. and Mrs. De Luca in the hall outside Allison's empty room. "She'll be back soon. They took her for a CAT scan."

"Emma, what happened? They said they found her in a basement?" She looked at Emma's face and saw the cuts and bruises. "Oh, Emma," she said, and started to cry.

Mr. De Luca wrapped his arm around his wife and put his hand on Emma's shoulder.

"I'm all right, really, and Allison's going to be all right, too," Emma said firmly.

A nurse slid another chair from the hall into Allison's room. The De Lucas sat down and were talking quietly to each other when Emma overheard the deputy talking to the nurse. She assured him that the doctor would be seeing Emma in a few minutes and that as soon as she was medically cleared, she'd be free to go with him.

Emma told them everything she knew and wasn't going to spend another minute being useless. Desperate to find a way out, she scanned her surroundings. Mr. De Luca was comforting his wife when Emma's plan bloomed. Against the wall sat a small table. Mrs. De Luca's purse was on top of it, and directly next to the purse was a set of keys. She walked over, turned her back to the table, reached behind her, and pulled the purse closer and closer until...it went over the edge. Emma's hand closed over the keys, stopping them from clanging together. She was already apologizing for knocking it on the floor as she concealed the keys against her hospital gown.

Mr. De Luca, being the gentlemen he was, reached over the side of his chair and picked it up.

"I'm so clumsy," Emma said. "I'll be back." She pointed toward the hall. "I have to find a restroom." She peeked around the curtain that served as a divider for the small rooms and didn't see the cop. With one hand holding the thin gown closed, she stepped out into the hall. The nurses' station was halfway down the long corridor on the right. Not far past that was her way out.

The nurse she remembered from earlier walked out from behind the desk, looked down at a clipboard, made a left, and was about to meet her head-on when a door opened on Emma's right. A woman stepped out, carrying a stack of pink pans, and blew past her. Emma sidestepped to the right and was through the door before it closed. She felt around for a light switch and was more than pleased when the light came on.

A couple minutes later, two men pushing a man on a gurney rushed into the ER. No one paid any attention to the woman in scrubs as she walked through the door, dodged around an ambulance, and disappeared into the parking lot. When she reached the second row of cars, she repeatedly pressed the key fob. A horn sounded off to her left.

Thirty-five minutes later, Emma parked the Cadillac in her driveway and walked around to the side of her condo to see if by chance she'd left the window unlocked. "Shit!" she said when it didn't budge. Now she'd have to pay a visit to Arlene, the head of the homeowners' association. As she cut through the small yards, she was reminded of how late it was, because none of her neighbors' lights were still on. She had to get into her condo and see what else was in those boxes. The pictures Luke kept talking about must be there, and she needed to see them. Emma knocked on Arlene's door and was surprised how quickly the woman's face appeared in the window.

"Arlene," Emma said when the door opened, "I'm so sorry to wake you, but I had no other choice."

The woman looked her over. "I don't sleep worth a damn anymore, anyway," she said, her gruff voice drifting off a bit when she got a better look at Emma under her porch light.

Emma tilted her head down a little to escape the woman's gaze. "I need to use my extra key to get into my condo. I locked myself out." She could only imagine what this woman thought about her scraped-up face and bare feet.

"Is everything all right, Emma?"

"Oh yeah, fine, everything's fine," she said, her head bobbing up and down.

"I'll be right back, or would you like to come in?" Arlene looked as if she would really prefer Emma to wait outside.

"I'm fine here."

Five minutes later, Emma gulped down a cold glass of coffee she'd left in the pot that morning. She rummaged through her bathroom cabinet, and when she found what she was looking for, she pushed the other bottles aside. As she tossed two white pills in her mouth, she caught sight of her face in the mirror. After the initial shock, she took a closer look. What she saw wasn't a wounded woman but one with a fire in her eyes that she hadn't seen there before. After everything that had happened since the beginning of summer, she didn't look defeated. No, she looked pissed.

When she returned to the kitchen, she got a carving knife and sliced the other box wide open. It contained mostly junk—a few baseball hats, suspenders, a wooden jewelry box with tie clips in it, a battery-operated coin counter, and a few old books.

More photos were in the box with the picture of her father and Luke. She spread them out on the floor to get a better look. They were black and white, and by the looks of the cars in the background, probably dated back to the fifties. She pushed them aside and dumped out the box she'd already opened a couple days ago. These were probably the photos that Luke kept talking about. After sorting through them, she pulled out all the pictures that Luke was in and then all the pictures she was in. She spread them out in a large circle and sat down in the middle of them.

Ten minutes had passed, and she hadn't found anything that could help her find Jeremy. It was a dead end, and she had no more ideas. She picked up the phone and called Kate's cell phone.

"Emma? They said you were in the hospital," Kate said.

"I was, but I got out. Any word yet?"

"No, they said they're doing everything, but what if they don't find him?" asked Kate, her voice shaking.

"They will."

"Did you see him? Is he all right?"

"Yes, he's OK. I don't think Luke wants to hurt him. He wants us all to be…family. Wants me to write a book with him in it."

"This is all my fault," Kate wailed into the phone. "I should have seen *something*."

"No, Kate, he's smart. He's been planning this for a long time."

"I'm at the police station. They're still questioning Phil. I told the police he had your car. He's the one who told us where you were."

"Yeah, and that's only because they forced him to," Emma said, remembering how he ditched her. "Try to stay calm. I'll call you later."

"Emma, wait," Kate said. "David remembers. Everything."

Emma's hand shook. Yesterday, that would have been the best news. Now, all she could think about was getting Jeremy back. "I have to go now." The phone slipped out of her hand and landed on the scattered photos. She blinked back tears and bent over to pick it up. That's when she saw it. Near the edge of one of the pictures she was in, she saw the corner of a wood structure. When she bent over, she realized what she was looking at. It was a gazebo. Peter had taken pictures of the day Luke was talking about. Emma fell to her knees and dug through the pile, looking for more pictures of herself wearing the same turquoise shorts. Within a minute, she was able to find five more of her wearing the same outfit. She lined them up and examined them. Several children were in each one, but nothing jogged any memories—not until she looked harder at one that Kate was in. Her sister looked to be about seven years old, and she was crying. She looked harder at the picture and saw herself, standing with her hands on her hips. In front of her stood two boys. One was pointing at her, and both appeared to be laughing. Kate was standing behind her. She remembered how as a child, she was always defending the underdog. Especially if the underdog was Kate. Then something else popped out at her.

Sitting on the ground, leaning against the gazebo, was another child. A boy. It was hard to make out his face, but he had a full head of wavy brown hair. When they were in that basement, Luke said that she told *them* to leave him alone and that he was good. He insisted that she had to have heard them, too. The other two boys in the picture must have been bullying her sister and Luke. The picture was old and a little beat up, so she brought it closer to her face. The boy sitting on the ground had his hands over his ears. Why would her sticking up for him have had such an impact that he'd remember it to this day? She was sure that she would never have remembered anything if she hadn't seen this picture.

She closed her eyes and went back to the farmhouse. Her breathing slowed, and she tried to replay the conversation she'd had with Luke. She pictured his expression and the anguish in his eyes.

Then she knew. The answer had been there the whole time. She slipped the picture into the pocket of the scrub top and went upstairs to her office. With her laptop under her arm, she came back down the stairs, slipped on a pair of running shoes, grabbed a flashlight, and slipped out the door without even locking it.

CHAPTER 16

• • •

Luke paced twenty feet from his truck. The constant movement helped burn off the anxiety. The way her eyes *spewed* distrust at him infuriated him to the core. He stopped pacing and listened. His head jerked toward the truck.

"No! Stay back!" he yelled into darkness. "Leave us alone!"

The whispers insisted on speaking their minds, and he couldn't stop them. Their grip had become stronger than he was, but he wasn't going to let them get near the kid. They would tire and go away if he could get a grip and calm down. He tore his eyes away from his truck and resumed pacing.

He'd seen it in her eyes. She was going to take Jeremy away from him... take it *all* away from him. *It wasn't fair!* He tried to tell her how it could be, how it *should* be.

In the distance, even the sounds of the night mocked him. An owl screeched, and along the river, the chorus of frogs croaked their disappointment in the dark.

• • •

The headlights went off as the Cadillac rolled to a stop. The moonlight alone was bright enough to illuminate the sign—The Belamy Park. It was a county park, and tax cuts had dictated its demise some years ago. To the right of the sign was the entrance to the long-ago-abandoned campground.

To the left was the road to the day park. With the flashlight in hand and the laptop under her other arm, Emma headed to where he had said it all began. Only she was taking the long way through the campground, not the way he'd expect.

The road curved to the right and then immediately narrowed as the individual campsites lined up on both sides. Even with the wide beam she used to navigate, the terrain was uneven, giving her already sore leg an open invitation to buckle under her.

Her foot caught the edge of a rut, and her ankle twisted. She yelled out, went down on her other knee, and dropped the laptop. Getting up was easier than she thought. Her will refused to let her body succumb to the pain.

The path to the day park was coming up somewhere on the left. She searched each clump of weeds, knowing it was in the general vicinity. The light hit something that glowed. It was overgrown from years of neglect, but the orange arrow on the marker was still there. The campground was on higher ground than the day park was, and to ensure he wouldn't see her coming, she switched off the flashlight. It was the only chance she had to possibly come up behind him.

The path descended at a gradual decline, and within minutes, the rushing water of the winding Clare River became more than just a faint sound to her left. If her memory served her right, the footbridge that went over the river was less than a few minutes away. She panned the area using the advantage of the higher ground, but with only the moonlight, she could see no sign of his vehicle.

The gazebo was straight ahead, before the bridge on the left. She paused every few steps to listen. The only sounds came from the river down below and the occasional croak of frogs. She shone the light on the bridge and decided against crossing it. The bridge wasn't nearly as long as she remembered it to be. It couldn't be more than forty feet, but as a child, it seemed more like a mile. It was chained off, and since a section of railing was missing on the right side, crossing it at night might prove treacherous.

Next to her stood the gazebo. She took the two steps up and stopped when she thought she heard something stir in the trees closest to her. She set the laptop down and turned around. The noise stopped.

After waiting a full minute, she was sure it had been nothing. She'd been so convinced that they would be here, and now she doubted her reasoning. There was only one more thing she could do before she made the long trek back to the car.

With the flashlight on, she stood on the bottom step. "I'm here, Luke! At the gazebo!" She listened. Nothing. "I heard them, too, just like you said!" Emma stepped back into the structure and slowly turned, sweeping the perimeter with the beam of light. After making two complete turns and fighting the sinking feeling in her gut, she was ready to walk back to the car.

"Emma."

She spun toward the voice and raised the flashlight. Luke's arm flew up to shield his eyes. Immediately, she lowered the light and hoped she knew what she was doing. She fought for control of her voice. "Luke. I knew you'd be here," she said in a feminine, disarming way.

His eyes were hard, fixed, giving away nothing.

"You said it all started here. That's why I came." She held the flashlight off to her side.

"You lie." He backed away.

Emma put her hands up. "No, I didn't lie."

"Not your words. Your eyes." He backed up a few more steps, his face fading into the shadows. "Back at the house when Jeremy called out to you, your eyes told me all I needed to know."

She stepped down from the gazebo. "I was only worried about him. That's all," she said, her voice cracking. "Where is he, Luke?"

He aggressively stepped toward her, planting his foot firmly on the ground. "That's all you really care about," he said, spitting the venomous words out of his mouth. His face twisted into an ugly grimace. "Do you think I'd hurt him?"

"No! I don't." She lowered her voice. "I just want to see him. Kate's missing him."

"Kate? She went behind my back. Checking up on me. At Phil's." He closed his mouth tight, his jaw muscles bulged, and his gaze intensified. His neck twisted to the right, and then he turned his back to her completely and stood in a defensive stance. "Did you hear that?"

She didn't answer him. She already knew beyond a doubt that it was nothing she could hear, but she needed to keep the dialogue going. "Kate was worried about you."

"No!" He shook his head. "That bitch lied, too!" He spun around to face her. "You're like Peter, both of you. One lie after another!" He turned away and threw his hands over his ears.

Emma ran to his side. "Wait. Luke, wait. Look." She pulled the picture out of her scrub pocket and pointed the light at it. "This picture. It's us. You, me, and Kate. This is the day you were talking about, isn't it?"

He looked at the picture, and his features softened, glowing with a fondness, a memory.

Emma lowered her head to catch his gaze. "When I heard *them*, right? The boys." She pointed to the picture and then at the two images that stood in front of her in the old photo. "They were teasing you."

Confusion filled his eyes, and then they met hers. "Boys?"

She looked down at the picture in her hand and saw the boy with the wavy brown hair sitting almost in this very spot, with his hands over his ears. The realization registered.

"Them," she said out loud.

The voices. The voices that followed him, probably for most of his life. He thought she had heard them, too, the day she told the boys to leave him alone. Their lives had been weaved together so long ago over nothing more than a misunderstanding. Her heart ached for the child in the photo. If only something had been different for him, somehow, maybe they wouldn't be standing here now. But they were, and she had to get Jeremy back.

"Luke, yes, I heard *them*. They were…bothering you."

He looked at her, pain rising in his eyes. "I don't *want* to listen to them, to do what they say. They *want* me to be alone."

"I'm here. Jeremy's here." She touched his arm. "Take me to him, Luke."

The tenderness in his eyes was genuine, but within seconds it gave way to distrust and then sheer fear. His hands went up over his ears again. "No! No!" He hunched over and backed away from her, mumbling incoherently.

"Don't listen to them." She grabbed his shoulders and shook him. "Look at me!"

Luke's eyes darted somewhere behind her into the darkness, and he shoved her away.

She landed on her back.

"No! Stop!" he said with nothing but panic in his voice. "Leave me *alone*!"

Emma got up and helplessly listened to him ramble. Her only chance of finding Jeremy was slipping away with Luke's sanity. She backed further away, and then off in the distance, a door slammed. A truck door? Emma spun around and pointed the light directly behind her. The woods were thick, but to the right there was an opening in the trees. She was halfway there when the flashlight caught something shiny. She came up on the spot and found herself looking at what was left of some kind of building. She pointed the light back toward the way she'd come and didn't see Luke.

She trudged through the high grass and stopped when she made it to the clearing. A parking lot. As soon as she held the flashlight up, she saw it.

In the far corner of the lot was a truck. She checked behind her—still no sign of Luke. At almost a run, she followed the beam of light to the vehicle. When she was about twenty feet away, the driver-side door popped open, and Jeremy slid off the seat.

"Aunt Emma?" he said, his voice calm.

"Honey, get in the truck. We're going home," she said, and looked behind her. "Hurry." She reached her hand around the steering wheel, feeling for the ignition.

"He took the keys with him," Jeremy said.

"That's all right. We'll walk then." Emma grabbed his hand and started pulling him, knowing the Cadillac wasn't too far ahead of them.

"Luke's saying weird things."

"I know, honey." She searched for the front of the park, but nothing looked familiar. It must not be as close as she remembered.

"Emma!" Luke's voice boomed.

Emma turned the flashlight off and pulled Jeremy to her. It sounded as if he was in front of them, blocking the shortcut to the car. She squeezed his hand and then pulled him in the opposite direction. If they had to take the long way, then the long way it was.

The river ran narrower at this end of the park before it got deeper and then widened, closer to the bridge. They stayed parallel with it, using the noisy water as cover, as they crunched over downed branches. The gazebo came into view, and Emma pulled Jeremy to the left of it, staying low. They crouched and listened. The path to the campground was straight ahead. Emma pointed toward it, and Jeremy nodded his head. They held hands and hurried toward the path in the dark.

Something moved in the trees up ahead on the left. And then it stopped. Without further warning it jumped out in front of them. Just a deer. It crossed the path and was gone. Emma tightened her grip on Jeremy's hand and pulled him toward the hill.

Less than thirty feet from their destination, a figure emerged. This one was not a deer. Emma stopped and put herself between Jeremy and the threat.

"You're leaving?" he said, his voice controlled now, his tone casual.

"We're going home. It's over."

He took two deliberate steps and was in front of her. "Home? Over?"

She kept Jeremy behind her as Luke circled them.

"No." The heat returned to his voice. "I counted on you. The story. There has to be a story! You know that!" He took one long stride, and they were face-to-face.

Emma nervously shook her head, trying to be agreeable. "The story, yes, write the story. Yes." She held the flashlight tight and was ready to plant it into his skull.

"Yes?" he asked. "Yes, what?"

"I'm writing the story. I am."

He leaned in and grabbed her shoulders. His eyes bore into hers.

It was easier to lie in the dark. "I brought my laptop. It's in there, the story, the beginning. I'll show you."

"All I see is a flashlight."

"It's in the gazebo. I can get it," she said.

He looked at Jeremy and said to her, "Go get it. We'll wait here." Emma froze.

"I really hope you're not lying," he said. "Go!"

On trembling legs, she made it to the gazebo and scooped up her laptop. She jumped off the steps and looked up. They were gone. "Jeremy!"

"Over here," said Luke.

The voice came from the left. The bridge. Luke and Jeremy were on the bridge. She moved toward it, straining her eyes until she found the small figure standing in the middle of the footbridge. She ducked under the thick chain that blocked the entrance, and was at his side in seconds. Jeremy reached for her hand.

She held out her computer to Luke. "Here, you can have it."

He took it from her and cradled it in his arms. "You really did bring it." The tenseness left his body, and he leaned back against the wood railing. "We can finish it, me and you."

"I'm cold, Aunt Emma."

"We need to get off this bridge," she said, and put Jeremy in front of her.

"Wait," said Luke, putting his hand on the back of Jeremy's neck. He handed the laptop back to her. "Now read it to me."

Hesitantly, she flipped it open. After a few seconds of waiting for it to load, she started to speak. "'They were connected, the boy and the girl, not by blood but by circumstance.'" She glanced up at Luke. He let go of Jeremy and was smiling, his eyes closed. "'Belonging was what they both sought, each in their own way.'" She reached her hand out to Jeremy. "'Both were bold and bright, looking for that place to shine.'" Jeremy took her hand. "'Time and space couldn't change their destinies.'"

They were ten feet away before Luke opened his eyes. The smile melted off his face, and his posture tightened as he stood straight up and fell into pursuit.

Emma maneuvered Jeremy away from the section of missing rail before she stopped and faced Luke.

He lunged at her. "Give it to me! It's mine!"

Emma turned to make sure that Jeremy was on solid ground before she lifted the laptop and tossed it into the air between them.

Luke reached up and clamped down on both sides of it with his hands. He pulled it to his chest and then reached for the rail with his left hand. His hand slid over the splintered wood, met with jagged edges...*and ran out of railing*. His body twisted as he tried to regain his footing before he met with open air.

With her hands over her mouth, she watched Luke as he held on to the laptop, seeming somehow unaware, and getting smaller and smaller before he disappeared into the river.

Her body wanted to rest, lie down, and just breathe, until her eyes met Jeremy's. "Stay there! This thing isn't safe!" Four steps from solid ground, something crackled and then snapped. The boards underneath her shifted. She landed on her right side as the ends of the plank under her crumbled near the edge and dropped away. On her hands and knees, she stayed low and crawled toward Jeremy. The boards shifted again, dropped a few feet, and then tilted. She slid closer to the edge and heard a horrible grinding sound as the old wood planks scraped and grated against one another. A wrong move would send her freefalling. Something slammed against her arm. She looked up and saw the chain.

"Grab it!" yelled Jeremy.

She wrapped her fingers around it and pulled herself the last few feet, landing on her back in the grass.

"You're right. It wasn't safe," Jeremy said, holding up a metal sign that was hanging from the chain. "It says, 'Danger, Bridge Closed.'"

The stars were brilliant and thick in the sky this far from the city. It had been a long time since she'd seen them like this, or maybe she just hadn't noticed. "You were so brave. You saved me."

"No, Aunt Emma, we saved each other."

• • •

The sun was shining by the time Emma stepped out of the police station. Lena was waiting for her at the curb. She slid into the car and rested her head against the window, unable to stop the what-ifs. Jeremy and Kate could have been hurt, or David and Allison could have been killed. They were *all* her family, and she'd never seen it as clearly as she did that morning. Luke wanted what she had and died trying to get it.

"Thanks for picking me up," Emma said.

"I'm just glad everyone's all right," said Lena. She gave Emma a once-over. "You *are* all right, aren't you?"

"Yeah. Well, close enough."

"And Luke—you think you know someone…"

"They found a shallow grave at the farmhouse," Emma said. "A woman. The police are still putting it all together."

"What about…Luke?"

"They're dredging the river," Emma said, "but nothing yet."

"I need to get you home," said Lena.

"I think that's what we all spend so much time doing," said Emma.

"And what's that?"

"Trying to get home. Putting all the pieces together. Luke Stone just went about it…in a different way. The only way he knew."

"I think you need some sleep, girl," Lena said.

"Yeah, but there's someplace I need to go first."

Lena smiled and made the left turn. "He's waiting for you."

CHAPTER 17

• • •

THE SANDY GROUND CRUNCHED UNDER Emma's feet as she traversed the narrow path. The woods were still thick but glistened with orange-and-red hues in the fading daylight. This was their final hurrah before the trees would give up their leaves and hunker down for winter. The unfortunate events of summer had been swept away by the content, balanced energy that now flowed through her.

The last curve of the trail came into sight, making her want to push harder. She increased her speed, knowing she was almost there. Her lungs hungrily took in the crisp air of autumn that had thankfully replaced the foul summer stench, during which time she could have lost everything. She'd turned a page in her life. It was exhilarating and scary, but she knew she could now let the past peacefully reside in only a small piece of her, and not determine her future.

The rhythm of the run quieted her soul, but the last leg of it always gave her a rush as she was spurred on by the challenge of navigating the steep hill. When she reached the top, she looked at the old stopwatch in her hand and then leaped into the air. "I did it! Beat my best time!"

David was sitting on the deck with a cup of coffee. He gave her a thumbs-up.

She settled down hard in the chair next to his and took the bottle of water he held out to her. "You're going to have a hell of a time catching up with me when you start running again," she said.

"We'll see," he said, and reached for her hand.

Her jesting mood turned solemn, and she lowered her eyes. "You were right about this house."

"That was huge," he said.

"What was?"

"Emma Simms admitting that I was right."

Her smile returned. "Baby steps, my friend."

With no more needing to be said, they watched as the sun set.

• • •

The last light of day offered a clear view of the minivan from his window. He watched her remove the sleeping child from his car seat and carry him to the house. Her posture curved and slumped forward, while her slender arms struggled to hold the child and unlock the front door. Someone like her shouldn't have to be alone. It was achingly painful being alone. There was only one thing he knew more about than loneliness. Betrayal.

Snapping back from a still-raw memory was a rude thing.

He squinted and saw it was now dark outside. He had no idea how long he'd been sitting there since he saw her go into the house. The curtains in her kitchen did little for privacy and only framed the clear view. They were sitting at the kitchen table now, in their usual spots, the toddler rubbing his eyes and eating something from a bowl. A warm feeling blanketed him as he watched the intimate scene.

He was drawn to it yet saddened by it, but he couldn't stop looking.

Their daily routine gave him structure and helped divide the days. Even though he hadn't heard her voice in days, it was still in his head. And so were...*they*.

It was the *way* she said his name. It wasn't luck that put him there that day to change her flat tire. No. It was a sign, nudging, pushing. Better days were coming.

Out of nowhere, headlights lit the street, and a car swooped into her driveway. A man got out, and before he even reached the front door, she opened it. His smile wilted as he saw her smile at the stranger. The same smile she'd given him that day in her driveway. They went into the house and closed the door.

Numbness seeped into every crevice of his body, crowding out the warmth that resided there moments ago. He scanned the windows of the aluminum-sided house for any sign of the intruder. As the drapes closed, he cursed.

About the Author

 L. M. KAYE SPENT MORE than twenty years of her career working in a locked psychiatric hospital helping patients return to their optimal level of functioning. These experiences were invaluable and gave her good insight into people's motivations for their actions. She has seen, firsthand, how the mind can be our worst enemy, sometimes causing more pain than the outside world could ever inflict.

Kaye lives in Michigan with her family. She is thankful for them every day and knows all too well not everyone is as fortunate as she is.

CPSIA information can be obtained at www.ICGtesting.com
Printed in the USA
LVOW10s1816120116

470290LV00002B/477/P